Praise for *The Imposter*

"Woods Fisher does her Amish research and it shines bright in her latest offering."

—*RT Book Reviews*

"Suzanne is an authority on the Plain folks, and that's important to readers when it comes to Amish fiction. She always delivers a fantastic story with interesting characters, all in a tightly woven plot."

—**Beth Wiseman**, bestselling author of the Daughters of the Promise and the Land of Canaan series

"Suzanne Woods Fisher's *The Imposter* is a heartwarming story of overcoming obstacles to find peace and a place to belong. The story will captivate readers who love the Amish culture and enjoy spending time in the Plain community."

—**Amy Clipston**, bestselling author of *A Simple Prayer*

"Suzanne Woods Fisher has written another delightful book that is sure to please fans of Amish fiction. Filled with endearing characters and wry wit, *The Imposter* is a wonderful story."

—**Kathleen Fuller**, bestselling author of *A Faith of Her Own*

"Suzanne Woods Fisher is at the top of her game in this richly rewarding tale of faith and love and the ties that bind. *The Imposter* is everything you want in a novel. I loved this first installment of her newest series."

—**Mary Ellis**, bestselling author of *Midnight on the Mississippi*

Praise for *The Quieting*

"Fisher is a talented author who knows what readers have come to expect from her novels and always gives them more."

—*RT Book Reviews*, 4-star review

THE BISHOP'S FAMILY #3

THE
DEVOTED

A Novel

SUZANNE
WOODS
FISHER

Revell

a division of Baker Publishing Group
Grand Rapids, Michigan

© 2016 by Suzanne Woods Fisher

Published by Revell
a division of Baker Publishing Group
P.O. Box 6287, Grand Rapids, MI 49516-6287
www.revellbooks.com

Printed in the United States of America

Library of Congress Cataloging-in-Publication Data
Names: Fisher, Suzanne Woods, author.
Title: The devoted : a novel / Suzanne Woods Fisher.
Description: Grand Rapids, MI : Revell, [2016] | Series: The Bishop's family ; #3
Identifiers: LCCN 2016022832 | ISBN 9780800723224 (pbk.)
Subjects: LCSH: Amish—Fiction. | GSAFD: Christian fiction. | Love stories.
Classification: LCC PS3606.I78 D48 2016 | DDC 813/.6—dc23
LC record available at https://lccn.loc.gov/2016022832

Scripture used in this book, whether quoted or paraphrased by the characters, is taken from the King James Version of the Bible.

This book is a work of fiction. Names, characters, places, and incidents are the product of the author's imagination or are used fictitiously. Any resemblance to actual events, locales, or persons, living or dead, is coincidental.

Published in association with Joyce Hart of the Hartline Literary Agency, LLC.

16 17 18 19 20 21 22   7 6 5 4 3 2 1

To the Salch family: Kim, Clayton, and A.J.
There's a little bit of you in every book.

Cast of Characters

David Stoltzfus—mid-40s, father to six children: Katrina, Jesse, Ruthie, Molly, Lydie, and Emily. Formerly widowed, now married to Birdy Glick. Owner of the Bent N' Dent store and bishop to the church of Stoney Ridge.

Ruthie Stoltzfus—17 years old, middle child to David. Bright, ambitious, restless, she's right on the cusp of leaving the Amish to pursue a higher education.

Luke Schrock—17 years old, brother of Miriam (Mim), son of Rose Schrock King (owner of the Inn at Eagle Hill). Smart as a whip, irreverent, loves to live on the edge.

Patrick Kelly—20 years old, Canadian Catholic, guest at the Inn at Eagle Hill. Eager to convert to Amish church.

Jesse Stoltzfus—19 years old, owner of the buggy shop, hovering on the precipice of manhood.

Dokdor Fraa—nicknamed Dok, but her name is Ruth Stoltzfus. Dok is David's sister. Raised Amish but left to go to college, then medical school, a doctor to the Amish.

Ed Gingerich—late 40s. Highly regarded neurologist (both professionally and by his own assessment) at the local hospital. A fascinating, exasperating love interest to Dok.

Matt Lehman—mid-40s. Police officer for Stoney Ridge. Has a desperate crush-from-afar on Dok.

Jenny Yoder—19 years old. Made her first appearance in Stoney Ridge in *The Lesson*.

Katrina Stoltzfus Miller—22 years old, oldest daughter in the Stoltzfus family, now married to Andy Miller. Two little children, a girl and a boy, and lives at Moss Hill.

Molly Stoltzfus—14 years old.

Lydie and Emily Stoltzfus—11-year-old twins.

Birdy Glick Stoltzfus—35, married to widower David Stoltzfus. Bird aficionado.

Thelma Beiler—touchy about her age, elderly widow to former bishop, Elmo Stoltzfus. Runs a farm called Moss Hill.

Hank Lapp—60ish, uncle to Amos Lapp of Windmill Farm. Former owner of the buggy repair shop. Made his first appearance in *The Keeper*.

Fern Lapp—50ish, wife to Amos Lapp of Windmill Farm. Arrived in Stoney Ridge in *The Keeper*.

Miriam (Mim) Schrock—19 years old, older sister to Luke Schrock. On-again, off-again love interest for Jesse Stoltzfus.

1

The bad thing about Ruthie Stoltzfus's job was that it barely paid minimum wage and she had no job security. She was only employed when someone from the Schrock family, who owned the Inn of Eagle Hill, was busy or unavailable, like now.

The good thing about her job was that it was across the road from her home. She liked to think of the now-and-then job as a hotel concierge-in-training, minus the hotel. The Schrocks referred to the position as a filler.

But as for what happened last evening . . . nothing ever—ever!—could have trained her for that. She was still shaky from the shock. The guests who had checked out of the inn yesterday had trashed the little cottage. Completely *trashed* it! Just as she was locking up after she had worked all day long to clean it up, she saw a man stagger over to her.

"Is this a motel?"

"Not really," Ruthie said. "It's a bed-and-breakfast." And then she noticed the man had a cut on his forehead. "You're bleeding."

He lifted a hand to his head as if startled by the thought. "It's nothing. Look, I need a room for the night."

She looked back at the main house. The lights were out. It was late and they'd gone to bed. But the guest cottage was empty, and she knew Rose would appreciate the income. Still, this man seemed odd. Not in a dangerous way, but he seemed dazed, a little confused. Drunk, maybe? She should send him on his way. But then again, what would he do if she turned him away? He was miles from town. "You'll have to pay cash, up front."

He reached behind him, then patted his pants, his shirt front, alarmed. "I don't seem to have my wallet." He reached into his pockets. "I'm good for the money. If you could just trust me. Just for tonight. In the morning, I'll take care of everything. I promise." His eyes pleaded with her.

In the end, Ruthie ignored her usual overriding caution and let him stay. She walked him over to the guest cottage, showed him how to use the kerosene lights, and left him there. As she closed the cottage door behind her, she felt a hitch in her heart. Had she done the right thing? Or the wrong thing. Birdy, her father's wife, often said that the Bible warned they might entertain angels as strangers in need. Nothing about this man seemed particularly angelic, but he definitely was a stranger in need.

Ruthie crossed the road and turned around, walking backward, as she climbed the steep driveway to her family's home. The light in the little cottage was already snuffed out. The man was probably in bed. She'd made her decision. She had to trust it was the right one, even if the stranger-in-need didn't end up paying for the stay.

She slept fitfully, tossing and turning. In the morning, she woke and dressed in a flash. She left a note for Birdy and her dad on the kitchen table, that she had to get to work early and would miss breakfast. She grabbed her shawl from the wall peg and rushed down the driveway. The cottage still looked as quiet as it did last night, though she wasn't sure what she had expected to find. Burned down? Exploded? *Don't be ridiculous, Ruthie*, she told herself. *You're letting your imagination run away with you.*

Rose was already in the kitchen at the main house of Eagle Hill as Ruthie walked right in. She looked up at Ruthie in surprise. "You're here early."

"There's a guest in the cottage," she said. "Late last night, as I was heading home—a man came and asked for a place to stay."

Rose straightened up. She looked out in the driveway. "Where's his car?"

"He didn't have one."

Rose got that look on her face, the one that seemed as if she knew this story wasn't going to end well.

"I might have made a mistake, Rose. He seemed to be in some kind of trouble."

"Did he threaten you?"

"No. Nothing like that. He was very polite." She explained the whole story.

Rose went to the window to peer at the cottage. "It's early. Let's wait another hour or so, then I'll take him some coffee."

"Are you mad at me?"

Rose swiveled around. "No. Not at all. Please don't worry, even if the man doesn't pay for the night. You were put in a tough spot and made a decision that felt right to you." She turned back to peer out the window, looking at the cottage, crossing her arms against her chest. "But maybe I'll have Galen take him the coffee."

An hour later, that's just what she did. Galen King, Rose's husband, a no-nonsense kind of man, took a pot of coffee

11

over to the man in the cottage. Not two minutes later, he returned with the untouched coffee tray.

"Is he all right?" Ruthie asked. "Should I call for a doctor?"

Galen set the tray down and slumped into a chair at the kitchen table. "Not a doctor. He definitely doesn't need a doctor." He swallowed. "He needs . . . the county coroner."

And that's why Ruthie couldn't stop shaking. The coroner arrived, and after he saw the cut on the man's forehead, his bleeding knuckles, and discovered there was no identification to be found, he called the Stoney Ridge Police Department. They dispatched their only two cars, sirens blaring, which alerted all kinds of townspeople to come out and see what on earth had happened at the Inn of Eagle Hill. A reporter from the *Stoney Ridge Times* said this was the biggest story to hit the town in two years, since someone had blown up Amish farmers' mailboxes with cherry bombs.

"Perhaps there's a link," the reporter said, sniffing for any clue he could find to flesh out his story. Hard news, in Stoney Ridge, was as scarce as hens' teeth.

"No link at all," Luke Schrock said with certainty. Rose's son, Luke, was Ruthie's on-again, off-again boyfriend, depending on how much patience she had for him. Lately, it was off-again. Luke seemed almost amused by the activity that was quickly filling up the front yard of his family's property.

Ruthie found Luke's attitude to be callous and would have told him so, but the reporter kept pestering her with questions. When the reporter overheard one policeman tell the other that Ruthie was the only one who had seen and spoken to the man, he cornered her. "What kind of weapon was used to murder him?"

"Murder? Who said anything about a murder?" How

awful. What horrible chain of events had Ruthie set into motion last night?

"It's obvious," the reporter said. "The bedroom window was open. The man was found on the floor. It's a cut-and-dry case, elementary crime solving. Someone came in through the open window, killed him, and left through the front door. And now"—the reporter muttered to himself, taking down notes—"we've got ourselves a John Doe, right here in sleepy Stoney Ridge."

The policemen were unrolling yellow crime-scene caution tape over the front door of the guest cottage. Ruthie knew one of the officers, Matt Lehman. He was talking to Rose, so she started toward them, hearing him tell Rose to call tonight's inn guests to explain that their reservation had to be canceled due to unforeseen circumstances. Then he turned to Ruthie and told her, twice, that she wasn't to talk to anyone about what she'd seen or done until she'd been questioned.

"Right," Ruthie said. "So don't say anything about the blood."

Suddenly the *Stoney Ridge Times* reporter was by her side again. "What blood?"

"The man's forehead was bloody."

Matt Lehman scowled at the reporter, led Ruthie to the backseat of his police car, and told her to sit there, say nothing, do nothing.

Luke Schrock watched Matt lead Ruthie to the car. "Don't say anything without a lawyer present, Ruthie! You have rights!"

Matt turned to Luke with a sigh. He was well acquainted with him. "She's not being arrested."

"Oh," Luke said. He waved a hand in the air. "Well, then, carry on."

Ruthie sat in the police car, arms tightly folded against her chest. *Murder*. She had let an injured man into the cottage, a criminal, probably, only to have him brutally killed in his sleep.

What did I do? she thought miserably.

A little later, Matt Lehman and the other policeman walked over to the police car to question Ruthie about everything she could remember from last night. It was surprising how many details her mind had taken in and filed away without realizing it. The stranger was surprised when she pointed out there was blood dripping down his forehead. He had seemed dazed and confused. Even still, he was very polite, very appreciative.

"Why didn't you ask for the man's name?" Matt said. "Why didn't you ask him for any information?"

For that, she had no answer. It was a set of circumstances that had flustered her, made her feel as if she just wanted to get the man settled in so she could go home. The main house was dark, she was alone, the man seemed like he needed to rest. Looking back, she realized how many mistakes she had made. But the stranger hadn't seemed dangerous.

"Who might have broken into the cottage to murder him?" she asked Matt, and he looked at her strangely.

"What makes you think he was killed?"

"The reporter said so. He called it a homicide."

"Aw, no," Matt said, turning to the other officer. "He's gonna get everyone twitchy."

The officer frowned. "They'll all be hearing things go thump in the night."

"But . . . *was* the man murdered?"

The two police officers exchanged a look. "We aren't sure of anything," Matt said. "Not until we get the coroner's report."

"What about the open window?"

"The innkeeper said there'd been a group in there the other night who trashed the place."

"That was true, but I was the one who cleaned up the cottage yesterday and I didn't notice an open window."

"Ruthie," Matt said. "Are you positive? Absolutely positive?"

"No. I guess not." She wasn't positive of anything anymore.

"Can you think of anything else? Anything at all?"

She squeezed her eyes shut, trying to make herself remember. Her cousin Gabby should have been the one here last night but had moved to Kentucky with her new husband, Dane. With Gabby's unique attention to detail, she could've given the policemen a blow-by-blow detailed report.

Her eyes popped open. "He had no wallet." Something else tickled her memory. "When he reached for his wallet, he pulled out a ticket stub. It was to a Lancaster Barnstormer baseball game." She recognized the logo because her brother Jesse often slipped off to go to home games. She was rather pleased with herself. Such recall!

The officers were not as pleased. In fact, they seemed rather disappointed as they closed their notepads.

Matt handed her a card. "If anything else comes to mind, give me a call." A stain of pink started up the sides of his cheeks. "Or you could have your aunt track me down."

"My aunt?" Her aunts lived in Ohio.

His cheeks went redder still. "The doctor."

Oh! *That* aunt. "You know Dok? How?"

"I've bumped into her a few times at the hospital." His face was now streaked with red blotches.

Oh. *Oh!* Matt Lehman was *sweet* on her aunt! How curious. As soon as the policemen finished with their questions,

Ruthie walked over to the porch of the farmhouse, where Rose King stood waiting for her.

"Are you all right?" Rose asked.

"I suppose so." Ruthie looked at the cottage, at the ribbons of yellow caution tape covering the door. "I'm so sorry. I should never have let that man stay here last night."

Rose put an arm around her shoulders. "You did what you thought was best. Innkeeping is all about dealing with strangers. I'm not sure what I would've done if I'd been in your shoes."

"But look at what it's turned Eagle Hill into. A human zoo."

Rose's gaze swept over the driveway to the cottage. A police car, a handful of horses and buggies, dozens of scooters, clumps of Amish men and women standing together, all curious onlookers. "Well, no doubt it'll all blow over soon."

Ruthie hoped so, but something deep inside her felt this was just the beginning.

~

It was a beautiful July day. Life had its twists and turns, but right now, it was smooth sailing. David Stoltzfus had never felt more content, more optimistic about the future. He felt light as air.

He gave the horse's reins a shake to back up the buggy, eager to return home.

Home. What a beautiful word.

Home to Birdy. His wife.

His wife. It still amazed him, to wake up each day beside this woman, whom he dearly loved and grew more attached to each day. It was a different kind of love he had for Birdy than for Anna, his first wife and the mother of his children.

Different, but in a way, it was more precious. He knew how fleeting life could be, how quickly things could change.

Yes, David thought, he had much to be thankful for: his calling to be bishop, his health, his friends, his family, and now his wife. Life had certainly thrown him some curves, and doubtless there would be further tests, trials, and tribulations. But just for now, on this beautiful summer day, it was to be enjoyed in all its fullness and with all its wonders.

He thought back to this morning, to holding his beautiful little newborn grandson in the crook of his arms. The baby was mewling away when Katrina passed the bundle to David and his crying stopped immediately. He opened his dark blue eyes and peered at him, as if he knew he already had a place deep in his heart.

A grandchild. His second. A boy! His first.

For a long while, he studied this little baby who stared back at him. He lay still, silent, his fists closed tight, his wispy hair fine as silk. David kissed the baby's forehead. He was sure no baby on earth held a candle to how beautiful his little grandchildren were at birth, not even his own six children. He watched the baby's pulsing scalp, counted his tiny toes and fingers. So miniature, so perfect. A miracle.

Too soon, Thelma Beiler, a beloved elderly woman with whom Katrina and her family lived at Moss Hill, insisted he relinquish the baby and return him to his mother. As he placed the baby in Katrina's arms, Thelma gently scolded him like a mother hen, practically shooing him out of the house. "You've got bishop work to tend to." And she was right. He had a full schedule and then some ahead of him.

As David watched Katrina rest the baby against her shoulder, a wellspring of emotion emerged within him, a memory so powerful and vivid that it made his eyes sting and he had to turn away. She reminded him so much of Anna. Maybe that's why people enthused about becoming grandparents: it brought up so many poignant memories, long buried.

The horse nodded her big head, making the harness jingle, snapping his attention to the present. A police car, lights flashing, siren screeching, was flying down the road past Moss Hill's turnoff. How odd. It was rare to see a police car over in this part of Stoney Ridge—it was made up almost entirely of Amish farms. And then his thoughts drifted to Luke Schrock and, perhaps unfairly, he automatically assumed the police visit had something to do with Luke. What might the boy have done now? Luke wasn't a boy, David thought to himself. Nor was he a man. He was stuck somewhere in between.

As he flicked the reins, clucking to the horse, Thistle, to turn left from the driveway onto the road, his mind traveled from Luke's frequent brushes with the law to the farms he passed, all belonging to church members of Stoney Ridge, and settled on the church that bound them together. Two years ago, the little church had weathered a great wound and survived. More than survived. It was thriving. The baptism class this last spring was the largest one in years. No families had moved away for over two years. In fact, the church's population had increased with new families moving in.

He stopped the horse for a moment to watch the pump-jacks atop Moss Hill, bobbing their heads up and down as they pulled oil from deep inside the earth. Those oil pumps—they were a blessing to this community. It astonished him, and humbled him too, to think the oil had been there, all this time, waiting to be discovered. More Amish families had leased their land after having it surveyed for oil traps.

Those oil leases had given Stoney Ridge a fresh wind. The church was able to pay off substantial bills, to build a reserve for future emergencies, and to offer aid to other churches.

The role of bishop still felt new and a little uncomfortable to David, as if he were wearing a coat that was much too big for him. The previous bishop, Freeman Glick, a tall and broad man, had a powerful presence. Even his long beard, gray and flourishing, conferred considerable authority.

David's beard was the opposite of Freeman's, short and trimmed, a little like his own presence, which was not at all authoritative. "Truth discovered is better than truth told" was his motto as a bishop, as a father. He believed in letting church members, including his own children, embark on their own journey to faith. The Lord God desired obedience, but only if it came from the heart.

He felt an unexpected sense of peace and well-being on this beautiful summer morning. A rare day!

Slapping the reins again to get Thistle trotting, he glanced in his rearview mirror and saw a tiny vehicle gain on him from behind his buggy. The driver extended his arm out the side, waving it like a flag. David slowed the horse to see if there was a problem.

The arm belonged to Hank Lapp, driving up the road in a bright yellow golf cart. "HELLO THERE, DAVID!" he yelled in his everyday voice as he passed the horse and buggy. "Somethin's brewing over at the Inn at Eagle Hill. I'm heading there now!"

Hank drove on past him as if it was the most normal thing in the world for an Old Order Amish man to drive himself around in a golf cart.

2

Jesse Stoltzfus heard the harsh shriek of a police siren and pulled himself out from under a buggy to see which direction the sound was coming from. It was a rare occurrence in Stoney Ridge and well worth taking a break from work. He wiped his hands on a greasy rag and stopped short when he saw his two apprentices, Sammy Schrock and Leroy Glick, stroll up the driveway. His black Labrador, C.P., two years old but still a puppy at heart, was already darting across the sheep pasture to greet them.

Jesse's spirits instantly dropped to the basement. These two boys worked at the buggy repair shop. *Work* might not be the right word. Puttered. That's the word. They puttered around Jesse's buggy shop.

Why, he wondered for the umpteenth time, did he ever start taking on apprentices? When the idea was first presented to him, over two years ago, he thought it would be a win-win situation. His buggy repair business needed an extra pair or two of hands and he would like to work fewer hours. Miriam Schrock had asked him to take on her brother Luke, the town's juvenile delinquent, with the hope that Jesse would be a positive influence on him. A sterling example, were Mim's exact words. "Everyone knows Luke is a difficult boy," she said, tears glistening on her sooty eyelashes. How could he say no to Mim, the girl who held his heart in the palm of her hands? He couldn't.

But he should have.

Luke was impossible to manage. Oppositional Defiant Disorder was the diagnosis given to him by the local doctor, Max Finegold, and Luke was delighted. "See?" he said, grinning. "It's not my fault."

To Jesse's way of thinking, Oppositional Defiant Disorder was an excuse that let Luke persist until he got what he wanted and avoid whatever he didn't want. Like work.

There was another apprentice, just as impossible to manage as Luke but for an entirely different reason. Yardstick Yoder had cornered Jesse into the apprenticeship, driving a hard bargain, insisting he wouldn't agree to be the Bent N' Dent's delivery boy unless he also learned buggy repairs. Jesse's father's store was trying to expand customer services, and Yardstick was the one to make deliveries, quick and speedy. He was the fastest boy in town. How could Jesse say no to that? He couldn't.

But he should have.

Optimistic to a fault, Jesse started the apprenticeships with high hopes for success: Yardstick Yoder, who had a strong work ethic, would settle into work at the store. Mim Schrock would feel beholden to Jesse for being kind to her difficult brother, Luke, who had no work ethic at all.

Sadly, Jesse's high hopes were mistaken.

Those two boys were oil and vinegar; they couldn't stand

being anywhere near each other—all because of Ruthie, his sister, whom they both had serious crushes on. Jesse spent most of his time keeping them occupied with tasks at opposite ends of the buggy shop just so they wouldn't irritate each other. Once, they nearly came to blows over something as ridiculous as the tune one of them was whistling.

And then everything changed.

His sister Ruthie concluded that Luke was a Person of Interest to her—a POI—and Yardstick was no longer a POI. Stunned by her cold rejection, Yardstick decided that the problem did not lie with him but with Ruthie and, by extension, with the entire Stoltzfus family. He quit the buggy shop, he quit the Bent N' Dent, and he took a job at the Hay & Grain.

Not to be outdone, Luke quit too. If the job was beneath someone as low as Yardstick Yoder, he said, it was certainly beneath him.

Personally, Jesse could not imagine what Ruthie saw in either one of them. It wasn't only that the boys never had much on their minds, but they did not seem to have the proper awe and admiration for the important task of buggy repair work. Not the way they should have.

Never again, Jesse decided, would he take on apprentices just to make a woman happy. Any woman.

Alas alack. His resolve was promptly challenged.

As soon as Birdy, his father's new wife, learned of the two vacancies, she paid a call to Jesse to ask if he would hire her nephew, Leroy, who sorely needed someone like Jesse in his life.

And he buckled.

And then Mim Schrock paid him another call, apologizing

for her brother Luke and pleading with him to take on her other brother, Sammy. "Before it's too late," she said, batting her eyelashes at him in that way that made his stomach feel like Jell-O. "Before Luke's influence over him is permanent."

Again, Jesse buckled.

It was another grave mistake in his brief management career.

Jesse had spent the last couple of years diligently improving the disastrous reputation of the buggy repair shop. He had inherited the business from Hank Lapp, a good-hearted but easily distractable man who was untroubled by matters of timeliness. Most of the Amish of Stoney Ridge, Jesse had learned, had taken their buggy business over to Gap or Leola. When he did a little mental calculation, he realized that Hank had lost himself a substantial revenue stream for no good reason other than laziness. Jesse wanted to convince local residents that they didn't need to go elsewhere for buggy repairs. He could use the help of good apprentices.

Unfortunately, he did not have good apprentices. He had less-than-average apprentices. Leroy Glick and Sammy Schrock were obsessed with fast girls, fast horses, and fast cars, and they left grease marks from their dirty hands on the freshly painted, pristine walls of the buggy shop. Even more irritating, he had found greasy fingerprints on the cupboard where he kept his private stash of snacks.

How often did he need to point out the rags to those boys? Yesterday was an example. "When you finish working on a buggy," Jesse had told them both, "wash your hands before you touch other things. What's so hard about that?"

"Not hard at all," Sammy said, brushing back his floppy brown hair. "I always wash my hands."

Both boys, aged fourteen, looked as though they had barely entered adolescence, other than a whisper of untended fuzz on their upper lips—something they were quite proud of.

Jesse turned to Leroy, who was enormous, a great pumpkin of a boy, as round as Sammy was thin. "Then is it you? Are you the one who leaves handprints on my cupboard?"

"Not me," Leroy said, lifting his hands to reveal greasy palms. He had to talk around a big wad of bubblegum in his mouth. "I wash my hands more often than Sammy. Twice as often. Maybe three times."

Jesse decided there might be something essential missing in those boys' brains. Something significant. An axle, a rod, a wheel. Something like that.

Today, as the boys sauntered up the driveway, late as usual, they stopped halfway up. Leroy did a little dance step and Sammy tried to copy it. Jesse whistled for C.P., but the dog ignored him, dashed between the apprentices, his whole body wagging with excitement. As far as dogs went, C.P. was not good for much. He wasn't the brightest, he wasn't the most obedient, he still chewed up any shoe left unguarded, but Jesse had wanted to believe he was, at least, loyal. Not true. Fickle, fickle dog.

Just as Jesse was about to shout to the apprentices to hurry up and get to work, another police car sped down the road, siren blaring. The apprentices stopped their dance jig and swiveled around to watch the car race along. Not a minute or two later, the siren stopped.

Leroy looked at Sammy, eyes wide. "I think it stopped near your house. It's down by Eagle Hill."

"Let's go!" Sammy said, and the two of them bolted down the driveway, C.P. on their heels.

24

Well, Jesse thought, watching them as they veered onto the road, to quote his predecessor Hank Lapp, *these buggies aren't dying. They'll still be there when you get back.*

He hurried to catch up with the apprentices and his fickle dog to find out what the ruckus was all about.

❧

Later that day, at home, Ruthie heard a knock on the door and went to answer it. Rose King, the owner of the Inn at Eagle Hill, stood on the porch with a tired look on her lovely face, dark circles below her eyes.

"Has something happened? Did the coroner finish the autopsy? It was a murder, wasn't it? Oh my goodness, oh my goodness." Ruthie's heart started pounding as she stepped aside to let Rose come in. All day long, she had felt rattled by the morning's gruesome discovery.

Rose waved off Ruthie's anxieties. "Slow down! First, I haven't heard anything. Matt Lehman told me the coroner's report will take awhile, apparently because he's backed up."

Thoughts collided in Ruthie's head. The coroner was backed up? A wave of nausea rolled through her as she visualized stacks and stacks of dead bodies in a cold morgue. She had never been comfortable around dead bodies, despite the fact that she had been to plenty of open-casket viewings and funerals in her seventeen years. No matter how lifelike the undertaker tried to make a corpse, it looked weird and smelled awful.

Rose sat down at the kitchen table. "There's a favor I need to ask of you."

"Anything. Anything at all." Ruthie couldn't do enough favors for Rose. She loved working at the inn. She loved it when new guests arrived. There was always someone new to talk to, something new to learn about.

"The inn's next guest has reserved the cottage for a month. I called and told him what happened, about the stranger who died in the cottage last night. I was sure he would cancel. Would you believe he wasn't bothered in the least? In fact, he's already on his way. If I turn this guest away, we'll lose a month's booking." She bit her lip. "Ruthie, we need the income. So I wondered, do you think he could stay in Jesse's old room until the cottage is given the all clear? Matt Lehman said it should only be a few days until the coroner is . . . well, until he gets caught up."

Another wave of nausea hit Ruthie at the vision in her mind of dead bodies. "I'll have to ask Birdy and Dad, but . . . I don't think they'd object." A thought occurred to her. "Does he have proper identification?" She wasn't going to make the same mistake twice.

"His name is Patrick Kelly. He's from Canada. He already paid me, in full, for the month."

"But he's coming alone? That seems odd when it's not hunting season."

"He's not interested in hunting. Not for game, anyway. That much I know." Rose hesitated. "He says he wants to become Amish. That's why he's coming to stay for a full month. He wants to immerse himself in the culture. That was the word he used. 'Immersed.' Like a teabag in hot water."

Ruthie knocked her forehead on the table, once, twice, three times. "Not another," she groaned. Why did anyone think he could, or should, convert to the Amish? So many people came to the Inn at Eagle Hill with the intention of becoming Amish. They poked around the countryside, visited quilt shops, and returned at the end of the day to wax romantic about their longing to simplify life. Ruthie listened to them, answered their silly questions, and masterfully hid a smug smile. She knew how these stories played out.

Three weeks ago, two sisters had arrived with the same determination as this Patrick Kelly fellow. The sisters peppered Ruthie with questions about her life as if she was an endangered species at the zoo, asked if they could attend a church service. "Why, certainly," she told them, barely able to swallow a smile. Imagine these two sisters, with highlighted hair and French manicures, sitting on a backless hard bench in a barn filled with horseflies . . . for three-plus hours! But then a heat wave rolled in, spiking the temperature with hair-curling humidity. The cottage had no air conditioning, no ceiling fan . . . and . . . *whoosh!* The sisters had a change of heart. They opted to leave early and head back to city life. Going Amish had lost its romantic appeal.

As far as Ruthie was concerned, there was *nothing* romantic about being Amish. She felt like a bird trapped in a cage, eager to break free and fly away. The only one who could understand how she felt was her father's sister Ruth, for whom she was named. Her aunt Dok, an emergency room doctor at the local hospital, was everything she wanted to be. Dok led a purposeful, valuable, significant life. A non-Amish life.

"So . . . ," Rose said, pulling Ruthie out of her muse of discontent, "will you ask your dad and Birdy? See if they're comfortable with having a stranger in the house?"

"I'm sure it's no problem at all," Ruthie hastened to say. "You know that Birdy thinks nobody's a stranger once you know their name."

Rose stood. "Tell Birdy that Patrick Kelly sounded . . . nice. Friendly. Not someone I would hesitate to host in my home, if we had the room for him."

Unlike the bloody soon-to-be-murdered mobster whom Ruthie had let in. She was sure that's what Rose was thinking but was too kind to say.

Rose took a few steps, then turned at the doorjamb. "Do you think you could ask Birdy about it as soon as possible? Patrick Kelly is due in this afternoon at the bus stop on Main Street. I told him someone would pick him up."

The clip-clop sound of a horse approaching up the driveway drew Ruthie to the window. "There she is now. Let's go ask."

What a day. It began for David Stoltzfus with the birth of his beautiful new grandson. A new life, just beginning. It was ending with the untimely, unfortunate death of a stranger, right across the street.

David couldn't shake a feeling of uneasiness. Certainly, the muddy circumstances that surrounded the man's death were to blame. There was no point in borrowing trouble, no point in assuming that it had been an actual crime, not until the coroner's report came back.

But on the other hand, the entire thing sounded suspicious. The blood on the man's forehead, the lack of any identification. His daughter Ruthie said she overheard the reporter say that most likely the stranger had been in a tussle, then whoever had injured him had come to the inn later to finish off the job.

If that were true—and David knew enough about such

SUZANNE WOODS FISHER

matters to not jump to conclusions on unfounded fears—but if that *were* true, could Ruthie be in any danger as the sole witness?

David was willing to let the Inn at Eagle Hill's guest stay at their home for the time being, but he also insisted on being the one to pick him up at the bus stop. After ten years as an ordained leader, he felt he had become a pretty good judge of character. If he brought a stranger into his home, one filled with young girls, he was going to make absolutely sure he felt comfortable with him.

He pulled the horse over to the side of the road to wait for the bus to arrive and thought about the other stranger who had created ripples of anxiety. So odd. No one knew who *that* guest at the inn was, where he came from, how he died. Or why he died.

He was grateful that Galen King was the one who went into the cottage this morning and not his daughter Ruthie.

Ruthie's face suddenly swam into view. Right now, he worried about her more than any of his other children. David had found a GED practice book in a trunk in the barn's tack room and had no doubt it belonged to Ruthie. Seventeen now, she was the one who was in the barn most often because she milked their dairy cow, and she was the one with the lively, active, insatiable mind. She was the one most intrigued by life outside the boundaries of the Amish world.

After Ruthie had finished eighth grade, David hoped she would work at the Bent N' Dent, but she took a job at Edith Fisher Lapp's chicken and egg farm. Ruthie assumed she would be collecting eggs and caring for the hens. Edith gave her the job of ending the life of old layers and preparing the hens for the freezer. That job only lasted one week but gave Ruthie nightmares for a month. She kept dreaming that chickens were coming after her to seek vengeance.

She worked for two weeks at the Sweet Tooth Bakery but had trouble sticking to the proper suggestions to use with customers. One of the bakery girls heard her discuss calorie counts with a customer instead of offering, "Better take two cinnamon rolls. They're going quickly." The customer did *ask*, Ruthie defended. She was let go.

Brief, but that short stint at the Sweet Tooth Bakery gave Ruthie a taste for working "out." She wanted to interact with as many non-Amish as she could. She loved the sound of foreign accents, the close-up glimpses of lives far removed from her own. When she heard there was a job available at the Inn at Eagle Hill, she begged David to let her work there.

David held himself partially responsible. Maybe more than partially. When he moved his family from Ohio to Lancaster County, he hadn't fully realized how distracting a place it would be for his family, especially for someone like Ruthie. Lancaster County was far less isolated, with far more interaction with tourists. Ruthie kept postponing baptism class (postpone? or avoid? he wasn't sure which) and David respected her wishes. He wouldn't interfere, but oh, *how* he prayed for her.

Even more so now that his sister, nicknamed Dok, had become such a big part of his family's life.

It was a great blessing to have reunited with his sister, but with every blessing came a burden. Dok and Ruthie had a special connection. He wasn't troubled that Dok's influence over Ruthie would pull her away from faith, but he was concerned that Ruthie would leave the Amish church and all that it meant: the security of community, the comfort and blessings of family. His sister was a woman of sincere faith, and she firmly believed that one didn't have to be Amish to live a life of faith.

There were many Amish who would disagree with Dok's perspective, many who believed that only the Amish were the true believers, but David wasn't one of them. In fact, he encouraged the youth to get baptized and join the church only if their whole heart was in it. The worst thing of all, he was convinced, was to be half Amish. To sit on a fence for most of one's life, partly in, partly out. Did not the Scriptures warn men of fence sitting? "So then because thou art lukewarm, and neither cold nor hot, I will spew thee out of my mouth."

He heard the approaching bus before he saw it. It rolled around the corner and came to a squeaky halt at the stop. The doors opened and one person jumped off. A young man. A very English-looking man, with short-clipped hair, khaki pants, a crisply ironed blue button-down shirt, a fat brown backpack slung over his shoulder. In one hand he held a birdcage with a large black bird inside.

That sight alone, David thought with a smile, would endear this young visitor to Birdy, his wife. Her childhood nickname had been bestowed on her because she was passionate about anything with feathers and wings. He hardly gave much thought to birds until he met Birdy, but now he spotted them everywhere and tried to identify them with the tools she'd taught him: size and shape, color pattern, behavior, habitat. He still couldn't identify much more than a bright red male cardinal, but he found himself enjoying bird-watching. On buggy rides, on walks in the woods. No matter how complicated life became—and boy, did it ever—Birdy had a way of reminding him of its simple joys.

31

The young man strode right toward David's buggy and went to the open window, shifted the birdcage to his left arm, and thrust his right hand out for a shake. "I'm Patrick Kelly. I've got a reservation at the Inn at Eagle Hill. That is, as soon as the police give it the all clear."

A little startled by the young man's direct manner, David reached a hand out to return his shake. "David Stoltzfus."

"The bishop?"

David nodded. "How did you know?"

"I've been a subscriber to the *Budget* for four years now. I've been reading about Stoney Ridge for a while." He pointed to the empty seat next to David. "Mind if I get in?" He walked around the horse and slid open the buggy door before David had a chance to answer. He tossed his backpack into the backseat and settled into the passenger seat beside David, resting the birdcage on his lap.

David ran through the identifying tools for this bird. Size and shape: bigger than a robin, smaller than a crow. Color: glossy black feathers, yellow-orange bill, yellow streaks on the sides of its head, fleshy wattles, bright yellow feet. Behavior: perched on a wooden rod. Habitat: a birdcage. Nope. He had no idea what kind of bird this was.

The bird made a few clucking noises, a whistle, then suddenly burst out with a very clear phrase: "This is the day the Lord hath made!"

David's jaw dropped. "It talks?"

"Yes and no." Patrick grinned. "She mimics. This is Nyna, my common hill mynah bird. One of the world's best birds for mimicking the human voice. I've taught Nyna to quote Scripture. That's the verse we were working on during the long bus ride from Canada. It's her longest phrase so far."

David laughed. "Wonders never cease. Imagine that! A bird quoting the Holy Book. She might be useful to keep people awake during church." If he had harbored any doubts about letting this young man stay at his house, they just evaporated. "My wife will be interested to meet Nyna the Mynah. She's a bird lover, a true birder. In fact, her name is Birdy."

"Oh boy." Patrick beamed. "This is great. Just great. I can't tell you how excited I am to be here. I've been planning this trip for years. Looking forward to it for a very long time. It's my defining moment."

David flicked the reins and clucked his tongue to get Thistle moving. "How so?"

"A few years ago, my parents took our family on a trip to Lancaster County." He shot David a grin. "My mother has regretted the trip ever since."

"It wasn't a good trip?"

"Just the opposite. It was the best trip of my life. That was the moment I decided I was going to become Amish. I was fifteen at the time, and my parents insisted that I wait until I . . . well . . . until I was a little older before I returned to Pennsylvania." He grinned at David. "So here I am." He looked out the storm front, straight ahead. "My parents have given me thirty days. But as far as I'm concerned, there's no turning back. I'm going Amish."

Well, well, David thought. *Interesting.*

It started out as just a ride home. Luke Schrock was passing by Ruthie Stoltzfus after she visited Moss Hill to meet her newborn nephew and offered her a ride in his buggy. He slowed down as they approached the turnoff to their homes. "How about if we drive up to Blue Lake Pond and talk?"

"Luke," Ruthie said in her crisp *don't-pretend-we-are-still-dating* voice.

"What? I just want to talk to you. We never get a chance to talk at the inn without Sammy or somebody buzzing around us."

She sighed. That was the truth. Privacy was an oh-so-rare luxury. "Fine. But we can't stay too long."

He drove past the turnoff to their respective houses and out toward the lake, turning onto a dirt road that led up to a very, very private lookout spot, a place the two of them had discovered on a hike last summer. She wondered if Luke had brought other girls here since she had told him she wanted to take a break.

"I just now noticed you're wearing my favorite-colored

dress. That shade of blue always makes your eyes look like the color of a tropical sea. I don't know how I missed seeing it when you got in the buggy. I must have been blinded by your dazzling smile."

Thinking that she didn't remember smiling at him, she watched him climb out of the buggy. Tall, tall, tall, a full five or six inches taller than her father or brother. Luke held himself with the squared shoulders of a prince. He had midnight black hair that curled at the edges under his straw hat, and laugh lines at the corners of his sapphire blue eyes. He was so strong, he picked her up out of the buggy and swung her around. And then they both laughed as Luke set her down.

"I've missed you!" he said.

Well, she'd been right here. He was the one who had disappeared for the last few days. "Where were you last night as I was coping with a bloody stranger at the inn?"

"I told you. Out with my friends." He kept his hands on her hips and his eyes on her lips. "So . . . tell me again why we're on a break?" In his eyes was a plea. She felt it more than she saw it. He just wanted it to be nice between them again.

The tops of Ruthie's ears started to feel warm. That meant they were turning pink, the only outward sign that she felt affected by him. She would never, ever, ever tell him about that betrayal signal. As far as he was concerned, she was in complete control of her emotions.

The truth was that all kinds of emotions swirled around inside her. So many that she kept them tightly stuffed down. Sometimes she felt as if her feelings were like a bottle of shaken soda pop. If the cap came off, she might explode.

She felt as if she were skydiving and never entirely sure her chute would open in time—a ridiculous analogy because she had never been skydiving and probably never would, but she had read about it once and realized that's exactly what it meant to be Luke Schrock's girlfriend: complete uncertainty of what was coming next and very worried about the landing. She had become the kind of girl she didn't even like: jealous and suspicious. It was one of the reasons she told him she wanted to take a break.

"I miss you so much, Ruthie," Luke said. "I miss *us*. This break we're taking—the one you said you wanted to take— I've used it to go out with a few other girls. They're great girls, not a thing wrong with them, but I only went out with them a couple of times before I lost interest."

Girls. How many had there been? Ruthie felt a miserable wave of jealousy. She was the one who wanted to break up; she knew it meant he would pursue other girls. They were both free to date others. The difference was that no one held her interest, not the way Luke could. She wiggled out of his grasp and took a step back. "And why," she asked, "are you telling me this?"

"I want another chance," Luke said. He swallowed, seeming to be overcome by genuine emotion, a rare thing. "I want you to be my one and only. Ruthie, you're the best person I know. You're the person who gets me like no one else gets me. You can't deny that we get along so well." He reached out and took her hands in his. "There's no way you can tell me all your feelings for me have died."

Oh Luke. There were things she missed about being his girl—his eyes shining with mischief, his irreverent sense of humor, his over-the-top romantic gestures. But there were things about him she didn't miss—that never-being-sure gut feeling that he might be spending time with other girls if she didn't go with him to parties. But the truth was that she hated the parties. Luke's life was an endless party.

"Of course my feelings haven't died for you, Luke." He was one of those guys impossible to stay mad at, which in itself was maddening. "And I do understand you. But, Luke . . . I'm not sure you understand *me*."

"Understand you? Of course I understand you. I've always understood you. You're beautiful and smart and witty. You like bonfires and buggy races and . . ." He searched for other words. "Books."

"Bonfires and buggy races?" She yanked her hands out of his. "Luke, that's what you like to do."

"But you do like books."

"Yes. But so do you." She looked him right in the eye. "I wanted a break because you were drinking too much. Have you stopped?"

He glanced down at the tops of his boots. "I'm not going to lie. I haven't stopped. Not entirely. I'm getting there, though. I know you think I can't change—"

"People don't change," Ruthie said. "They only get more so."

"That's not true. Have a little faith in me, Ruthie. For you, I'll do anything. And you have to admit that you miss us being together too." He leaned toward her and took her hand, cupping it with both of his and holding it close to his heart. "Just a little?"

To be honest with herself, there were things about Luke she would always be attracted to. In particular, his essential "I don't care what anybody thinks-ness." But was that enough?

"A little. But not everything. Especially not the drinking." She reclaimed her hand. "It's getting late. I need you to take me home."

He nodded, then helped her into the buggy. She was startled and—what a surprise!—disappointed that he was giving up so easily.

⌒〜⌒

Leroy Glick tapped Jesse on the shoulder, leaving a greasy handprint on his freshly washed and ironed blue shirt. Jesse was particular about his clothing. The two apprentices were always tapping him on the shoulder with their dirty hands, and it immensely annoyed him.

"If you want to ask me a question," Jesse had said countless times, "you can always use my name. You don't have to put your dirty hands on my clean clothes."

Leroy would look at his hands, surprised to discover that they were filthy, apologize, but it never changed. Sometimes, most times, Jesse felt he was fighting a losing battle.

"There's someone who wants to see you," Leroy said, chewing a large wad of pink bubble gum—a disgusting habit. "He's outside."

Jesse put down his wrench and wiped his hands on a cloth. He had been involved in a particularly delicate operation—adjusting the taillights on a buggy with a switch panel on the dashboard. He didn't like to be interrupted during delicate operations. They required his full attention.

"Jesse, he knew my name."

"Who?"

Leroy pointed to the door. "That guy. He knew my name."

Jesse pointed to Leroy's coveralls. "Think that's why?" After daily arguments between the apprentices about whose coverall was whose, Jesse had taped a piece of masking tape with their names written on each one.

Jesse went outside and blinked a few times while his eyes adjusted to the bright sunlight. A young English fellow was walking around the old sisters' buggy, peering inside. "Are you looking for me?"

"I am if you're Jesse Stoltzfus, the highly regarded buggy repairman of Stoney Ridge."

Jesse felt a little taken aback by this fellow's forthrightness. Swooping in on top of that feeling came one of pleasure. He did not mind receiving a compliment or two. "I am. I'm Jesse."

"I'm Patrick Kelly."

"So what can I do for you?"

Patrick looked at the buggy. "I'd like you to teach me how to drive a buggy. For pay, of course."

Jesse barely suppressed an eye roll. Another whacky tourist. "Two towns over, there's a Mennonite who gives buggy rides for tourists."

Patrick shook his head. "That's not what I want."

"Well, you don't have to pay me. I'll take you out on a ride. Or I can get my apprentices to take you." Those two needed a great deal of practice to improve their social skills. They could be appallingly rude. The other day they told Edith Fisher Lapp that her buggy wouldn't need new shock absorbers so often if she just lost some weight. Edith was outraged and complained mightily to Jesse.

"No, no," the fellow said. "I'm not being clear. I want to learn how to drive a buggy myself. I need lessons. Regular lessons. That's why I want to pay you. I realize you have an important job to do here. I want to make it worth your time."

Jesse tilted his head. "Why in the world would you want to learn how to drive a buggy?" Why would anyone bother if they weren't Amish?

39

"Because I'm planning to become a convert to the Amish church."

Jesse swallowed a laugh. Later, he would have to tell his sister Ruthie about this guy. So many people thought they wanted to become Amish, until they actually came to an Amish community and saw what it really looked like, up close and personal. Within a few days, 100 percent of Amish wannabes left for home. One hundred percent. "You know, my dad's the bishop."

"Right. David Stoltzfus. He picked me up at the bus stop yesterday afternoon. I also need someone to tutor me in Penn Dutch."

"You're trying to learn the language?" This fellow was a funny duck.

"Yes. In thirty days. So I need someone who would be very determined, very hard on me. Someone who won't cut me any slack. Any suggestions?" His gaze swept over Windmill Farm, ending at the sheep pasture. "I don't have time to waste."

"My sister Ruthie. She's as tough as they come. By day two, you'll be begging for mercy."

"Excellent. Just the kind of tutor I need."

Jesse rubbed his chin, deep in thought. "Have you told my dad about your plans to convert?"

"Yes, sure. Absolutely. He said we could talk more about it as I settled in. In fact, I'm staying in your room. While the Inn at Eagle Hill is . . ." He searched for the right words.

"Under police investigation." Jesse scratched his head. "Well, I suppose I could teach you how to handle a horse and buggy in thirty days." Who knows? Maybe this fellow would end up being the first Amish wannabe who actually converted.

"I'll pay top dollar."

That changed everything. Jesse smiled at Patrick Kelly. "Well, then. I definitely think we could make some kind of arrangement."

Ruthie set the bucket underneath Moomoo, their sweet and docile Jersey cow, and sat on the milking stool. She wiped Moomoo's teats with an iodine solution, dried them, and leaned her forehead against the side of the cow as she pulled to start the flow of milk. Morning and evening, this mindless routine in the barn gave her time alone to think.

It was a strange thing about being a teenager. You were supposed to be figuring out your life, but you had no idea what that could mean. Or how a decision you made today could affect your life in ten years, or twenty, or fifty. Or what to do when you had an inkling that something was wrong.

Like . . . why did she think Luke was hiding something about where he was the other night, when the stranger died at the inn? It wasn't anything he said, it was the way he averted his eyes when she asked him where he'd been. Those blue eyes of his always seemed to swim with a secret.

Was Luke with another girl? Probably. But that couldn't really be considered cheating after she told him she was no longer his girlfriend. She had no claim on Luke and made sure he knew that.

She heard someone call her name and lifted her head above the cow's back. It was the inn's displaced guest, Patrick Kelly. He stood in the open barn door with the afternoon sun streaming down behind him, making his appearance almost . . . angelic. She smiled at such an odd impression. She wasn't

41

sure what an angel would look like, but she had assumed he would be dramatic looking. And that definitely did not fit Patrick's description. The very opposite!

His was a finely chiseled face: high sculptured cheekbones, a long narrow nose, wide-spaced brown eyes with thick, long lashes, rimmed by dark brows that matched his short brown hair. He had a lean, lanky build—so unlike the stocky, muscled German men in her church. His skin was milk pale, so different from the perpetual suntanned look of an Amish farmer.

Even his hands were unusual. Most Amish, man or woman, girl or boy, had thick fingers, shaped and honed by hard work. Patrick had long, tapered fingers, and his palms were without calluses. She had noticed how soft and smooth they were when she shook hands with him last evening. Those soft hands, they struck her as an odd thing for a man.

Plus, he must be crazy. Why would anyone—anyone!—convert to Amish when they weren't born Amish? It *was* crazy. She had almost laughed out loud when she heard him tell the family what his plans were last night, but fortunately, she caught herself just in time.

She felt a little guilty about wanting to laugh, as if she was trying not to laugh at a funeral. He seemed so earnest, but what a ridiculous notion! If her brother Jesse were at last night's supper, they would have made a bet to see how long it would take, or what trigger, before Patrick packed his bags to head home. One hot day spent harvesting field corn? Two? Or maybe the first Sunday morning three-hour church service on a backless bench. He'd be on the next bus to Canada. Gone!

Ruthie made herself *think* the comment and not say it. That would be her new rule, going forward, starting right at that moment. She was going to try to keep her critical opinions to herself. As her dad often reminded her, *Mer kann denke was mer will, awwer mer daerf net zu laut denke.* *Think what you please but not too loud.*

Patrick Kelly walked around to where Ruthie sat by the cow. "I was wondering if you might be willing to give me lessons in Penn Dutch."

Ruthie had to look over her shoulder to see him. "And a hello to you too."

He smiled. "My apologies. I can be a little task oriented. I'm eager to get started. There's no time to waste."

"Why me?"

Gliding the flat of his hand along Moomoo's bony spine, he walked to the front of the cow so she didn't have to keep craning her neck to see him. "Your brother Jesse recommended you."

"You've already met Jesse?"

"Yes. He was top on my list of people to meet in person. He's going to teach me how to drive a buggy."

She had to swallow a smile. "You have a list of people to meet?"

"Yes. Does that seem odd?"

"No, not at all." Yes. This guy was weird.

Weird, but in sort of a charming way.

But then again, there was that bird.

Nyna the Mynah. After dinner last night, he coaxed the bird to talk and it spewed out short Bible verses. Birdy, Lydie, Emily, and Molly were over the moon about it. Ruthie thought it curious—in her orbit of friends, she couldn't think of any guy who would have the patience to teach a bird to mimic words. Yes, Patrick Kelly was . . . weird.

"What do you think?"

She took her time answering as she finished milking, focusing her attention on the cow. "That brings up another point. If you do convert to the Amish, what are you going to do for a living? Everyone works hard, you know." She pulled the pail from beneath the cow. Steamy wisps from the hot milk, fragrant and fresh smelling, floated between them.

"I'm not at all concerned about that." He stared at her, saying nothing, and she waited for a feeling of awkwardness to set in at the lengthening silence. But it didn't. The oddest sense of ease flowed between them, and something told her such a situation wasn't an unusual occurrence for him—this tendency not to fill every moment with words. "For now, I've saved up enough money to last for the duration."

What did that mean? The duration. She was just about to ask when he added, "I'll pay for the lessons. I don't expect you to give up your valuable time without compensation."

Why not? Right now, it felt good. Or not good, exactly, but unusual and interesting, which might be the most she could hope for this summer . . . other than the distressing homicide at the Inn at Eagle Hill. But there didn't seem to be anything more she could do about that particular situation. She poured the milk into a large stainless steel container. "I guess so."

"Oh boy." Patrick grinned. "That's great. Just great! There's no time like the present. Let's start today."

4

The morning sun shone brightly, hinting of a hot afternoon. David Stoltzfus arrived at the Bent N' Dent and unlocked the door, breathing in deeply the smells of fresh-dried herbs and spices that permeated the store. His favorite smell. No, better than that. It was his favorite place.

One of the things David enjoyed about running a store was its reflection of everything he loved about being Amish. A store was the hub of a community's wheel. In less than 1,000 square feet, he tried his best to provide anything and everything that might be needed, which meant that every inch, floor to ceiling, was utilized.

It was all based on the goal of being helpful. To David's way of thinking, being helpful was an act of grace. Tangible evidence of the loving, kind character of God. That was why he was very open to most—but not all—of the ideas of his son Jesse, along with Hank Lapp, as they sought to expand customer service. A home delivery service was one of the first plans that actually worked—unlike the used self-serve frozen yogurt machine, jerry-rigged to work by aid of a generator, that kept shooting liquid yogurt out the top. Hank Lapp was no longer allowed to make unsupervised purchases for the Bent N' Dent.

The original plan was for Yardstick Yoder, fastest boy in Stoney Ridge, to make those deliveries. It worked quite nicely for a short time, until Yardstick was offered a job making deliveries for the Hay & Grain at triple the hourly wage that he made at the Bent N' Dent. David was sorry to lose Yardstick as an employee, especially because his Bent N' Dent customers were quickly hooked on the home delivery concept. More often than not, David ended up being the delivery boy. In a good way, he touched base with many families he would normally see only on Sundays. In a less-than-good way, it meant he was often home later than expected. Fortunately, Birdy was a very forgiving wife.

She was more than forgiving. She was a wonderful wife, a faithful companion. Just last night, she was in her favorite chair, mending the hem of Lydie's dress, as he sat at his desk, thinking through a sermon based on Genesis 1. He read aloud verse 21: "'And God created great whales, and every living creature that moveth, which the waters brought forth abundantly, after their kind, and every winged fowl after his kind: and God saw that it was good.'" He swatted an annoying mosquito that kept circling and buzzing around him. "Really? Every creature?"

"Yes," Birdy said firmly, without looking up from her mending. "We are all creatures from the same Creator. Mosquitos and great whales have their place in the goodness that God has provided."

The goodness God has provided.

Birdy was right—that was what the Bible said: *And God*

saw that it was good. Even mosquitos—a creature David despised. When he thought of the creation of the animal world, he generally thought only of those creatures that inspired marvel and mystery—the sight of a bald eagle soaring in the sky, the bright colors of a graceful monarch butterfly bouncing around the kitchen garden. Never once had he considered a mosquito to be a creature of awe. Terror, annoyance, but never awe. Never part of the goodness God provided.

It dawned on David how he tended to classify the created world according to his conveniences, his likes and dislikes. He rethought the focus of his sermon, to encourage his church members to see everything as interconnected and complementary in the world of God's goodness. Without realizing it, Birdy provided that kind of inspiration to him. He had asked God for the gift of a wife. God had given him a gift beyond anything he could imagine asking.

He started the coffeepot brewing for the old codgers who should be arriving soon. He checked the messages on the answering machine in his storeroom office, hoping to hear something from Matt Lehman about what caused the death of the stranger at the Inn at Eagle Hill.

Nothing.

David settled into his desk in the storeroom, filling out some orders, when his sister Dok peeked her head through the partially open door. "Have a minute?"

"For you, always." He pulled out a chair for her. It still amazed him that his sister was in Stoney Ridge—of all places!—and that they had been reconnected after years of silence and separation. Her Amish upbringing made her a favorite among the hospital staff—as soon as they realized she could speak Penn Dutch, a nickname emerged: Dokdor Fraa, Penn Dutch for "lady doctor." It was shortened to Dok, a handle that David's own family quickly picked up because it made it easier for all to distinguish between Ruthie, his daughter, and Ruth, his sister for whom she was named.

This morning, Dok was dressed in blue scrubs, which was not at all unusual, even when she wasn't at the hospital. David was often caught by the irony of seeing his sister in the modest, nondescript garb. Dok, who so wanted to be independent from anything Amish, was still most comfortable in a type of uniform. "Want a cup of coffee?"

"Yes, thanks. By the way, how are you managing your ulcer? Any new pain or discomfort?"

David poured her a cup of coffee and handed it to her with a frown. "Are you here as a doctor or as a sister?"

She smiled. "Both. Always."

Something was on Dok's mind, but he knew not to press. She would tell him in her own sweet time. He waited patiently, watching her settle into the chair across from him and stretch her legs out. In her midforties, his sister was quite a lovely woman, with a delicate, heart-shaped face. A sweet Valentine face, he realized, that belied her feisty spirit. Her hair was strawberry blond, like Ruthie's and Emily's, with eyes that were blueberry blue. She had the Stoltzfus strong nose and high cheekbones, much like his own.

She leaned back in her chair and tented her fingertips. "David, something happened a few weeks ago at the hospital. Something that I've been waiting to discuss with you until after it was all done."

"Go ahead."

"A patient came into the emergency room. A ninety-three-year-old woman with dementia. She had fallen and twisted her ankle badly."

David nodded.

"She's Amish. From your church. Lives with her sisters, also quite elderly, who watch over her."

His mind ran through possible identities and came up with one face. "Ella?" He was aware that she had hurt her ankle and was using a walker, but it wasn't a serious injury. "That happened a while ago."

"Yes." Dok rapped her fingers on the desk. "Her primary care physician was notified."

"Dr. Finegold?" Max Finegold had a medical practice down the road from the Bent N' Dent. The Amish went to him, but reluctantly.

"Exactly. Dr. Finegold. He insisted that Ella be sent to a nursing home. He said she wasn't safe. I objected, strongly. I explained that she has her sisters' help and, by remaining in her home, she would be in familiar surroundings. I didn't think he should take her away from everyone and everything that was meaningful to her. I suggested that he order some physical therapy. Maybe some occupational therapy too."

"What did he say?" David didn't really need to ask. He could guess. Max Finegold was always at odds with the Amish way of handling illness and injury, birth and death.

"He said, and I quote," she lowered her voice to a growl, "'She doesn't need physical therapy. She's not going to remember how to do anything.'" Her voice returned to normal. "And then he started to fill out an order to have her sent to a nursing home."

This part of the story he was not aware of. "So . . ."

"So I told him that it was time for him to retire. That he'd gotten too old to learn."

David's brows lifted. "And how did he take that suggestion?"

"He slammed down his pen and told me that he agreed with me. And that if I think I'm so all-knowing, why don't I buy his practice so he can move to Florida and golf year-round." She grinned. "He might have used more expressive language."

Oh, boy. David folded his arms across his chest. "What happened then?"

She shrugged. "Well, a few days later, I bought it from him." She glanced at him. "Stop staring at me like that."

David didn't know what to say. He couldn't believe what she had just said. "You bought his practice?" Max Finegold's practice? His office was just down the road from the Bent N' Dent! Why, from David's office window, he could see when Dr. Finegold's car rolled in or out, or watch his patients come and go. It was *that* close in proximity.

"Yes. You don't seem particularly pleased."

"It's not that. I'm just . . . stunned."

"I'm not hanging up my spurs."

"Had you been thinking about starting your own practice?"

"Not really. I guess it was an impulsive act, but it had something to do with Ella. And with all the elderly people who come into the hospital with a problem. The hospital tackles them like *they* are the problem. Like aging isn't normal. I've seen so many people yanked from everything familiar and sent off to nursing homes. I prefer to keep them in their homes, to make adjustments so they still have their independence, their sense of dignity and belonging. I want to make lives meaningful in old age. The Amish . . . for all they do wrong, I think they do old age right." She paused, watching him. "You still look skeptical."

"Not skeptical. Still stunned, still absorbing this news. I thought you enjoyed working in the emergency room."

"I have enjoyed it. I've seen more and learned more in a few years than I could ever learn in office practice, but I'm growing a little weary of the hectic pace."

"It might not be all that different out in the country. Dr. Finegold always complains about those middle-of-the-night house calls."

"Maybe . . . it's not just the pace. I'm tired of not knowing my patients. They come in, I treat them, send them to their regular doctor for follow-up. I never have a chance to follow the patients to their homes, to see how they're doing. Maybe having a private practice would be more satisfying for me. I just feel as if . . . maybe there's something missing."

That was an expected confession to hear from his sister, because that was the very reason she had chosen to work in an emergency room. She used to say it was less complicated. It pleased him to hear her flip-flop on this issue. Something was calling her back to her roots. "Community."

"I guess that's the word for it, but don't get all bishop-y on me."

He smiled. She was prickly, this sister of his. She'd always had a mind of her own, one that didn't follow all the beliefs of the church. But you knew where you stood with Dok. You always knew what she was thinking. If you asked her a question, be ready for an honest answer. So like his daughter, Ruthie, her namesake.

"So what are your thoughts?"

"I think . . . you'd be a wonderful asset to Stoney Ridge.

It's so important to have a doctor who can understand Amish patients and care for us in a way that respects our convictions and way of life. The way you were treating Ella, for example. You understood what kind of support she would receive at home. Dr. Finegold meant well, I'm confident of that, but he had trouble accepting us. There was always tension between him and his patients. He felt they resisted his efforts to treat them well. They felt he tried to prolong biological life past the time God allotted."

"No doubt I'll have some of the same tension. It's the kind of training we get in medical school—to pursue every possible avenue to heal a patient."

"Yes, but it's important to ask the patients if that's the avenue they want. Not all do. Dr. Finegold didn't listen to his patients' wishes." He smiled. "I'm sure you will."

"If I do get the patients." Ruth looked down at her hands, folded in her lap. "So how do you think the Amish of Stoney Ridge will accept a female doctor?"

David leaned back in his chair and steepled his fingers together. "This church, it's always surprising me. Just when I think they're very conservative, something happens that makes me think they're very progressive. My guess is that it will take some time, but as they come to know you and trust you, you'll win them over."

"It would help to have my brother the bishop come to me as my patient."

David smiled. "I can do that." He leaned forward and put his feet firmly on the floor. "Dok, you have a great advantage here. Don't overlook what you can bring to your patients because of your background, not in spite of it."

She watched him for a long while, seeming to contemplate

his advice, and then got up to go. At the door, she turned around and looked at him again. "Well, do me a favor and add this new venture to your prayers."

"Done," David said. "Always." She didn't even have to ask.

Dr. Ruth Stoltzfus had told her brother the truth, but not the whole truth. Was that so wrong? She knew that David had made some assumptions about her: One, that she had come to Stoney Ridge merely by accident, a few years ago, when a position was offered to her. Two, he thought she was purchasing Max Finegold's practice because she was longing for community, harkening back to her Amish roots.

Both accounts were incorrect assumptions. The truth was that she had come to Stoney Ridge to be nearer in proximity to Ed Gingerich, a neurosurgeon who also happened to be the man she loved. And he was the reason she had been unceremoniously fired from her position as an emergency room physician at the hospital. She had covered for a mistake made by Ed late one night over Memorial Day weekend, when the hospital was on a skeleton staff and he was on call as a favor to a general surgeon. A young nine-year-old Amish girl had been brought in by her parents with severe stomach pains. Dok diagnosed it as a possible infected appendix and sent a message to Ed to have the tests confirmed and, if necessary, get surgery scheduled. But the emergency room was so crowded that evening that she was busy with another patient when Ed finally came in to the ER. He decided it was only a bellyache and sent the girl home.

The girl returned later that night with a burst appendix. She had very nearly died.

Ed went to Dok the next morning, begging her to take the blame for him. He had promised her that there would be no repercussions if she admitted that she had made an incorrect diagnosis during a hectic night in the emergency room. "Unintended errors happen all the time in the emergency room. Everyone expects them now and then. But if I were to admit it?" he said. "My career would be over."

She believed him.

That was a terrible decision.

The head of the hospital called her in and told her she was being terminated. As a courtesy to her, he wouldn't report her error. Her mind raced ahead, trying to process the news. The only reason for that feigned mercy, she knew, was because the parents were Amish and wouldn't threaten a lawsuit. Emergency rooms, he explained, were the top hospital departments responsible for malpractice suits. He paused for a moment before continuing. "You understand, of course, that although we understand human error is the root cause for these kinds of things, we can't tolerate it. It might be unfair to expect perfection, but nevertheless, that is what my job is all about. Expecting perfection from all my departments, even the emergency room." He stood. "I'm sorry, Dr. Stoltzfus." He walked to the door and opened it. "Human Resources wants to see you now. They'll have you finish up some paperwork and escort you out."

It was at that moment that her situation truly sunk in. Sunk was just the right word for it too. She *was* sunk! And livid with Ed.

"Ed," she rehearsed in her mind, "you've drawn me into something that was wrong. You've made me lie and I never lie. And now I've lost my job despite your promises that I would be spared."

The last phrase struck her by its forcefulness, as if something inside her knew this promise was as empty as all the other promises he'd made to her. In particular, the promise he had made about wanting to marry her.

Ed was waiting for her outside the head of the hospital's office. "Well?" he said, looking at her expectantly. "Did everything go as planned?"

"Not really. I was fired," she said flatly.

Ed was filled with pity. And colossal relief. But no regret. No remorse. Dok could see it in his eyes. He was safe. She, on the other hand, had lost her job, her reputation, and her integrity. She was infuriated with him, but it was only one of a thousand emotions whirling around inside her: anger, fear, despair, frustration, indignation, outrage . . . followed by guilt and, mostly, shame at her own foolishness.

What was the matter with her? Why would she, a woman known for being independent and strong-willed, allow herself to be caught in this kind of situation? Because . . . the man was Ed Gingerich. The most fascinating, intelligent, exciting man she'd ever known. What made her feel that stomach-churning longing for one person and not another? It was an exasperating puzzle.

And that's why she didn't tell him what she had mentally rehearsed—because she realized that the blame belonged to her alone. Ed was one of the most influential doctors on staff at the hospital. Nothing would have happened to him, even if he had told the truth. She was the fool for listening to him. But there was something about Ed that was hard to resist. If he asked her to do something for him, she would do it. In fact, she had just done it. She was the fool, not Ed.

"Honey, I'll make it up to you."

"No. I don't want you to."

He breathed a sigh of relief, misunderstanding her intent. "You're amazing. What did I do to deserve you?" His cell phone went off and he reached for it, his attention diverted. "I'll call you later?"

She maneuvered around him to walk toward the Human Resources office. "You do that," she said.

She was walking out to the parking lot with a big box of her things in her arms when she bumped into Matt Lehman, a police officer who was well known at the hospital.

"Let me get that for you," he said, taking it out of her hands before she could object. He set it in her passenger seat. He kept his eyes on his shoes and cleared his throat. "I don't suppose you'd have time for a cup of coffee?"

Oh Matt. He had a ridiculous adolescent-like crush on her that she tried her best to discourage. "Matt, now's not a good time."

He glanced at the box of belongings and connected the dots. "Dok, Max Finegold is serious about wanting to retire to Florida. He told me so this very morning. Small towns need doctors." He took a step closer to her. "When Dr. Finegold offered his practice to you, he wasn't kidding. He told me he thinks you're the one for it."

She looked at him, and he met her gaze directly. "Did he say that?"

"In a manner of speaking."

"What did he say exactly?"

A slow grin spread over Matt's face. "He said that you're

always meddling with his Amish patients and you should put your money where your big mouth is."

A short laugh burst out of Dok. "That sounds more like him." It sounded like her too. She was the world's worst meddler. A trait she'd inherited from her mother, the one and only Meddling Mammi.

"He has a point. Seems like you would understand the Plain People in a way Max never could. Or other doctors. I've seen it myself. You have a way with them." He leaned across the space between them, his fingers still tucked in his belt loops. "It appears you might be ready for a change. And I know I already said this, but small towns need doctors. You'd be making a big contribution."

She sighed. He'd found her Achilles heel. She was driven by an inner compulsion to make a contribution, to have something to offer this world. She fiddled with her car keys, thinking through Matt's remarks. What other options did she have right now? She could probably get her old job back in Ohio, but that would definitely mean the end of a relationship with Ed and she wasn't ready for that. She might be furious with him for throwing her under the bus, but she wasn't ready to throw the relationship out the window. A feeling came over her, of things falling into place, coming into focus. Maybe . . . this might just be the path she belonged on. "So how do I get in touch with Max Finegold?"

Matt reached out and touched Ruth on the arm, gently, as a friend. "Let me help."

5

The twists and turns of life, David mused, as he drove the buggy past his sister's soon-to-be medical practice. He could never have predicted such a blessing, to him, to his family, to his community. Never would have thought to ask for it! And maybe there's a lesson in that. "You have not because you ask not," the apostle James declared. Maybe David should try to expand his prayers, and ask for more. More evidence of God's work of redemption, more hearts turning to him, more signs of his church learning to love their neighbors as God loved them. His spirits lifted at the thought.

A life partner for his sister, Dok.

Now, that was a prayer he hadn't considered to pray yet. He had always been impressed by her medical career, by her calm confidence, her ability to make hard decisions under pressure—something he struggled with. But he worried she was lonely. Of course, she'd never admit such a thing. But everyone needed someone. Es is en Deckel fer alle Haffe. *There's a lid for every pot.*

Maybe, he realized, wanting to belong was the reason Dok

had come to Stoney Ridge in the first place. She must have known David was living here. She must have. And maybe that was what kept her here too. Close but not too close, to David and his family.

That thought lifted his spirits too. But he was still going to pray for a life partner for her. A man who would love his sister in the way she deserved to be loved.

To be a country doctor, one who actually had patients, Dok would need to embrace house calls. She wanted to be the kind of doctor the Amish needed. They used medical services, but with reluctance, caution, and with one eye on the bottom line, financially. If necessary, a house call could determine whether a patient belonged in the hospital or not. And that meant she had to say goodbye to her beloved energy-efficient Prius and look for some kind of sturdy vehicle that could get through snow and rain.

She stopped by a car dealership on the way home from work—there was only one in Stoney Ridge—and was surprised to find Matt Lehman, in full uniform, talking to the sales manager. She watched their interaction for a moment and realized that Matt was questioning the sales manager in an officious way, taking notes. Was the guy ever off duty?

Matt spotted her and his whole demeanor stiffened as if the Queen of England had arrived. Was it her imagination or did he flush slightly?

Matt was a good friend to her, very good. They had met a few years ago on a Sunday at the local Mennonite church. Whenever he had a reason to be at the hospital's emergency room, which was often as a police officer, he made sure to find out if she was on duty. Then he would look for her, bringing her a decaf caffè latte (her favorite) from a nearby coffee shop. Sweet, sweet man, great friend, kind and thoughtful, but definitely not her type. As in, he was not Ed Gingerich.

And that thought was something that shamed her. Why didn't she want to be treated well by a man? What was wrong with her? She seemed drawn to the Ed-types like a moth to the flame and dismissed the Matt-types. Something was definitely wrong with her.

Her mother had a theory, though her mother was never without a theory. Tillie Yoder Stoltzfus believed that Ruth always kept one foot out the door of wherever she was or with whomever, ready to move on if things got too complicated.

There was some truth to that.

But look at me now, Tillie Yoder Stoltzfus! I bought a medical practice. I have a permanent mailing address. I . . . have staying power.

She hoped.

She lifted a hand in a casual wave to Matt and went down a long aisle of pickup trucks, trying to decide if a pickup truck might be the best choice. Or an SUV? She didn't want something huge, but nothing too small, either.

As she wandered up another aisle, Matt came looking for her. "Hi there, Dok."

She waited until he walked up to her, a shy smile on his face. "Are you here on police business?"

"No. Actually, I was seeing if there might be a van I can rent for a camping trip to Yellowstone I'm taking with my cousins in a few weeks."

"Any word about the murder case at the Inn at Eagle Hill?"

"Murder case? Why does everyone keep calling it a murder?" Matt frowned. "There's nothing conclusive yet about the guest's death. Anything that's floating around is pure conjecture. Nothing but rumor. And I'd appreciate it if you would let others know that."

"Sorry. I didn't realize that." She was a little surprised by the tinge of annoyance in his voice. "I'll pass the word."

Softening, he said, "So, it happened. You did it. You bought Dr. Finegold's practice."

"Yes. Effective immediately. Dr. Finegold is probably sitting on a beach in Florida. I've hung my shingle and am open for business." She leaned forward and lowered her voice to sound authoritative. "And I would appreciate it if *you* would let others know that."

He grinned. "I'll pass the word." He gazed around at the trucks. "Are you looking to buy a truck?"

"Maybe." She started walking down the aisle, looking over each car and truck. "I'd like something that can get me through a snowstorm in the middle of the night."

"Why?" Matt's eyebrows lifted. "To make house calls?"

She nodded, peering into a blue truck's cab.

"I'm impressed."

"Hold on to that thought until I actually have some patients. The Amish are slow to embrace anything or anyone new, especially a female doctor."

"I always thought your nickname was a step toward acceptance." He shrugged. "It's like . . . getting anointed."

"I have my brother to thank for that." She adored David, always had. Ed might have been the reason she came to Stoney Ridge in the first place, but David was the reason she had stayed. And his children too. And now Birdy. She loved them all. She *felt* loved by them all. It didn't occur to her that she had missed being a part of a family until she accepted David's invitations to come to his home. The very first time, Christmas, a few years ago, was as nourishing as a drink of cold water on a hot summer day. She hadn't realized how dehydrated her soul had become.

"So . . . Ed Gingerich must have been disappointed that you left the hospital."

Matt didn't like Ed and made no secret about it. Then again, Matt made no secret of anything he felt. Unless it was official police business, of course. Then he would act as if he was guarding state secrets. But she respected that quality in him. "Let's just say that Ed's feelings are not something I considered in making this decision."

Matt grinned.

"Stop looking so happy," Dok said, calmly looking back at him and smiling as she made her way down another row of larger cars and trucks. "These are so big." She walked in a wide circle, frowning. "I'm looking for something easier to manage. Reliable, dependable, determined." She turned toward Matt and froze. "I think I've found what I've been looking for!"

He put his hand to his chest. "You mean . . . me?"

She pointed to the silver SUV behind him. "I was talking about the car."

Yesterday, there wasn't a cloud in the sky. This morning, gray clouds hung heavy over Stoney Ridge, threatening a summer storm. The sky matched Dok's mood as she unpacked a box of medical supplies, wondering if they'd ever be used, if she'd ever get shelves built for them. She couldn't afford to hire any office help yet, but it didn't really matter. So far, her only patient had been her brother.

She did have one appointment today, but she wasn't sure why the woman was coming to see her. Nora Miller had left a voicemail on her phone, saying she planned to stop in today.

Nora's daughter was the nine-year-old girl who had nearly died at the hospital from a burst appendix. Dok felt a spike of concern as she wondered why Nora was coming to the office. The hospital would have no doubt let Nora know that Dok had been terminated after the error. She knew how influential a woman like Nora, imbued with a matriarchal dignity, could be among the Amish community. Dok doubted that Nora would say anything of overt blame to others, but she fully expected her to quietly discourage anyone from coming to her practice. That would be the Amish way. Quite frankly, she didn't blame her.

The rain was pouring, beating the roof, when Nora Miller arrived around eleven in the morning. Dok hurried out to the waiting room to greet her. Nora set her wet umbrella on the porch and walked into the small waiting room, looking around.

Nora was as round as she was tall. She was only in her midforties, but her center part was nearly bare from years of twisting her hair into a tight knot behind her head. The hair roots had been destroyed. But the hair that was left mingled gray and brown along the edge of her cap. She was taciturn, soft-spoken, with her hands folded against her apron. "How are things going for you?"

Dok's gaze swept the empty waiting room. "Slow." A long silence followed.

"I came to discuss Malinda with you."

"Make yourself at home," Dok said. "Take a chair, any chair." They were all available. "How is your daughter?"

"She's fine, just fine. She's young. The youth recover quickly." Nora sat down in one of the chairs, crossing her thick ankles out in front of her. "I know that the mistake over my Malinda's appendix wasn't yours."

Dok sat beside her. "How do you happen to know that?"

"Because I remember it clearly. You were examining Malinda, and you asked me questions about her. You asked me if she complained very much and I told you no. Never. Then I heard you say to yourself it must be an inflamed appendix. I heard you say it. Then you told the nurse that you wanted Dr. Gingerich to take a look at her, soon, before the appendix burst. He was the one who decided it was nothing more than a tummy ache. Not you."

Thank goodness. Someone knew the truth. Dok let out a deep sigh. "Thank you, Nora."

"You lost your job over this."

What was the point of denying it? "I did."

Nora was quiet for a long moment, then she slapped her hands on her sturdy knees. "I'll spread your name around."

"Thank you," Dok said, and she had that feeling again. The feeling that, against the odds, all this might work out after all. Overhead, the clouds parted, this storm moving on.

As she watched Nora Miller climb into her buggy and drive off, she sensed she was looking at a woman who knew exactly who she was and what she was meant to be in this world. Dok felt—what was it?—an envy for her.

It wasn't unusual for Hank Lapp to drop by with interesting scraps of news or humorous incidents to report. Jesse's landlady, Fern Lapp, a woman with a knack for taking charge of people's lives like a house afire, seemed to have a sixth sense for knowing when Hank was heading over to Windmill Farm, and usually had a generous slab of pie or fresh-baked muffins waiting for him.

But it was a little strange to have him come by every single day that week to update Jesse on new details emerging about the murder at Eagle Hill. Hank had heard the rumors at the Bent N' Dent, where he spent the abundance of his spare time, which was substantial. "LATEST NEWS," he told Jesse and the wide-eyed apprentices who were supposed to be polishing spokes on the wheels of Edith Fisher's buggy.

"Hank, it's not necessary to shout," Jesse said. "We can hear you fine."

"So can all the neighbors," Luke Schrock added. He had shown up out of nowhere.

Sometimes Jesse's buggy shop felt like a gathering place for all those with a surfeit of spare time. It was a troubling thought.

"Sorry," Hank said, but old habits die hard and his voice started to rise in volume with each new juicy phrase. "The dead man committed a burglary with his friends, got in an argument with them, parted ways, and hid out in Stoney Ridge. He was planning to turn himself in to the police as an informant in exchange for amnesia."

"Amnesia?" Jesse said. "I think you mean amnesty."

"What's amnesty?" Leroy Glick asked.

"Pardon," Luke said, grinning. "A free pass. My favorite thing."

That did not come as a surprise to Jesse. Luke liked to think of himself as a subversive. Casually Amish, he called himself. The phrase would make his father cringe.

Hank wasn't finished and didn't appreciate being interrupted. "NOW HOLD ON! Best part's still to come. His buddies found out and came back to do him in. Broke into the cottage and killed him. IN COLD BLOOD."

"Who's the source for this information?" Jesse asked.

"My colleagues at the store."

The old codgers, he meant. The retired men who spent winter afternoons in the store, sitting in rocking chairs by the woodstove, and summers out on the picnic benches, playing checkers. "Hank, you know they just make things up."

Hank jabbed a finger in the air. "Perfectly plausible sequence of events."

"Don't you think you should wait for the cause of death from the coroner?"

Hank's tall forehead crinkled in confusion. "WHERE'S THE FUN IN THAT?"

"He's right!" Luke said. "The Inn at Eagle Hill hasn't seen this kind of excitement since that lady who was afraid of spiders."

Jesse remembered hearing about that particular guest. A woman with a serious case of arachnophobia. She was an Irish woman who was unusually skittish, the afraid-of-her-own-shadow type. When she called to make a reservation, she had asked Rose specifically if there were any spiders in the cottage. Any at all. Rose assured her that the cottage was spick-and-span, spider-free, but Luke couldn't resist the bait. He had placed spiders, easily collected in the barn, in strategic locations all through the cottage—in the refrigerator, in the bathtub, in her bed. Each time this guest found a new one, she shouted hysterically for someone to come kill it.

In the afternoon, the woman sat on the small cottage

porch, reading a book. Luke climbed up on the roof above her and quietly lowered a gigantic fake tarantula, rigged to a fishing pole, to gently land on her shoulder. Ruthie said you could hear that lady's bloodcurdling scream coming all the way from the Inn at Eagle Hill. She had packed up and left.

Whenever Jesse thought about the Inn at Eagle Hill, his thoughts rambled over to Mim Schrock. Actually, he thought about Mim Schrock nonstop. His ardor for her, over the last two years, had doubled and quadrupled. And it seemed as if Mim was growing fond of Jesse. Well, fonder. He thought there might be a chance for him, especially when Danny Riehl moved to Prince Edward Island with the start-up of a new Amish community.

But Jesse wasn't sure where things stood between Danny and Mim. She wouldn't say outright that it was over between them. Not over, she told Jesse, but not together. She needed time, she said, to think.

To Jesse, that indicated she was hoping things would still work out between them, despite the distance. What else could it mean? Mim had gone to visit Danny a few weeks ago, and he envisioned the two of them running along the sandy shoreline of Prince Edward Island, hand in hand, barefoot, laughing. Probably laughing about him, stuck in a buggy shop with her little brother for company.

Stop it! Jesse told himself. His imagination was his worst enemy.

Maybe Mim was using the time on Prince Edward Island to decide that she didn't really like island living, or starting a new settlement, or Danny.

A window-rattling boom interrupted Jesse's Mim-musing, and everyone looked at Luke, even the apprentices.

"It wasn't me!" he said, hands lifted in the air. "I've been here the whole time."

The boom came from the house, and Jesse bolted over to it just as Fern opened the kitchen door, waving her apron as smoke billowed out behind her. "Fern! What happened?"

She seemed annoyed but unalarmed as she continued to wave smoke away with her apron. "That stove. Amos hasn't cleaned it out in months and the flue clogged up."

Hank, Luke, and the two apprentices came up behind Jesse.

"We'll take care of it right now," Jesse said.

Fern stopped waving long enough to sweep her gaze over the five of them. One of her eyebrows went up—a bad sign. "I don't need five of you messing up my clean kitchen." She pointed a long bony finger at Luke and gave him a look that could cut a steak. "He'll do. The rest of you—" she eyed each of them except Hank—"have work to do."

Talk about the lifting of eyebrows! As Luke Schrock was singled out by Fern, his eyebrows shot up to the top of his forehead. He looked colossally worried.

How about *that*? Luke Schrock was afraid of Fern Lapp.

Luke Schrock was in trouble again.

Yesterday morning, the town of Stoney Ridge woke to find newly installed stop signs placed at every single intersection, even on sparsely traveled roads. Previously, there had been only two stop signs in town, both along Main Street. Now there were over twenty-five. The morning rush hour traffic, composing largely of milk trucks driven by impatient drivers eager to get to the dairies for the day's delivery, inched through town.

Because the town of Stoney Ridge was unincorporated, no one quite knew who had approved the new stop signs or who was to blame. There was no mayor or city government, only the sheriff's office. So that's who people complained to. The police officers were as baffled as everyone else.

Working on a hunch, Matt Lehman came looking for Ruthie's father. Together, they went to the Inn at Eagle Hill and asked Rose to take a quick look into some of the outbuildings. In the last one Matt peered into, an old shack used for storing hay, he found the crude makings of a sheet metal shop, including pieces of sheet metal, soldering tools, stencils, and paint to replicate red traffic stop signs.

Back at home, Ruthie overheard her father explain to Birdy what he and Matt had discovered. Apparently, last night Luke and his devoted following of lowlife friends had quietly installed the stop signs throughout the town.

"Just for kicks," Luke had said, when Ruthie's father asked why he did such a thing. Luke seemed untroubled by the fact that he would probably be charged with a misdemeanor.

"The thing is . . . they were really quite masterful," Ruthie's father said. "Luke had replicated those stop signs down to the exact kind of bolt. They were identical to the county signs. It's too bad he can't take that brain of his and use it for something productive. He has the ability to aggravate the police department in spectacular ways."

Ruthie agreed wholeheartedly. She had tried and tried to convince Luke to take the GED with her, but he scoffed at it. He said he didn't need a piece of paper to tell him he was a genius. When she pointed out that the GED might be useful in persuading other people—such as a future employer—of his brilliance, Luke said he already had big plans in motion. He was always on the point of doing something, on the point of going somewhere.

So Ruthie took the test alone one Saturday morning in May, after studying for it in the barn all spring, and the results had arrived in today's mail. Her hands shook as she opened the envelope and read the scores:

Science: 610
Mathematics: 590
Social studies: 750
Language arts: written 780
Language arts: reading 790

She needed a score of 2,250 to pass. She had a score of 3,520. She added the numbers four different times, just to make sure they were correct.

She had *passed*.

On her *first* try! She, Ruthie Stoltzfus, had the equivalent of a high school diploma.

She could do anything now. *Anything!* Go to college. Find a job. Travel. Anything.

The world was her oyster.

Her aunt Dok was the only one with whom she planned to share the news of passing the GED, the only one who would understand how monumental this piece of paper was, the only one who would celebrate its significance with her. Whenever Ruthie was around Dok, she felt this world of otherness open up to her. Other options, other choices, other ways of living.

So, that afternoon when she stopped by her aunt's new practice, it came as somewhat of a blow when Dok didn't automatically congratulate her but instead asked her why she had taken the test. "Did you want to see how smart you are? Because you didn't need a test to tell you that."

"No, not at all. I took it because, well, because I want options."

"For what? What is it you want to do with your life?"

"I want . . . to matter."

"That's a wonderful goal, Ruthie, but how? And why? What's driving that desire? If you leave home, do you have a plan? Do you have money saved up?"

This conversation wasn't going at all the way Ruthie had hoped it would. Her aunt didn't even crack a smile as she read the scores. Instead, she folded the paper carefully, slipped it into the envelope, and handed it back to Ruthie, who now regretted showing her the results at all. Instead of answering her aunt's questions, Ruthie flipped them around. "So how did you know what you wanted to do with your life? I'm constantly trying to figure it out."

"I'm not sure I had it figured out. Certainly not when I was seventeen." Dok leaned back against her desk. "At that age, I was chiefly motivated by making my mother mad." She lifted her eyebrows. "And it worked."

Ruthie was stunned. "*That's* why you're a doctor? Just to make Mammi mad?"

"No, but that was why I went to college. The decision to go to medical school came later, after I realized I couldn't go back to the life I once had."

"Go back?" Ruthie was stunned. "Why in the world would you have wanted to go back?"

"Because making my mother mad wasn't a very good reason to leave the Amish. In fact, it was a pretty immature decision."

"But . . . you're a doctor! You're important."

Dok tilted her head. "Ruthie . . . work is important. But it isn't work that makes a person important. That's something that has to be settled between you and God." She reached out and put a hand on Ruthie's shoulder. "Maybe it's just too soon for you to try to figure things out. Maybe that's why you feel uncertain of what to do. Just remember that God has a plan for your future. Wait, Ruthie. Watch and wait for God's timing. You'll know it when it comes. I wish I'd realized that truth when I was young, like you. I'd have been far more careful about the choices along the way, instead of those that seemed important or self-satisfying at the time.

Decisions you make now can be very . . . far-reaching. Good ones and bad ones."

Ruthie sensed her aunt wanted to say even more but was holding herself in check, and frankly, she didn't want to hear any more. She felt deflated. She glanced around her aunt's office—it was a disaster. Boxes waiting to be emptied, desk piled with books and papers and file folders. "Looks like you're pretty busy."

Her aunt's gaze drifted around the room. "I don't even know where to begin."

Ruthie walked to the doorjamb, then spun around with an idea. "I could help. Just get things put away. I've got some time today." Until the Inn at Eagle Hill was given the all clear to reopen, she wasn't needed there, and the *last* thing she wanted to do was to work at the Bent N' Dent. If her dad knew she had free time, he would expect her behind the cash register.

That offer brought the first bright, honest-to-goodness smile on her aunt's face, the one Ruthie had expected to see when she showed her the GED scores. "Yes! Yes, yes, yes. I would love the help."

Ruthie got right to work, cheered up. For the moment.

Ruthie set up a rigorous daily schedule of tutoring Patrick Kelly in Penn Dutch. Partly, she believed this was the best way to learn a language. Partly, she wanted the money. She might not have a plan figured out yet for her future, but she knew a fat savings account would be essential to success.

She gave Patrick fifty vocabulary words to memorize each day, quizzed him, and corrected his pronunciation with impatient annoyance. He had studied German in high school so there was a foundation to work from, but as a dialect, Penn Dutch sounded different, vowels in particular. "Patrick, listen carefully. You keep making the *u* sound as an *uh* sound. It needs to be *u* like *ewe*. You need to listen and practice."

"Immersion."

"What?"

"That's how to learn a foreign language. Total immersion. That's what I'm trying to do."

"Well, then. Immerse yourself. Stop talking in English."

A look of panic hit him. "I . . . can't. I would hardly speak. I can barely understand Penn Dutch."

"You have to try."

"But I am trying!"

"Not hard enough. Try harder. Like now." She opened a children's book. "Repeat after me: Eise verharde nemmt viel Hitz." *Much heat is required to harden iron.*

"Eise verharde nemmt viel Hitz."

"Da elephant is gros un groh. Eah's oarich shtaut un sadda shloh." *The elephant is huge and gray. He's very strong and sort of slow.*

Patrick repeated what she had said, then his face crinkled up in confusion.

"Da monkey find sich so di haym mitt en banana draus in di baym." *The monkey feels at home with a banana out in the trees.*

He stared at her intently, and she could see he was thinking very hard about what she said.

"Oh boy. Ruthie, the thing is, I'm not sure these particular phrases would be ones I would need to use very often."

"Stop talking in English!"

At just that moment, David walked into the kitchen. "Ruthie, hab Geduld!" *Have patience.* "You sound a little tough on your student."

Ruthie looked up in utter surprise. "Patrick wants me to be tough. He told me he plans to be fluent by the end of the month."

Patrick nodded. "She's right. I want her to be tough on me. Full immersion."

She threw her hands up in the air. "Kannschtt du Pennsil-faanisch Deitsch schwetze?" *Can you speak in Pennsylvania Dutch?*

Patrick's eyebrows lifted in panic. "Unwohl." *Not well.*

"Nau is awwer ball Zeit!" *Now is the time!*

Patrick paled.

"Ruthie, I don't think yelling at him is going to help him." David took a green apple from the bowl on the kitchen counter and sliced it into slivers, then sprinkled the slices with ground cinnamon. He put the apple slices in two bowls, one for himself and one for Ruthie and Patrick. "Immersion. In a way, it's like learning to listen to God, isn't it? Immersing yourself in prayer. Developing an ear. Daily practice. Practicing daily."

Patrick reached for a handful of slices. "Maybe it's a little like learning obedience."

David lit up. "Yes. Exactly that, Patrick. You haven't heard God until you've heeded God."

Oh no. That was one of her father's all-purpose sayings. Ruthie sensed a sermon was about to unfold.

Her dad took a bite of apple, chewed, swallowed. "You might have just helped me work out a sermon illustration."

Patrick was clearly intrigued. "How so?"

Ruthie had to cut this off before the two of them got carried away into a long and boring theological quagmire. When would her student ever learn? "Pennsilfaanish Deitsch!"

Patrick panicked. "Oh boy . . ." You could see his mind strain and search for words. "Gfalle! Es . . . hot . . . mer . . . gut . . . gfalle." *I was well pleased with that.*

A smile lifted the corners of Ruthie's mouth, ever so slightly. "Besser." Ruthie didn't mean to sound so mad at Patrick. In fact, she was actually starting to enjoy him. She sensed something different about him but couldn't pinpoint what.

He wasn't handsome, certainly not the way Luke Schrock was handsome. He had a broad forehead and a Roman nose and a long throat with an Adam's apple that was a tiny bit too prominent. But it was a likable face. The honest brown color of his eyes, the crinkles at their corners, the cleft in his chin, the thoughtfulness over that high brow.

She gave her father a smug look. "Er is alli Daag am besser warre." *He's improving every day.*

"If his mental health can take it."

"Don't worry about me, David. I told Ruthie that I was willing to do whatever it takes. And I'm tougher than I look."

Ruthie's smile faded and she pounded the table with her fists. "Pennsilfaanish Deitsch!"

Patrick nearly jumped out of his chair. David walked past him, patted him on the shoulder and whispered, "Amazing to think you're paying for this privilege."

As the horse and buggy crested the hill, David saw the blue-dark outline of the ridge. Above it hung the gibbous moon. He didn't usually notice such things—those were the details of life that gave Birdy such joy. Maybe she was rubbing off on him? He slowed the horse down to a walk, then to a stop. How long had it been since he'd stopped to gaze at the night sky above? It seemed years. Beneath a starlit sky, it was all too easy to forget there was anything pressing in, anything demanding his attention.

He was driving home from the Sisters' House after what he had hoped would be a brief check-in on Ella, whose health was fading. Those old sisters were night owls and kept him far too late, but he couldn't pull himself away. Not only did they have riveting stories, but they gave him black-as-coal coffee without a single warning of how it would affect his stomach ulcer. The real stuff! Not decaf. Life was too short as it was to miss out on good coffee, they said. And it was delicious. Strong, too, which was probably why he was wide awake after midnight. But best of all, he felt as if he were eighteen years old again when he was with those lively old sisters.

Thistle shifted her weight and suddenly David realized a man was walking down the road, toward the buggy. "Patrick, what are you doing out at this hour?"

Patrick seemed just as surprised to see David. "It was so hot that I couldn't sleep. I thought I'd just walk a while in the quiet of the night."

"Hop in. I'll take you home." Patrick was walking in the opposite direction, but David didn't feel right about leaving him alone, so he didn't pose it as a question. The boy seemed tired. No, not tired. Worried. David knew that look because he wore it so often himself. "Everything okay?" he asked as Patrick climbed in the passenger side of the buggy.

"Everything's fine," Patrick said, in a too-quick way that

made David think everything wasn't fine. "Lately I've just had trouble sleeping."

"Too much on your mind?"

"No. Not really. I think it's because . . . time is passing so quickly." His voice was thick with feeling. "I don't want to miss anything. The stars at night. The first birdsong in the morning. Catching the first hint of dawn as it rises above the ridge behind Eagle Hill."

David understood Patrick's reasoning. "When I was your age, I milked cows for a neighbor. There's something about getting up and going out in the middle of the night that gives an edge to your start of the day. I used to feel as if I had those nights all to myself." He felt a unique intimacy with God during that year and often wondered if it had to do with those predawn hours. No distractions. No demands. The whole village slept, he alone was awake.

"Yes. Yes, you understand. It's almost like time slows down." Patrick settled back onto the buggy's bench, relaxing a little. "Before I knew I wanted to become Amish, I thought I might become a monk. I think they know what they're doing when they get up in the middle of the night to pray."

A monk. A life set apart, devoted to vows made to God: obedience, chastity, poverty. Interesting. A monk's life held a certain appeal, David thought, but not so much the chastity part. He felt a renewed contentment with the life God had given him. "I'm curious about the expectations you had for the Amish. Do they line up with what you're observing on your walks?"

"Pretty much," Patrick said. "The Bent N' Dent was a surprise."

"How so? Don't tell me you thought the Amish lived entirely self-sufficient lives." The misconceptions about the Plain life amused David. One woman came into the store last week and wondered if the Amish ate only raw food. When David asked her why she assumed such a thing, she said, with absolute confidence, it was because the Amish had no stoves. David pointed to the woodstove in the store and the woman was amazed. Later that evening, he repeated the customer's conversation with Birdy and she hooted with laughter. "Someday," Birdy said, "I want to write a book called *We're Not as Dumb as We Look*." David said he would start writing down conversations with non-Amish customers for her.

Patrick fanned himself with his hat. "I guess it's what was in the store that surprised me. So many products of processed foods. Canned goods, cereal boxes, cake mixes. Even a freezer full of frozen prepared foods." He shrugged. "I guess I just hadn't thought the Amish would heat up Stouffer's frozen lasagna like anybody else."

"Summertime, especially, can be very busy for the farming families." But it occurred to David that over the last two years he had, indeed, stocked the store with more and more prepared products. Why was that? Because customers requested them.

Patrick laughed. "And I really didn't expect to see a pizza delivery man arrive at an Amish house!"

Ah. He would be referring to last night's dinner at the Stoltzfuses' home. Birdy had been helping Katrina all day and asked David to bring something home from the store. He had completely forgotten and ended up calling for a pizza delivery.

"Mostly though, I was shocked by the Sunday tradition."

"Church is only held every two weeks. Next Sunday will be an off-Sunday."

"I know about the every-two-weeks tradition. But I thought Sunday was a do-nothing day for the Amish. A day set apart."

"Yes, that's what all Sundays are supposed to be. Off-Sundays and church Sundays. The Sabbath."

"But what about the quilt shops that were open? I saw tour buses stopping at farmhouses."

David's eyebrows shot up. "Certainly not to Amish homes."

"I'm pretty sure they were stopping at Amish homes. Starting at the Fisher Chicken & Hatchery. Hank Lapp was in the roadside stand as I passed by, selling eggs."

"You're sure it was Sunday? Maybe you had it confused with Saturday?"

Patrick gave him a funny look. "Oh boy. I hope I didn't get it mixed up. I don't think I did. But maybe . . . No. No, I'm sure I had it right."

David was silent.

"My church back home was the same way."

"What way was that?" David asked. Patrick attended a Catholic church, a very orthodox one, he had said. What would that have in common with an Old Order Amish church?

"The priest tried to make everyone follow the Sabbath, but no one really did. Other than an hour or so at church in the morning, it was a day like any other."

A day like any other? David felt uneasiness stir as he drove up the steep driveway to the house. It worsened as he put Thistle in her barn stall and gave her a handful of oats as a thank-you for a later-than-usual night. Patrick's frank observations swept away any lingering delight of the evening with the old sisters and left him with a bothersome case of caffeine-induced insomnia.

7

With Birdy's permission (which took very little persuasion because she thought Nyna the Mynah was thoroughly winsome), Patrick brought his bird in its cage into the kitchen during afternoon tutoring sessions with Ruthie, hoping the bird would pick up some Penn Dutch. Ruthie was baffled by his devotion to that bird. It was the noisiest thing. Lots of needless ear-piercing whistles and screeches, followed by shrieks of random Bible verses: "Jesus wept!" "Pray continually!" "Rejoice!" "No other gods!" "Do unto others!"

In the kitchen, Ruthie cut up apples, dusted them with cinnamon, and put them in a bowl. Then she poured two glasses of iced tea. "Why do you like that bird so much?"

"Nyna? Because . . . she speaks truth."

Ruthie let out a laugh. "You teach it—" she corrected herself "—you teach *her* every word she knows!" Patrick must have spent hours teaching Nyna the Mynah to mimic him.

Patrick smiled. "She can say, 'Gut Tag' if she's in a good mood."

"That's why you brought her along to Stoney Ridge? To teach her Penn Dutch?"

"Sort of. Mostly, I didn't want to leave her behind."

Ruthie took a sip of iced tea. "So what did you leave behind?"

He didn't answer for a long moment, which, she was learning, was typical of Patrick. He thought carefully before he spoke. But then he said, "My parents. My friends. My car."

She reflected on his answer as he set Nyna the Mynah's cage on a stool in the corner. It was a life condensed to short, concise words, a little like Nyna herself. Staccato-ese. And Ruthie's own life in such terms—what would she leave behind if she walked away from being Amish?

My family. My home. My sense of well-being.

That last phrase bubbled out of nowhere, but it literally took her breath away. It was a revelation. If she were being brutally honest with herself, it filled her with anxiety to think of what life might be without the safety net of family, home, and the security that came with being Amish.

But was that any reason to stay? Fear of the unknown?

She watched Patrick coax Nyna to mimic him. He had absolutely no fear of the unknown. She had to admit, he was growing on her. She liked his openness, his transparency. He was refreshingly honest about himself.

So different from Luke, who was always hiding things.

And along with Patrick's candor was the fact that he didn't seem particularly charmed by Ruthie. He seemed impervious to her. Or, at the very least, indifferent. She admired that in him too, because most of the young men she knew in her church were tongue-tied and struck by bouts of profound immaturity around girls of their age.

"Why didn't you bring your car along?"

He turned toward her. "Part of the adventure is living without it."

She leaned her elbows on the table and propped her chin in the palm of her hands. "I suppose I've led a very boring life. The biggest adventure I've ever had is when Dad took us all to Niagara Falls. In a bus. But it was rainy and foggy and we couldn't see the waterfalls."

"I'm almost never bored," Patrick said. "In fact, I can't remember ever being really, truly bored."

"So you've had lots of adventures, then?"

He seemed surprised by the question. "Almost none. This summer, it's my first true solo adventure."

She swept the kitchen with a glance to make sure no little sister was within listening distance and leaned across the table. "I drove a car once. A friend of mine keeps one hidden." She didn't say whom.

"But that's against the rules."

Ruthie wiggled her eyebrows. "Exactly." A recurring motto of Luke's floated through her mind: If you come across a rule you don't like, just change it.

Patrick smiled, amused. "You think it's that much fun to drive a car?"

"Yes."

A slow grin spread over Patrick's face. "Try driving from Ontario, Canada, to Pennsylvania during a steamy hot July, stuck in the back of a car, with a huge shedding dog that has horrible breath. Then you'll see how fun a car can be." He reached out and took a slice of apple. "But maybe the fun of it is knowing you're not supposed to." He chewed his apple slice, swallowed, then said, "Maybe it's as simple as the grass is always greener on the other side of the fence."

She suddenly felt annoyed. And aware of how immature she must seem to him. A cliché! She was a cliché. How *embarrassing*.

But Patrick seemed oblivious to her embarrassment. "Everyone has been so kind to me here. A total stranger."

"Yeah, well, don't get too syrupy. You haven't been here very long."

"True, but I'm committed. At least for this month. My parents want me to return to finish up college. I'm hoping I can change their mind."

She leaned back in her chair. "You said you wanted to know what it's like to be truly Amish, right? Not just what the tourists think it means."

"I did. I said that. I meant it."

"Good. Then, you should come to a frolic."

"I've read about the youth gatherings. The volleyball games, the barbecues."

"Well, that's not exactly the kind of frolic I meant." She reached out to fill up her glass with more iced tea.

"An Amish party, right?"

That, Ruthie thought, was an oxymoron. She frowned as though searching for the right words. She seesawed her hand back and forth in the air. "Yes and no. It's not churchy, if that's what you mean. It's when the community all pitches in to build someone an outbuilding or a shed or a barn. If you're still here in the fall, I'm sure you'll be included in corn shocking." She'd like to see what he thought of Amish living after those soft hands of his were sliced up by the sharp edges of corn husks.

But he looked like she had just handed him the moon on a silver platter. "Count me in. When and where is the next frolic?"

Ridiculous! This guy really was one of a kind. She resisted

the urge to say that if he thought she was a tough taskmaster, then just wait until he got bossed around by the men at a barn raising. "Dad announces any upcoming frolics at the end of the church service." She gave him a smug look. "So you can work yourself to the bone for someone else, and all you'll get for your kindness and labor is a hearty meal."

"But they'd do the same for you, wouldn't they? For your family. For the Schrocks. For everyone. That's what the community does for each other, right?"

She must have looked confused, because he hastened to add, "It's based on the book of Acts, about people taking care of each other. 'Every man according to his ability.' Acts 11:29. But I'm sure you know."

"Love never fails!" squawked Nyna, and Patrick's attention instantly turned to praise his bird.

Ruthie might have known that reference from Acts, but she'd forgotten until Patrick reminded her. She found herself growing increasingly irritated by his romantic notions of being Amish. He refused to see it for what it was. But what irked her most was that he saw things she didn't see.

She tore a piece of paper from the notepad, a bit more firmly than she needed to, and ended up ripping it in half. She frowned and pulled out another piece of paper, then handed it to him. "Why are you staring at me?"

Patrick's cheeks went pink. "Did I say something wrong? It seems like I made you mad."

"No." Yes. "If you don't learn Penn Dutch, then you'll never know when and where to show up for a frolic." She raised the bar on Patrick. "You are no longer allowed to speak in English. Not a single word."

That kept him quiet.

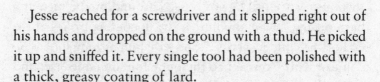

Jesse reached for a screwdriver and it slipped right out of his hands and dropped on the ground with a thud. He picked it up and sniffed it. Every single tool had been polished with a thick, greasy coating of lard.

"I distinctly remember that you said to polish the tools," Leroy said, looking offended, when he and Sammy arrived at the buggy shop for work. "I distinctly remember it. Polish them until you can see your reflection in them. So clean you can comb your hair from it. That's what you said." He reflected for a moment. "We did think it was a peculiar custom."

Sammy nodded. "We thought it was strange. But we did what you asked."

"Clean and polish! With mineral oil. Not *grease* them with bacon fat."

"So that's where my can of lard went," came a certain voice, sharp as a pinch. Fern stood at the door, listening to the lecture Jesse was giving to his clueless apprentices about using common sense.

It wasn't easy to discern, because Fern's facial expressions were not widely varied, but Jesse thought she might have tossed him a rare and catlike smile of sympathy. On the other hand, it was the same expression she used to convey "what goes around, comes around."

It was nearly midnight. Standing there at the crest of the steep driveway, Ruthie had one of her odd moments when she felt as though she were on the precipice of discovering something important. What that might be—a calling, an adventure, a true love—who knew? Ruthie didn't like those moments at all. They only seemed to escalate the longing she felt for whatever *it* was that she was on the precipice of. What was *it*?!

Those were the thoughts that were humming messily around her head as she quietly made her way down the gravel driveway, until she saw a bobbing flashlight come toward her. "Luke?"

"Hello there, Ruthie."

She jumped at the voice. "Patrick!" She exhaled, heart thudding, yet also pinging a little at the sight of him as he approached her. "I didn't expect to see you." She popped him in the upper arm like she used to do to her brother Jesse, but the gesture felt far more intimate with Patrick. "What are you doing out so late?" She had made an elaborate effort to sneak out of the house, even to quietly tiptoe past Jesse's room— where she assumed Patrick was sleeping—and carefully step over the telltale squeaky floorboard. Down the hall, her father could hear that squeaky floorboard like it was a fire alarm.

"Just stargazing." He turned the flashlight off and looked up at the black velvet sky. "Where I'm from, there's an ambient light from the city that kind of erases most of the stars. It's easy to forget they're there." He lifted his head. "It's hard to sleep when there's so much beauty to absorb."

Ruthie looked up at the sky. Yes, a clear night of bright stars was nice, but it had never kept her from sleeping.

"What exactly are you looking at?"

Patrick pointed toward the blanket of night sky in the gap. "Polaris," he said quietly, and she tried to follow the trajectory of his finger. "Also known as Polestar and Lodestar, but better known as the North Star. It holds nearly still while the entire northern sky turns."

"Like the hub of a wheel."

"Yes." Patrick smiled. "Just like that. The sky turns like a wheel and Polaris is its hub, always marking true north."

True north. She liked the sound of that. "Which one is it?"

"First, find the Big Dipper." He traced it with his finger, and she tried to follow along.

"I don't see it."

His hand moved, his arm brushing her shoulder. "Pretend the Big Dipper is the palm of your hand. Wait. Hold on." He unwrapped her fingers. "Cup your hand, but don't make a fist. Just pretend you're holding a mug or a bowl." He lifted her cupped hand in the sky. "At the top of your fingers, you'll find the Little Dipper. That can be a little harder to find. See it?"

"Oh, okay. Yes, I see it."

"Now track down to where your fingers meet the palm of your hand. It's the end of the Little Dipper's handle. That bright star is Polaris."

She saw it then. The North Star. Polaris. True north.

"It always sits over the North Pole. The closer you get to the North Pole, the higher it will be in the sky."

"So if you're down by the equator, it would sit low on the horizon."

"Yes!" Patrick laughed. "Exactly right, Ruthie. You're a quick study. Its position is constant. It never moves. A navigational marker. People could use it to sail the seas or cross the deserts without getting lost. When slavery existed in the United States, slaves used the North Star to light their way to freedom."

She eyed Patrick curiously, storing this information away. Then she turned back to the night sky, black and blank but for the stars and a sliver of a new moon.

It seemed to occur to him that he was holding her hand because he suddenly dropped it and stuffed his hands in his pants pockets. "It's really not so hard to find, once someone shows you where to look."

Their gazes caught, and a hot flush started along the top of Ruthie's ears. She was glad for the darkness. "No, you're right. Once you know where to look, it's not hard to find." True north. Was that her *it*? The thing she was waiting for?

She stared until her neck ached. "The night sky . . . it's so vast. It makes me feel incredibly insignificant."

"Really? I have the opposite reaction. To think that this third planet from the sun, nestled in the Milky Way Galaxy, one galaxy among billions, is the object of God's attention. Why? Why us? He could have given us one star to admire, but he's given us billions. And planets too. Did you know that one of the rings of Saturn is braided? No one knows why. Perhaps just to show us God's infinite creativity. It's mind-boggling. It makes me feel very, very significant."

"It makes me feel very, very, very small."

"I see."

But how could Patrick see? She doubted he was ever confused. He seemed so sure about everything, so certain, so clear.

"Where are you going?" he asked.

"Where am I going?"

"It's late. Nearly midnight. You look like you're on your way somewhere."

A familiar sound of a horse's clip-clop mixed with the clackety sound of iron-clad wheels crunching on the road announced the arrival of a buggy to the bottom of the driveway. Earlier today, against her better judgment, Luke had talked her into going with him to meet some friends. "It'll help you get your mind off of that stranger in the inn," he had told her, and that was just the encouragement she needed. She glanced at Patrick. "I'm going to a . . . youth gathering."

Patrick's eyes met hers with the faintest lift of his eyebrows, as if she were a puzzle he was trying to piece together. The effect was unsettling. "Well, don't let me stop you."

"Do you want to come?"

He shook his head. "Not tonight. I'm a little tired. Maybe next time, though." He did look tired. Pale, with dark circles under his eyes. Hot, too, for it was a muggy night. His hair fell in tangled strands over his forehead, curling slightly at the ends as he gazed upward. She fought an impulse to brush the hair back out of his eyes, to touch him with the same gentle touch that he would give to his bird. "Thanks for not insisting we talk in Penn Dutch."

Her eyes went wide. "I forgot!"

He laughed, before stepping around her to walk up the driveway. "Next time, I'll go with you. I'd like to meet your friends."

She watched him for a while. He was a strange one, that Patrick Kelly. *Unflappable* was the word that came to mind. She wished she were unflappable. Unable—or unwilling?—to be flapped. She heard Luke's horse whinny and hurried down the hill to meet the buggy.

"Your chariot awaits, my lovely damsel," Luke said, slurring the words.

She stopped abruptly. "You're drunk."

"Nonsense."

She looked at the shine of booze bright in his eyes. Booze-shine. She knew that look well on Luke. "You're gutter-drunk and I'm not going."

"Nonsense. That's ridiculous. I'm church-sober."

She snorted. His version of church-sober meant mildly intoxicated.

He stared down at her a moment longer, then heaved a deep sigh. He wrapped the reins around the brake handle and swung out of the buggy. "Don't get on your high horse. I just got the party started a little early, that's all." He tapped her nose with his finger and tried to wiggle his brows at her. "Who were you talking to?"

"None of your business."

In his other hand was a bottle. He held it out to her. "Do you want a drink?"

Ruthie shook her head. "Your drinking has dimmed my enthusiasm for alcohol."

"Aw, come on, Ruthie. Don't be like that." He reached out for her, but she backed up and he nearly fell over.

"I told you. I'm not going with you. You're mistaken to think I would want to go anywhere with you when you're like this."

He gave her a smile. "Look at it this way. I've made all the mistakes, so you don't have to." He drained his bottle and tossed it in the road, causing it to shatter.

She was already irritated with Luke for showing up drunk. No, that was inaccurate. She wasn't irritated, she wasn't annoyed, she wasn't "out of sorts." She was flat-out, full-steam, blow-your-top *angry*. "What is wrong with you? I have three little sisters who walk barefoot everywhere. You're going to clean up every last shard. Or I will get—"

A strange look came over Luke. He folded up as if someone had let the air out of him and bolted for the side of the road, one hand holding onto the mailbox post, as he threw up the vodka that had soured the contents of his belly.

Ruthie took a few steps, then looked up at the house. Lamp-shine spilled from Patrick's open bedroom window in a soft yellow pool. She wondered if he could hear the terrible gag-ging, choking sounds that came from the road. Grateful he hadn't accepted her invitation to come tonight, she did won-der what he would have done, or said, if he were witnessing Luke's . . . disgusting humiliation.

Nothing could be further from what Patrick thought it meant to be Amish. But what did he think it meant? What drew Patrick to them?

The peace in their hearts, she supposed. But what was so peaceful about watching Luke Schrock throw up? Nothing. Nothing at all.

After Luke's stomach emptied, he slowly straightened, wiped his mouth with his shirtsleeve, ran a hand through his mussed hair. She picked up his hat and handed it to him. "I'm going inside."

"Ruthie, wait." She could see the throb of the pulse in his throat. "I'm sorry."

She sighed. "I know. You're always sorry, Luke." She started up the hill and he fell into step beside her, his stride long-legged and only a little wavery now.

"Wait." He pulled on her arm, a little too sharply, and she pulled it away. "Wait. I really am sorry. I won't do it again." He crossed his heart to emphasize his sincerity.

"Okay," she said, not believing him. She glanced over at the mailbox, splattered with the contents of his stomach. And the broken bottle glass that littered the road. "You'd better get a bucket of water and clean that up. And a broom too."

"Absolutely." He gave her a dazzling smile. He was feeling

better. "Wouldn't want to shock Molly when she runs to get the mail." He walked to the horse.

"Now, Luke. Now. Before you meet up with your friends and drink more and forget everything."

"My, my, aren't you getting a bit sharp-tongued in your wise old age."

"I'm not old and I'm not wise. I'm just tired of this." She pointed to the mailbox. "Use soap and hot water on that."

Luke swept his hat off his head and bent over at the waist in an exaggerated bow. "Consider it done."

In the morning, Ruthie woke early and hurried down to the mailbox with a bucket of hot soapy water and a scrub brush to clean up Luke's mess before anyone else found it first.

She had forgotten about the broken bottle, shattered shards of pieces on the road. Luke! No doubt, he was sleeping off his binge, happily unaware of the effect his foolishness had on others.

"Here, let me help."

She hadn't heard Patrick come up behind her and jumped at the sound of his voice. In his hands were a brush and a dustpan. "Don't want you cutting yourself with the glass." He bent down and started sweeping the broken vodka bottle into a neat pile.

And that was the moment when Ruthie's great fondness for Patrick Kelly began.

Matt asked to meet David and Dok at the Bent N' Dent late in the day. Official business, he told them. He handed Dok the coroner's report. As she rifled through it, Matt told David that the stranger at Eagle Hill, known for now as a John Doe, had died of a heart attack.

"But what about the blow to the head?" David asked.

Matt shrugged. "The coroner wasn't sure what caused it, but he ruled it out as the cause of death."

"What about his identity?" Dok said. "Have you gotten any closer to that? Someone must have reported a missing person by now. It's been days."

"Working on it."

"In other words . . . no leads?"

"Nothing yet. We're still working on it. On my way back to town, I'll stop at the Inn at Eagle Hill and let them know they can open up for business."

Which meant, David realized, that Patrick Kelly would no longer need to stay in Jesse's bedroom and could move across the road, as originally planned. He felt a tinge of disappointment. He had liked having Patrick around. He might be young, only twenty, but he was quite mature and extremely well read. Twice now, they had stayed up late having a theological discussion about the effects of the Reformation. Raised as an orthodox Catholic, Patrick had been exposed to very different views about the Reformation than most Protestants. Some parts of being Amish were quite close to Catholicism—the emphasis on confession, for example. And some parts were radically different—adult baptism versus infant baptism, the worship of the Madonna, praying to saints. Patrick was full of questions, brimming with curiosity. David relished their talks.

Matt leaned against the counter. "So, Dok, how goes private practice?"

"Slow."

That was an understatement, David knew. He'd been her only patient, all week long.

"Give it time."

"Time is something I happen to have an abundance of right now."

A streak of red started up Matt's cheeks. "Maybe, then, we could get lunch sometime." He cleared his throat. "Or dinner."

She handed him back the coroner's report. "Matt, it's never a good idea to mix business and personal life." She went to the door and lifted her hand in a casual goodbye.

"But . . . we're not in the same business," Matt said. "Not at all."

She either didn't hear Matt or pretended she hadn't. After the door closed behind her, Matt looked back at David. "Why won't she go out with me?"

"I don't know."

"Any advice?"

Advice? On how to date his sister? He laughed. "Only this—if you give up too easily, you're clearly not The One."

Ruthie arranged a dozen long-stemmed red roses in a vase. Luke Schrock had sent them to her as an apology for his behavior the other night. "It will never happen again," he wrote in the card. "Just say you'll forgive me."

She forgave him. She always did.

There was something about Luke that made it impossible to stay mad at him for long. He was fascinating but reckless—and not in a good way. He had sworn his undying love to Ruthie since they were in seventh grade, but something always made her hold back from fully returning his feelings. It wasn't because she didn't have feelings for him. She did. Strong ones. She cared about Luke, at times she even thought she might love him, especially those times when he was sweet and thoughtful and attentive. He was an amazing, lavish gift giver. He remembered romantic details: her birthday, the color of her dress on the day he first saw her, her favorite flower—a red rose.

Her feelings about Luke were a mess. She was a mess. She was a jumble of messy feelings. Alles fashmiaht. *Everything is messy.*

But not when she was around Patrick. There was a stillness about him that made her feel calm too. He was sort of enigmatically happy, with a tranquility that drew her to him like an ant to a picnic. He was refreshing, like a summer rain shower that cleared away the oppressive and muggy air.

She'd never spent time around a boy before who didn't seem to care at all what she thought of him. Most boys, including Luke—especially Luke—sought some kind of reaction from her. Patrick was the same before she showed up and exactly the same after she left him.

For the first time in her life, she found herself making minor adjustments to attract a boy's attention. She wore a green dress during yesterday's tutoring session because Patrick had casually mentioned that green was his favorite color. Tonight she stayed up much too late, reading in the living room, waiting until he returned home from stargazing. How ridiculous! He walked in the house, said hello and goodnight to her, and went straight to his room.

She'd tried hard to interest him, only to find that nothing seemed to affect Patrick Kelly. He was friendly and polite to her, but kept a slight air of distance and and detachment. Dare she think it?—he clearly did not feel any attraction to her. None in the least.

Really, she knew almost nothing about him. He took an interest in everything, asking question after question, but he didn't volunteer much about himself. Her mind reeled back to their tutoring session earlier today. He had diligently mastered the lengthy list of vocabulary words she'd given him. She handed him a new list, this time with one hundred words—he told her to be a tough taskmaster!—and said, "You fit in as though you'd been around here for years. And we're not always an easy bunch to get along with."

"Thank you," he said, with that straightforward look of his that made her stomach feel fluttery. "Time is short. I don't want to waste a moment."

"Oh?" Ruthie was immediately interested. Here was the perfect opening to discover more about him. But just then her father arrived home to announce that the cottage at the Inn of Eagle Hill was deemed ready to be back in business, and Patrick vaulted upstairs. He hurriedly packed up his backpack, thanked David for extending hospitality, grabbed Nyna the Mynah's cage—which got her squawking in indignation—and moved across the road. He didn't seem one bit bothered to leave the Stoltzfus home. Grateful for the time with them, but almost eager to be on his own.

What would happen to their Penn Dutch tutoring sessions? Patrick didn't mention a word about them. Were they over?

She felt a zing of disappointment.

David went out to the garden to find Birdy picking tomatoes in the tomato patch. He'd never thought he'd see this patch of soil looking the way it did. Neat, tidy rows; green, healthy plants. It was Birdy, all Birdy. He watched her for a few moments before he interrupted her. She looked like a young girl, with the blue scarf wrapped around her head and tied under her chin. He began to think, not for the first time, of how extraordinarily blessed he was to find this late-flowering love.

She lifted her head when she heard him call her name and responded with a bright smile, such a beautiful smile. It lit her from head to toe.

"Matt Lehman said the stranger who died at the inn had a heart attack. Natural causes. The cottage was given the all clear, so Patrick packed up and moved over."

Birdy's face fell in disappointment. "I suppose that means he's taking Nyna the Mynah with him."

"Yes, but you can hear her squawk from here." Frankly, David would not miss Nyna the Mynah's nocturnal one-sided conversations. He took off his straw hat and wiped his forehead with one arm. "Let's go canoeing at Blue Lake Pond."

"Now?"

"Yes. Now. For one brief afternoon, all is well in Stoney Ridge."

She beamed, positively beamed. The joy on her face moved his heart, every time.

"I'll go get the girls."

"No, no. Just you and me. The girls are fine. Ruthie said she would watch them." He walked up to her and helped her to her feet. "Just you. And me." He leaned over to kiss her gently on her lips.

"On a Saturday afternoon? When the tomatoes need picking and the laundry is waiting to be taken off the clothesline?"

"Especially then."

She grinned and kissed him back. "I'll meet you by the buggy in five minutes."

Not much later, they arrived at Blue Lake Pond and hitched Thistle to a post in the deep shade. David lifted the canoe off the top of the buggy. He and Birdy hoisted it onto their shoulders and lowered it into the water. It was an old canoe, one David had as a boy but hadn't used since they came to Stoney Ridge. They paddled the canoe slowly around the pond, exploring lovely nooks and crannies along the shoreline, chatting about family news.

"I was over at Katrina's this morning," Birdy said, "helping Molly give the baby a bath."

David knew how Birdy loved babies, how she longed for a baby of her own. "Does holding the baby help? Maybe, satisfy the desire for one of your own?"

"It's lovely to hold him, but it's no substitute for having our own baby someday." She dipped her hand in the water. "I dream of it every day."

Every day? It was a thought that rarely occurred to David, only when he considered Birdy. He could barely keep up with the six children he already had, and now two grandchildren.

Every day? She dreamed of having a baby every single day. He had no idea.

Lord, he silently prayed, *I need to pray for my wife's deepest desire to be fulfilled. Every day.*

They sat back in the warm sun and drank in the stillness of land and water and sky. The air was windless, the trees were absolutely motionless.

"It's so quiet," Birdy said. "Even the birds are silent. It reminds me of that moment, in church, just before the Vorsinger trills the first note. It's like we're in an outdoor sanctuary, one that's hushed with reverence."

Leave it to his Birdy to find a way to worship a majestic God in an old canoe on a second-rate pond. She viewed all of life in quiet wonder. Birdy taught David that he had been set down in a world of wonders: rivers and trails, birds and beavers. "A lot is going on," Birdy often reminded him, "when you don't think anything is."

He loved this woman. Sometimes, it seemed as if he'd been frozen for the last few years and was only now beginning to thaw. "Birdy, have you ever seen the ocean?"

"No. Someday, perhaps."

Someday, definitely. He would love to watch her face as she dipped her toes into the sea for the first time, breathed in that salt-tinged, oxygen-rich air. She would love it.

"So you've been?"

"Yes. Years ago." He looked over the side at the placid water, watching a water bug skate over the surface of the pond.

"With Anna?"

He looked back at her sharply. How did she know? "Yes."

"David, I like to hear about your memories with Anna. You rarely mention her name. I don't want you to feel as if you can't talk about her."

She had told him such things before, but he still felt uncomfortable sharing memories of his first wife with his second wife. It was one thing to have the children talk of Anna as their mother—something he encouraged—but for him to speak of her as his wife felt completely different. Uncomfortable. Memories of Anna were . . . private. If he shared them, he felt as if they might lose their effervescence, like opening a bottle of carbonated pop.

"You get a certain look on your face when you're thinking of her, as if you're lost in another world."

He reached out for her hand. "Maybe I seem to be in another world, but I'm not lost."

She smiled.

"At times it might not be easy for me to bring my past up, but you are always welcome to ask me anything."

"Anything?"

He nodded. "Anything."

For a long moment, they gazed at each other, until a curious look came over Birdy's face. "Can you swim?"

"Yes, of course. Can't you?"

"I'm an excellent swimmer. I had to be to keep up with those brothers of mine."

"Why do you ask?"

She pointed to their bare feet. David looked down and realized the bottom of the canoe was filling up with water. They were sinking! And far from shore.

She started to chuckle, then laugh out loud—deep down

belly laughter. David watched her for a moment. He was not a man prone to levity. Often, he took life so seriously that others encouraged him to lighten up. But Birdy had a way of releasing joy in him. Holy joy. Her laughter was contagious and David couldn't help but join in. Laughing, laughing, laughing. Laughing until his sides ached. He grabbed the paddles and turned the canoe around to paddle toward shore.

"We should just give up and swim to shore," she said between gulps of giggles, tears streaming down her face. "We'll never make it."

"We'll make it," David said confidently, though he paddled faster and harder than he had thought was possible.

Jesse grabbed his favorite clay pitcher to fill with water for C.P.'s dish and stopped short. A strange odor wafted up. He sniffed his pitcher, then ran a finger inside it. He rubbed his fingertips together. Gasoline. Someone had filled it with gasoline! He stormed out to find his two apprentices, sleeping in the sun. "Who did this?" he roared. "Which one of you filled my pitcher with gasoline?"

The boys jumped up. Sammy looked puzzled, while Leroy looked sheepish. "I did it," Leroy admitted. "It was Fern's fault. She told me to mow the front lawn. The mower was out of gas, so I went to the tank, but I couldn't find anything to catch the gas. So I found that thing and it was empty. I thought I'd use it. It was all Fern's fault. Blame her."

Jesse was incredulous. "Can't you see that it's a water pitcher? My favorite water pitcher?"

"Don't worry, I'll wash it." Leroy shrugged his shoulders. "Or you could get another one and we can use this one for gasoline."

Jesse couldn't just go and get another one because this pitcher had once been his mother's. But there was no way this ignorant boy could understand that. He couldn't see that this water pitcher was important to Jesse because he couldn't see longer than his nose. How was anyone ever going to be able to break through Leroy Glick's thickheadedness?

Normally, he took the boys along when he delivered a repaired buggy. They would follow him in Jesse's buggy, partly so that they could observe customer satisfaction and also so that he could get a ride home. Today, he couldn't handle being around them for one more moment. He harnessed his own horse, Sir Galahad, to the repaired buggy traces and told his useless apprentices that he would be gone for an hour or two. He gave them specific tasks to do, repeated them for clarification, doubting all the time that they would complete them.

Jesse had to travel through town to get to the Sisters' House, to deliver their buggy with its reflector bolted tightly on the back, and happened to notice the Sweet Tooth Bakery as he drove up Main Street. On the way home, he decided, he would stop in and treat himself to a cinnamon roll, maybe two, to improve his mood before returning to the simpleton apprentices. After leaving the buggy at the Sisters' House, he rode Sir Galahad bareback, stopped at the bakery, and tied him to the hitching post. This was a good idea to salvage his mood.

This was a bad idea to salvage his mood.

In a hurry, Jesse Stoltzfus exhaled, frustrated. The wait inside the bakery had nearly reached to the door when he had arrived. He had already waited ten minutes—watching the glass case as only four cinnamon rolls were left, then three, then two. Finally, he was at the counter, ready to order. The door opened with a gust of hot humid air. "Wann en Gaul eigschpannt is, mach mer die Lein fescht." *When a horse is hitched up, one should tie the line securely.*

He turned around slowly, curious as to whom the beguiling voice, low and musical, belonged. Guckich. *Gorgeous.* That's the only word he could think of to describe this young woman. His mind spun as he realized he knew her, and from the look of horror that filled her face, she recognized him too. Jenny Yoder, a girl he had known in Ohio. Swallowing with effort, he suppressed an unmanly shudder.

They went to school together for a few years, before she moved and he'd lost track of her and her older brother Chris. But he'd never forgotten her. She had been *that* annoying.

"Why . . . Jesse Stoltzfus!" She managed a smile that almost appeared genuine. "What a coincidence . . . seeing you . . . here. In Stoney Ridge."

"Jenny. Hello. And you're right, it certainly is a coincidence. I wasn't expecting to see you either." Ever again.

"Your hair." She sounded amazed. "It's still the color of carrots."

Jesse tried to come up with a tart retort but drew a blank. Frustrating! He turned his attention back to the counter clerk. "I'd like that last cinnamon roll."

Jenny Yoder gasped. "Oh no. I just got into town and I've been dreaming of Sweet Tooth Bakery cinnamon rolls for days. Weeks. Months!"

The clerk froze as she reached into the counter for the last roll, then glanced up at Jesse with a question in her eyes. *Are you going to be a gentleman?* the look said.

Nope. Too bad for Jenny Yoder, Jesse wanted to say. Come back tomorrow. "Yes, well . . . I . . ." He turned to look at

Jenny. For an instant, her expression faltered and he was startled again by her appearance. That . . . loveliness.

Then her lips formed a tight curve. "But don't let that stop you."

Normally he wouldn't. However, Jesse liked having the upper hand, especially when it came to Jenny Yoder. "It is most kind of you to concern yourself with me, Jenny, but I am, in fact, more interested in the low-fat bran muffin. That cinnamon roll could feed a family of four." He was aware of the smugness of his tone. And the frown on Jenny's face. Her expression told him she knew exactly what he was doing, which only increased his satisfaction.

"You could share it," the bakery clerk suggested. "I can cut it in half and you can share it."

"Nonsense," Jesse said. "Let the portly girl have it." That wasn't kind and it wasn't true. Jenny wasn't at all portly. He pointed to a very dry-looking bran muffin in the case.

"Excellent," Jenny said, uninsulted, accepting the cinnamon roll from the clerk.

Jesse took the bran muffin out of the bag and took a bite. It tasted like it looked. Horrible.

Jenny was at the door, turned, and leveled her gaze at Jesse, unblinking. "By the way, your horse is gone."

He strode to the window and looked at the hitching post. Sir Galahad had left without him.

"That's what I was trying to tell you when I came into the store. You hadn't fastened the reins in a tight enough knot." She took a bite out of that sweet, gooey cinnamon roll, slathered in icing and laced with cinnamon, and her eyes swooned. "Appeditlich," she said through a mouthful. *Delicious*. "Better than I even remembered." She gave him a breezy, queen-like wave of her hand as she walked out the door.

9

As she crossed the road for the third time that day, Ruthie was embarrassed to realize she kept making up excuses to run over to the inn in hopes of bumping into Patrick Kelly. She had started across the road twice and turned back, until she finally found an ironclad excuse to head over. In her hand was a long list of new vocabulary words, including phrases that he could use in everyday conversation: Di grabba greisha "caw, caw, caw." Ich vinsh so geahn 's veah gaych di law. *The crows scream "caw, caw, caw." I earnestly wish it would be against the law.*

She smiled at the irony of the phrase, considering Patrick had the noisiest bird in Stoney Ridge as a pet.

She found Rose taking laundry down off the clothesline on the far side of the house. "I thought I'd stop by to see if you needed any help with the cottage."

Rose finished folding a towel and dropped it into the large wicker basket by her bare feet. "With this particular guest, there probably won't be much to do on a daily basis. He seems like a very self-sufficient young man."

Ruthie glanced over at the cottage. That was a very good description of Patrick. Utterly self-sufficient. Frustratingly so.

"I would've thought it might bother someone to stay in the cottage after the stranger died, less than a week ago. But Patrick Kelly seems to be a very practical young man. It didn't faze him."

Ruthie looked down at her toes. "Rose, I am sorry about that stranger. I just didn't know what to do."

"Oh Ruthie, please don't worry about that night." She handed her a stack of towels. "You're going to meet a lot of people in need in your life. You should feel confident that your instinct was a good one. He wasn't a dangerous man. He was a man who needed help." She reached out to pluck some clothespins off a pair of pant legs, folded them, and dropped them in the basket. "In a way, I'm glad the stranger passed away feeling safe and wasn't left to wander the road during the night. It was just . . . his appointed time to die." Rose bent down to pick up the basket, filled to the brim with folded, dry laundry with its lingering scent of sun and soap. "Would you mind taking those towels to the cottage?"

Ruthie could barely contain a smile. "I'd be happy to." Extremely happy.

She practically skipped her way to the cottage. She knocked on the door, but there was no answer. She tried the door and found it unlocked. She hesitated. She had gone into this cottage dozens of times when she filled in for Mim Schrock at the inn—delivering fresh towels, taking out the rubbish, changing sheets . . . so why was she nervous? What was wrong with her! She was just leaving a stack of towels for the inn's guest. And a list of vocabulary words. Nothing more.

She pushed the door open, a little skittish after talking about the stranger's death. "Patrick?"

No answer, other than a "Jesus wept!" squawk from Nyna the Mynah, sitting on a perch in her cage.

Ruthie stepped into the cottage and set the towels on the table, along with the vocabulary list. The room smelled stuffy, so she unlocked the window over the kitchen sink and hoisted it up, letting in a spray of fresh air. The scents outside were the scents of summer, triggering a memory of walking hand in hand with her mother one morning. She stilled, lost in that moment, feeling a sharp pain of missing her.

Losing a parent, suddenly and unexpectedly, was what she and Luke had in common. Maybe it was the bond that glued them together, the thing that made it hard to just dismiss him as a lost cause. She understood his emptiness.

A huge part of Ruthie's life felt unfinished, incomplete. There were so many questions she would have liked to ask her mother, ones only meant for a mother. She liked Birdy, loved her, but it wasn't the same, and her sister Katrina was too busy for her.

Nyna let out a squawk, jerking Ruthie back to the present. She peered around the rooms, unabashedly curious. It was spotless. The bed was made. Next to the bed was an open Bible, with underlines and notes all over the page. How strange! No Amish person in her church would dare write in a Bible, unless it was to record births and deaths. She didn't touch anything, but she did look to see what Patrick had been reading that day and what was so important that he underlined it, twice.

"A man's heart deviseth his way: but the LORD directeth his steps." Proverbs 16:9. At least, Ruthie thought, he read from the King James Version. Then she squinted to see what note he had written in the margin, in surprisingly sloppy penmanship, as if he'd written it while riding a scooter down a gravel road.

Let things come to me instead of rushing at them as I usually do.

Curious! It was hard to imagine Patrick Kelly as someone who rushed at things. At anything. He moved slowly and cautiously.

Though, in a way, maybe he did rush at things. Coming to Stoney Ridge, wanting to convert to be Amish, trying to learn Penn Dutch in less than thirty days, spending time with Jesse to learn how to handle a horse and buggy.

So maybe he was someone who rushed at life instead of letting it come to him. Was that so bad? She admired that quality about him. She, on the other hand, sat and watched everything with a critical eye. A faultfinder, Luke said of her once, and she couldn't deny it.

Nyna the Mynah watched her every move, staring at her with an accusing look that spoke volumes. A look that might as well be saying, "Trespasser! How dare you!" Ruthie felt a twinge of guilt for poking around Patrick's room. More than a twinge. She felt as if she had read his diary and that was just wrong. She felt ashamed of herself. She had never read her sisters' diaries, not even Katrina's, and that was the only diary that held any interest to her. She left the cottage quickly and walked down the driveway.

"Ruthie!"

She spun around to see Luke coming toward her, trotting

out his charm as a matter of course. "Did you get my roses to apologize for the other night?"

"For the other night? Or for the next morning, when I cleaned up your mess?"

A hint of confusion ran through his eyes, and Ruthie realized he hadn't given a second thought to cleaning up after himself. Then he quickly swung back into charismatic character. He straightened his back and gave her the smart bow of a butler. "I can only offer my humblest apologies."

"Save it, Luke." She started for her house, leaving him to follow or not.

He fell into step beside her, his stride long-legged. "Come on, Ruthie. I just got a little carried away. My good judgment left me."

Alcohol, she thought, had done it to him again. "It always does."

He crossed his heart. "I'll swear off the devil's brew, if that's what it'll take to make you happy."

She stopped. "Are *you* happy, Luke?"

He tried to wiggle his brows at her. "I'd be happier if you'd stop acting so prickly all the time." He smiled at her, but she didn't smile back.

"Do you have any plans beyond weekend back-acre parties?"

He tapped her nose with his finger. "There's no call to go looking down that disapproving nose at me. You've enjoyed plenty of parties yourself."

"A few. Not plenty. That was all I needed to see how tiresome you and your friends can be."

"Oh, Ruthie, don't be like that."

"Like how?"

"What's gotten into you lately? You used to be fun. You're so serious all the time. So quick to judge."

"It just seems like there should be more to life than living from party to party." She crossed her arms over her chest. "Do you ever read the Bible?"

He laughed, then his smile left his face as he glanced at the cottage. "Does this have to do with that guy? Saint Patrick?" His mouth pulled into another smile, this one with a touch of meanness in it.

"So have you stopped drinking?"

"Absolutely. I'm done. Clean and sober."

She eyed him suspiciously. "Just how long have you been clean and sober?"

"I don't know. What day is it?"

"Wednesday."

Luke counted it out on his fingers. "Two."

"Two days? That can't be right."

"Two hours."

Enough. She spun around and walked up the driveway. Stomped. As usual, interaction with Luke left her in a riled mood.

Jesse ended up walking to Windmill Farm from the Sweet Tooth Bakery in the slanting heat of a summer afternoon, thinking of clever retorts he should have aimed at Jenny Yoder. So why was she back in town, anyway? The July sun burned on his neck and he felt drips of sweat stream down his back.

He walked down the main road for a mile or two, hoping someone would come by and take pity on him. Alas, not a single buggy drove past. Finally, he gave up and took a shortcut through a cornfield and then a cow pasture. He hopped over the rail fence, back onto the road. It was a seldom-traveled road, leading from nowhere and heading to nowhere. Up ahead, he saw something shiny on the gravel road. He stopped to pick it up—a cell phone?—and pressed a few buttons to see if it was working. Dead battery. He took off his hat and wiped his forehead, his thoughts drifting off to wonder what his apprentices were doing in his longer-than-scheduled absence and if they had located his hidden transistor radio to listen to the Philadelphia Phillies game. Probably. That's where he wanted to be right now. In his buggy shop, listening to the game, tinkering on buggies.

Jenny Yoder. Of *all* people. His oldest enemy. By a fluke of fate, she was back in his life.

They went through a few years together in a one-room schoolhouse in Ohio. She arrived out of the blue, in the third grade, and shared a desk with Jesse for the next four years. The two of them made up the entire grade, year by year— third, fourth, fifth, sixth—and there was not a minute when the two of them did not resent sitting stuck together like a two-headed calf. Admittedly, Jenny was smart. Worse, she was clever. She kept him on his toes in school, but she also had a superior, queenly attitude that never failed to irk him. Professor Pompous, he had nicknamed her.

Her family life was always a little vague, and she kept it that way. The most Jesse could ever figure out was that she and her brother Chris were raised in a foster home by a kind old Amish woman named Deborah, and that's why Jenny went to an Amish one-room schoolhouse.

Then, one summer, old Deborah passed to her glory and Jenny and Chris disappeared. No one knew what had happened to them. Jesse figured the state of Ohio had scooped them up and deposited them in another foster home.

So why was Jenny Yoder in Stoney Ridge, of all places? Hopefully, she was just passing through. Just long enough to abscond with his cinnamon roll.

Even now, half a dozen or more years later, Jesse couldn't account for the depth of passion, of the worst sort, that had risen up in him when he realized that young woman in the bakery was Jenny Yoder. You'd think he'd be more mature by now . . . but apparently not.

He tried eating the bran muffin, but it chewed like birdseed and tasted like sawdust, so he heaved the muffin into a huge, straggly blackberry bush along the road and heard an odd clunk, as loud as a rock—his muffin—hitting something metal. He peered into the blackberry bush. There was a car in there. He looked back at the road and saw a sign of tire tracks veering off the road and into the bush, tracks that looked fairly new. The rain they'd had the last few nights had turned the side of the road into puddles. He parted the bushes and saw a sticker on the windshield. The car was a rental and it hadn't been here long. He took a deep breath and peered inside. No one. Phew. Then he tried the door handle and flipped the trunk. Inside was a small suitcase.

Should he look inside?

Definitely not.

Jesse turned around and walked back to town to find Matt Lehman.

Later that night, Ruthie slipped downstairs to talk to her dad when she knew Birdy was upstairs with Emily and Lydie.

She appreciated Birdy, had grown fond of her, but she missed time with her father. Now and then, they used to have late-night talks after her sisters had gone to sleep. You could ask him anything; nothing was off-limits. An "open-door policy," he called it. Doubts, complaints, questions—he listened carefully, took her thoughts seriously, and never acted shocked or judge-y. Of all the things she loved and admired about her dad, the open-door policy was her favorite. She stood at the doorjamb until he looked up from his desk and noticed her.

He gave her a fond smile. "What's on your mind?"

"What does Proverbs 16:9 mean?"

David reached for his Bible and opened it. "'The heart of a man deviseth his way: but the LORD directeth his steps.'" He leaned back in his chair. "It means that whatever we think might be the right direction for us, the right path, God has the final say." He closed the Bible. "What makes you ask?"

Come clean, Ruthie. "I was putting towels in the guest cottage at the inn and Patrick Kelly's Bible was open. I didn't mean to snoop, but I . . . did. That verse was underlined twice, and then he wrote in the margin: 'Let things come to me instead of rushing at them as I usually do.' I wondered if that's what the verse meant."

"Setting aside the invasion of Patrick's privacy, I think you might be missing the point. Patrick wasn't simply restating the verse, he was applying it to himself."

Oh.

"It was an example of how faith intersects life. Patrick was letting the Scripture speak to him. To change him."

Again, oh. Such a thought hadn't occurred to her.

"Patrick told me that he spends a lot of time meditating on God's Word."

She glanced up quickly at her father. Was he aware that she was intensely interested in anything Patrick said or did? But her dad didn't seem to have a hidden motive. She spoke quietly. "I thought reading the Bible was enough."

"Certainly, it's a start. But reading the Bible without letting it sink deep into our hearts and souls isn't enough." He looked at the ceiling, as if searching for the right words. "It's a little like the manna that came down from the heavens each day for the Israelites to gather, to sustain them, while they were wandering in the desert for forty years. When the manna was kept, it spoiled."

"Other than on the Sabbath."

"Aha! You've been paying attention to my sermons. Yes, you're right. Other than on the Sabbath. And perhaps that means that reading the Bible without letting it affect us is like trying to keep the manna—it ends up rotting."

She collapsed into a chair with a heavy sigh. "I don't get it."

He held up his well-worn Bible. "It has to be devoured, consumed, ingested. Not just read. It has to go deep inside of us and make a difference in how we respond to circumstances, to people. To change us from the inside out. What's the point of having a head full of Bible verses and a heart full of emptiness?"

"So what's the difference between reading the Bible and meditating? Or what's the difference between meditation and prayer?"

"Great question," he said. "Certainly, it all begins in prayer." He opened his Bible and turned a few pages. "Here it is. Psalm 77:11–12. 'I will remember the works of the LORD: surely I will remember thy wonders of old. I will meditate also of all thy work, and talk of thy doings.' Look at the verbs in this passage that teach us how to meditate: remember, meditate, talk. The focus of our attention is on God. There is a change, a shift, and we are suddenly in an entirely different world. This happens while we are in prayer."

"And you're saying that meditation is part of prayer."

"In a way, yes. It's all part of the same conversation with God. Reading the Bible, prayer, meditating on his Word." He laced his fingers together. "They all work together to shape our heart."

Then the twins came tumbling down the steps to say goodnight and the moment was over. Ruthie quietly slipped upstairs to her room.

It was a Sunday afternoon, an off-Sunday. One of David's favorite days.

The conversation he had with Ruthie about the Israelites, manna, and the Sabbath stuck with him. He had always considered the Sabbath to be one of God's greatest gifts to man. Certainly, it was made for man, to cause him to rest, worship, and re-center on God, his work, his presence in one's life. A day of not doing, of not working, of renewal. The very word "Sabbath" had its origins in Hebrew as *sabbat*, was adopted by the Greeks, and eventually morphed into the Latin word *sabbatum*. It meant to rest. Stop. Quit. Cease.

Ceasing, David thought, was just the right word.

Isaiah wrote that "the everlasting God, the LORD, the Creator of the ends of the earth, fainteth not, neither is weary." God needs no rest. He rested on the seventh day because he had finished his creation.

David believed that a person's heart was reflected in how he honored the Sabbath. If the Sabbath were neglected, that meant that something else was "hallowed" or put in the holy place.

It was fair to say that he hadn't been greatly alarmed by Patrick's observations on that late-night buggy ride—curious and perplexed would be closer to the truth. But he also wasn't quite sure what to do with the information Patrick had indirectly supplied. Very likely, Patrick was mistaken. Hopefully, he was.

But what if he wasn't?

David shook his head in disgust. Why did he have to look for trouble? Why couldn't he just appreciate the way things were, right now? His mother, now living happily in Ohio with her new husband, told him she had named him after King David the Warrior, but he must have misunderstood her because he acted more like David the Worrier. He was always fretting over something.

Still he decided to drive down the roads and see for himself if any stores or roadside stands were open on this Sunday afternoon.

There was so much about the ministry that David loved— leading the church in worship, sharing the joy of baptism and weddings, shouldering the burdens of burials. But this part he loathed—the bishop's role becoming a stern father scolding errant children. Briefly, he considered giving the task to his deacon to ferret out those who had shops open on the Sabbath, but he knew that wasn't appropriate in this situation. It wasn't an issue of not taking the Ordnung seriously. Those issues belonged to the deacon.

This was a heart issue. A bishop dilemma. At best it was a casual use of this holy day, set apart from all the others; at worst it was a calloused one.

Lord, he prayed, *please don't make me be that kind of bishop. You know how difficult it is for me to be that kind of father to my own children—to set down rules and see that they are obeyed. I want to lead, Lord, not to scold.*

But as he drove down the road past Edith and Hank Lapp's chicken and egg farm, he saw the window open on the wooden roadside stand. Inside was Hank, feet up on the counter, sound asleep. David pulled in Thistle's reins and dropped his chin to his chest. *I hear you, Lord. I see.*

He climbed out of the buggy and walked over to the egg stand. Hank was in a deep sleep. His jaw was slacked open, he was snoring like a grizzly bear in midwinter. "Hank," David said softly.

No response.

"Hank," he said a little louder. "Hank."

Nothing.

"HANK!"

That worked. Hank jerked awake, dropped his feet to the floor, rocketed upright. "One dozen for two bucks. Two dozen for three bucks! Best eggs in the county!" Then his eyes focused—his good eye, actually—and he realized it was the bishop who stood before him. "David . . . ," he sputtered. "The thing is . . . Edith's hens were in a happy mood this week and laid an abundance of eggs. Edith thought it would be best to try to sell them to the tourist buses going down the road . . . otherwise they'd go bad. It's just a onetime Sunday. Not a regular thing like them quilters is doing." He pointed a thumb down the road. "That's who you should be going after. Them quilters."

There were so many things wrong with Hank's excuses that David didn't know where to begin. Blaming Edith, for one. A little like Adam blaming Eve in the Garden of Eden for giving him the fruit to eat. Another error: rationalizing the eggs would go bad if they waited a day to be sold. It boiled down to a missed opportunity for a sale. Rather than thank God for the abundance of eggs, Edith and Hank felt the burden of the blessing. And then accused the quilters.

But to make sense of this to Hank Lapp, he needed to think the way Hank thought.

"Hank, if someone were to purchase your eggs today, what would they do with them?"

Hank blinked rapidly as if it were a trick question. "They'd have to get them home, into the cooler."

"Maybe they want to make a cake for Sunday supper, but they realize they're out of milk. So then what would they do?"

"Run down to the Bent N' Dent and get a carton of milk."

"But the Bent N' Dent is closed today. However, let's say there's such a demand for milk on Sunday afternoons, because so many folks are buying your good eggs, that I decide the store should remain open. Then what?"

"I see where you're going, David. Other folks might shop on Sundays."

"Yes, and then maybe we would decide that church should be shortened up a little so we can get the shopping done. And as long as we're out shopping, let's get other errands taken care of too." He glanced over at Thistle, patiently waiting for him. "My horse needs new shoes. It'd be nice if the blacksmith could take care of that on Sunday, so I don't have to take precious time out of the workweek. And then there's buggy repairs. That, too, would be nice to have taken care of on Sunday, but Jesse may need help managing those repairs. Those apprentices of his, well, you know they aren't overly blessed with intellectual horsepower. You may need to help Jesse out."

Hank gasped. Buggy repairs—that was talking his language. "I like my Sunday afternoon naps!"

"Exactly. And all this happened because you sold eggs on a Sunday."

Hank breathed in and out. "I told Edith this was a blamed foolish idea!" He started packing the cartons of eggs into a box. "I told her. She doesn't listen. But is she the one who's facing the bishop? No. She's off visiting her sister. Women are always getting me into trouble."

David had to swallow a smile as he climbed back into the buggy. *Convict them one by one, Lord.*

But if Hank Lapp was any indication, they were going to need a nudge to get back in the right direction. Maybe more than a nudge.

10

David waited for the right moment to drop the bomb. The house was empty, and he was nonchalantly looking for a snack to tide him over to supper as Ruthie sat at the table, absorbed in preparing a lengthy Penn Dutch vocabulary list for Patrick Kelly. "Ruthie, the school board paid a call this morning. Danny Riehl is going to stay on at Prince Edward Island. They'd like you to consider taking the teaching job this next term."

Ruthie's head remained bent over her work. "No. Absolutely not. Never. Not in a million years."

"I don't understand that. You love learning."

She sighed and put her pencil down, then turned around to face him. "I do. But I don't like teaching."

"You're teaching Patrick."

"That's different."

"How so?"

"It's only for one month. And he's paying me a lot of money. Even still, the whole process of teaching tries my patience." She lifted her hands in a helpless gesture. "You might not have noticed, but I'm not a particularly patient person."

"Actually, I have noticed." Everyone knew about Ruthie's short fuse. "What would you like to do for work? The Inn at Eagle Hill isn't steady work."

"I've been giving that topic a lot of thought." Slowly, she pulled an envelope out of her Penn Dutch–English dictionary and handed it to him. "I took the GED. And . . . I passed."

He opened the envelope and read the scores. "You did more than pass. You sailed through it." He smiled at her. He wasn't surprised she did so well, not at all. Ruthie had a fine mind.

"You're not mad?"

"Not that you passed. I'm only disappointed you felt the need to hide it from me."

He saw her subtly guarded mask drop and her expression change to discouragement and confusion. A memory, more a feeling than a vision, flashed through his mind. He remembered what it felt like to be seventeen or eighteen, about the time his mother was applying daily pressure to make him get baptized. The closer and closer the day drew, the further and further his interest in baptism grew. He understood some—not all, but some—of Ruthie's inner turmoil.

Ruthie propped her elbows on the table and held her head in her hands. "Dad, I know what I don't want to do. The problem is that I don't know what I *do* want to do. Other than . . . I know I want to keep learning. Is that so wrong?"

David swept a hand toward the living room, where he had a full wall of a bookshelf, filled with books. "I understand. I feel the same way."

"It's different for you. You're a bishop. You're supposed to know everything."

"Honey, do you really think I wouldn't be reading books if I weren't in leadership? Of course not. I love to read. I love to learn. So do you. No one wants to change that part of you. It's the best part of you. It's the way God made you. It's a gift he's given you—your curiosity, your intelligence."

"I don't want to teach school."

This wasn't working. He needed to try a different approach. "Have you ever heard of the Dead Sea?"

She squeezed her eyes shut in that *oh-no-a-sermon-is-coming* way.

He persevered, nevertheless, well conditioned to that look from his children. "It's actually not a sea but a stagnant lake near Jordan and Israel. The Jordan River flows into the Dead Sea, but nothing flows out of it. Because of that, water depletes only through evaporation. Water in the Dead Sea is six times as salty as the ocean. Nothing can grow in it. No seaweed, no plants, no fish." He paused, hoping she would mull over the parallel he was trying to make, and noticed dirt on the floor that he must have tracked in from the barn. He grabbed a broom and dustpan from the kitchen to sweep it up. "Do you understand what I'm getting at?"

"Yes. You're trying to make me take the teaching job."

David finished sweeping the dirt into the dustpan with deliberate movements and straightened up, regarding his daughter with an exaggerated display of patience. "No. I would never do that. But I do want you to consider the Dead Sea as a picture of what happens when we don't use our gifts. They're meant to be shared with others. If you only take information in, then you're using your gift for selfish reasons."

She was silent.

"Consider the teaching job, please. Pray about it."

"Dad, teachers need patience. I have none."

He smiled. "Pray about that too."

It was an auspicious day, warm but not too warm, with blue skies and a gentle breeze. Hank Lapp was at the buggy shop, flopped in a chair in the shade, talking about the weather to the apprentices, who were listening to him with rapt attention, as if hearing that it might rain later on today was a shocking news flash. Why, Ruthie wondered, did people talk about the weather so much? Anyone could see for himself, just by looking out the window. It might appear to be a bright, sunny day right now, but there were a few clouds gathering in the distance, and the breeze was really quite brisk, and that might mean a shower later on. A simple deduction.

Then Hank gave his own weather deduction and Ruthie had to cover her mouth to stifle a laugh. "Wann ich so lass fiel, noh meen ich watt Rege am kumme." *When I feel so listless, then I think rain is coming.*

When was Hank Lapp ever *not* listless?

Suddenly, Hank vaulted to his feet and sniffed the air. "Fresh cherry pie! Out of the oven. Let's go, boys!" He started toward the kitchen of Windmill Farm and the two apprentices dropped their tools and followed along, like two tigers on the trail of a gazelle.

C.P., stirred from his nap in the shade by the clamor of tools dropping on the floor, perked up his ears, sniffed the air, and charged after them. Jesse sighed. "Hank Lapp's olfactory sense is top-notch. Too bad there isn't employment for being a sterling sniffer." He watched the three of them as they bolted toward the farmhouse like there was a fire.

C.P. weaved between their legs and made a general nuisance of himself. The dog slipped into the farmhouse with them, then the door opened again and the dog was banished to sit on the porch.

It *was* lovely, the scent of Fern's cherry pie drifting gently in the wind, silently inviting others by making their mouth water in anticipation. One of the great pleasures of life, Patrick had said the other day, as Birdy was browning beef for stew on the stovetop while Ruthie tutored him in Penn Dutch at the kitchen table. "Such good smells," he had said, inhaling deeply. "There are certain smells of the Amish that warm the heart."

"What?" Ruthie said. "Like what?" The sour tang of manure instantly came to mind.

"Like the aroma that comes from a pail of warm milk, straight from the cow. Or how about the sweet smell of freshly mown hay? Now there's a scent I wish I could capture and put in a bottle. Send it to my suburban-dwelling parents."

Those generous remarks had startled Ruthie, like so many of Patrick's observations about her people. He saw beauty in such commonplace things, sights and smells she had been immersed in and never gave a second thought.

She gave an affectionate stroke down a horse's muzzle and watched Jesse try to unscrew a stubborn bolt in a broken reflector on the back of a buggy. "So how are buggy lessons working out for Patrick?"

"Patrick? He's very conscientious." Jesse peered around the buggy to answer her. "But not very coordinated."

She smiled. She'd noticed the same thing about Patrick. Just the other day, the same day as Birdy's beef stew making, she tossed him an apple to eat and he completely missed it.

It ended up hitting him in the mouth and he cut his lip with his teeth. She had felt terrible. "Jesse, what would you be doing if you weren't Amish?"

"Doing?"

"Yes. Doing." She sat down on the ground and hugged her knees to her chest. "Do you think you would go to college?"

Jesse arched his back in a stretch. "If I could choose any life, at any time, I would sail a ship across the ocean to the farthest corners of the world. Or go west with the pioneers into the open prairies."

"Let's narrow it down to contemporary times."

"Oh. Then, I'd be an astronaut. No doubt about that. I'd be heading to Mars."

She gave him a curious look. "So, you see yourself as an adventurer."

"Yes."

"Then why are you working in a buggy shop with two simpleminded apprentices?"

"Because this is where I'm meant to be." He frowned. "And trying to teach those two anything is a daily adventure."

"Don't you feel as if you're made for something more? Like, you should be doing something really important with your life. Not just stuck—"

Jesse's head snapped up and she realized, too late, she had offended him. She spoke without thinking, as if the words had been rising inside her like hot steam in a kettle.

"Not just stuck in a buggy shop, you mean?"

She wanted to go back to where they'd been a moment before, the familiarity, but worried the moment had passed. "I didn't mean to imply there's anything wrong with repairing buggies."

"Good," he snapped, in a crisp *you've-hurt-me* tone. "Because I do see my work as important." His voice softened. "The buggy repairs . . . they help everyone get where they need to be safely. And teaching those two numbskulls some skills that might benefit them in life . . . that means something to me." He reached down to pat his dog, C.P., who had slunk back to the buggy shop after Fern's rude banishment from the farmhouse. "Ruthie, I understand that you're feeling frustrated about what to do with your life. I've felt that way too. Most everyone has. I can't tell you what to do, but don't lump all the right things, the good things in your life, with that pile of frustration."

She looked up at her brother's eyes, almost the same color as her own—blueberry blue, a Stoltzfus trait. "What do you mean?"

"After Mom died, I didn't care about anything, especially about being Amish. I got pretty full of myself, thinking I could pick and choose which rules I liked and which I didn't. I hurt a lot of people with that way of thinking. It took someone believing in me, thinking I had something to offer, that made me see our way of life in a different way. I started to appreciate what it meant to be part of something bigger than myself."

"Who?"

He tipped his head toward the farmhouse. "Fern Lapp's School of Reform for Wayward Boys."

A laugh burst out of Ruthie. She hadn't realized Fern had made such an impact on her brother, but now that she thought about it, she could see it was true. Jesse *was* different, less self-centered, not at all lazy like he used to be, and more caring too. "The thing is . . . I just want to matter."

"That's just it." Jesse picked up a buggy wheel in need of repair. "See these missing spokes? It might not seem as if they matter. In fact, the wheel could keep going for a while longer. But soon, the weight of the buggy will start to take a toll on this wheel. More spokes will break and the rim will be unbalanced and start to bend out of shape. Every single spoke is needed to keep the buggy balanced. Each one matters.

"Every part of the equation influences the whole. You're part of our equation, Ruthie. You do matter. If you weren't a part of us, we'd have a missing spoke."

Ruthie knew all about missing spokes.

Jesse grabbed a rag and wiped his hands. "I'm going in for some cherry pie before it's all gone." He threw the rag on the top of his workbench and looked at her. "You coming?"

"No. There's somewhere I need to be." She picked up her scooter and rolled down the driveway, not really sure where that somewhere she needed to be was, but she was leaving Jesse with what she had come for: a lifting of her spirits.

Now that David's attention had been alerted, he kept bumping into more and more evidence that church members were neglecting the Sabbath. He learned that young Willie King had agreed to work at a farmers' market in Lancaster on his off-Sundays. When David asked Willie King why, he said he was paid time and a half.

And this was a family who had recently received a bonus from an oil lease signing. Why did Willie King need more? Why did his parents, Ida and Ora, need more?

Why did any of them keep needing more?

It came down to the same issue, in David's mind. The

more money people had, the more they wanted. Longed for, lusted for. He remembered a buggy horse he'd had as a boy, nicknamed "Hay Burner." This Thoroughbred had such a high metabolism that its appetite could not be satisfied. That one horse took twice the feed as a normal workhorse. That's what was happening in Stoney Ridge. Prosperity was turning people into hay burners.

There was nothing David could do about Willie King. He wasn't baptized, not yet a church member, and his mother just threw her hands up in the air, as if she couldn't do anything to change his mind. "I've talked to him until I'm blue in the face," Ida King said.

The problem, David felt, was not what she said but the example she led. While she might have told her son not to work on off-Sundays despite higher pay, she had recently signed an oil lease and promptly used the signing bonus for a new, slightly used buggy. There was nothing wrong with her old buggy. It was just . . . old.

And then David found himself caught in a tight spot. Jesse's buggy business was starting to thrive. It had taken him years to get that business sorted out from the mess of Hank Lapp. He had practically taught himself how to make repairs, how to develop a solid reputation for timeliness and reliability. If David were to start putting pressure on the church to reduce expenditures, Jesse's business would be the first to suffer.

How could he do that to his own son?

He hung his head. Sabbath-keeping seemed so simple, so clear, but it wasn't quite as easy as it looked.

He found himself filled with a tension, even dread, that he hadn't expected. He sat back in his chair, suddenly fatigued.

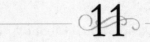

11

No one had ever told David what the best part of grandpar-enting was: it conjured up all those tucked-away memories of his own babies, minus the bone-tired fatigue of sleepless nights. David dropped by Moss Hill as often as he could to see his grandchildren. Little Anna was two years old now, the spitting image of his daughter Katrina. Strawberry red hair with a peaches-and-cream complexion. Newborn Benjo had more of Andy's coloring—olive skin, with a patch of dark fuzzy hair on his tiny head.

Birdy had packed up a hamper full of food for Katrina, to encourage her to rest and enjoy her newborn. As David set the hamper on the buggy seat, he wondered how Birdy was able to give so much to others when her own heart's desire went unfulfilled. On his drive to Moss Hill, he turned that thought over in his mind, as he had done countless times before.

Birdy never complained, but he knew she longed for a child of her own. As each few months passed, their hopes for a baby diminished. If he brought the subject up, Birdy would insist that she already had a quiver full of children. And she was an extraordinary stepmother. She seemed to know how to give each child what they needed from her. Not more, not less. Birdy never talked down to his daughters; she always took them seriously. She had the most mother-like role with the twins, and a very friendly relationship with Molly and Ruthie, Jesse and Katrina. But wouldn't it be wonderful if she could have a baby of her own? Their child. His and Birdy's.

He thought of the example of the psalmists, almost demanding God's attention. "Awake, O Lord." "God, listen to my prayer." "Have mercy on me." Audacious demands! With the kind of familiarity of an irate child speaking to a parent. Yet it struck David that such intimacy didn't offend God at all, but pleased him. He looked up at the sky. *Lord*, he prayed, *you are a promise keeper. You promised you would give us the desires of our hearts. Give Birdy the desire of her heart, Lord. If it's your will, let us have a baby.*

On this humid summer morning, David walked right into the farmhouse of Moss Hill and scooped up little Anna as she ran to him. He breathed in deeply, smelling the satisfying aroma of hot brewed coffee.

"I was hoping for a cup of coffee," he said.

Thelma, sitting at the table with Katrina, lifted an eyebrow. "How about a cup of chamomile tea?"

Ugh. He hated this meal-monitoring business. The women in his life were in cahoots, determined to keep his diet bland, beige, and boring. But then, where would he be without their vigilance? Popping Tums throughout the day, gripping his middle whenever he felt shots of pain. Or worse. He should be grateful for his wife's and daughters' surveillance but, oh! how he missed that cup of coffee in the morning. "No thanks. Already had one." Chamomile tea might be easier on his stomach ulcer, but it sailed right past his taste buds. He went over to the Moses basket in the corner of the room to see how little Benjo was doing and found the infant sound asleep. "He's grown, I think."

"Since yesterday?" Katrina smiled. "Not likely."

"How did he sleep last night?"

"Awful. He has his days and nights mixed up."

He turned and looked around the small house. "Weren't you going to have a mother's helper?"

"I had one lined up, but she changed her mind."

Thelma lifted a piece of paper. "We were just making a list of possible mother helpers." She frowned and picked up the pen. "But there aren't many options."

David saw Andy come up the driveway from the mossery. "I'll be right back. I wanted to ask Andy a question." With Anna in his arms, he walked down the hill to meet his son-in-law. When Anna saw him, she wiggled out of his arms to run to her father.

Andy might not be her biological father as he was Benjo's, but he was, in every way, Anna's father. When he had told David he wanted to marry Katrina, a single mother with a six-month-old baby, David questioned him about all kinds of things, but he made a point of asking how Andy would feel as more children arrived. He knew that Andy was desperately in love with Katrina, and he knew he adored Anna. But would he feel differently about Anna then? Favoritism could be toxic in families.

Andy had responded by pointing to the large kitchen garden next to the house, with its neat rows of tomatoes, beans stalks, sprawling pumpkins, spiky carrot tops. "The way I see it, any fellow can plant seeds. It's the way the seeds are cared for, tended to, nurtured, grown, and harvested that makes the difference. Anna will belong to me just the way our other children will belong to me. I'm the farmer in this family."

After that conversation, David never had another doubt about Andy. He never needed to.

Anna's squeals of joy jolted him back to the present. Andy lifted her high in the air, then down low, then up high again like a human swing.

"Morning, Andy."

Andy stopped swinging Anna and settled her onto his hip. "Good morning to you. I saw you drive up. Time for coffee?" He cringed. "I mean, um, tea? Water? Juice?"

David laughed. "Never mind. Katrina already offered. Actually, I just stopped by to ask you a few questions." They walked toward the house, matching strides. "Is the oil company still sending out more land agents?"

"Yes. They seem to keep coming. They're convinced that the oil traps on Moss Hill indicate more undiscovered oil in the region."

"And more leases are being signed?"

"Yes. I heard of two, just last week. The Noah Zooks and the Henry Smuckers."

David nodded. The leases brought in an initial signing bonus—usually ten to twenty thousand dollars, but the big money began rolling in when the oil wells were drilled and pumps installed. Each homeowner received a royalty percentage of the oil. For Moss Hill, it was a staggering amount. The first year, especially, the royalty check amount was beyond anything they could have imagined. Hundreds of thousands of dollars! That was the start of the turnaround for the church of Stoney Ridge. The first year's income was entirely donated to the church and helped wipe out heavy debts that had been piling up. David had hoped that Moss Hill would be a sterling example to everyone in the church. How to manage riches? Hold on to them lightly.

David felt a familiar niggling of distress . . . something he kept trying to throw off, but it kept returning to him, like a boomerang. As they reached Thistle and the buggy, he stopped. He'd gotten the information he came for. "I'd better head over to the store."

"Hold on a moment. I had something I wanted to discuss with you too. The end of the three-year lease will be coming due in a few months. The land agent has already asked about renegotiating. We're in a strong position. That oil trap has been a steady producer. Nothing like the first few months, but it's still going strong."

"I'll be in prayer over renegotiating." He climbed into the buggy and clucked to Thistle to back her up. He waved to Andy and Anna as he passed by, reading from the expression on his face that he hadn't given Andy the answer he wanted.

Yes, David pondered as he drove down the hill, that oil trap might be a strong producer of crude oil, but what else might it be producing in the church of Stoney Ridge?

Jesse smelled the corn fritters the moment he woke, the fry-oil scent in the air, the sweet corn aroma wafting down from the farmhouse. He bolted out of bed and changed his clothes, then hurried over to Fern's kitchen, throwing a casual wave at Amos as he tossed hay to the sheep in the pasture.

It came as a shock when he found Jenny Yoder standing by the stove, stirring a simmering pot of oatmeal.

"You," Jesse said in a flat voice.

"You," Jenny said in an equally flat voice. She added a dollop of butter and wiped her fingers on her apron.

"Why are you in Fern Lapp's kitchen?" His timing, as so often occurred with Fern, was unfortunate, as she was not ten feet away in the family room.

"Because Jenny lives here now."

"What?" Jesse must have sounded horrified because Fern pinned him with a look. "But how do you even know Jenny? She's from Ohio!"

Jenny ignored him and pulled some bowls out of the cupboard, like she knew exactly where everything belonged. Why was that?

Fern read his mind. "I thought you knew. Jenny's older brother Chris married Amos's youngest daughter, Mary Kate." She smiled at Jenny, or as close to a smile as Fern ever got. "She's family."

Jesse sank into a chair, buffaloed by that news. "So she's actually living here."

"I can hear you," Jenny said, putting a bowl of oatmeal down in front of him. "It's rude to speak of people as pronouns if they're standing right in front of you."

That, he decided at once, proved to him that this was the same Jenny Yoder he had known throughout grades three through six. Always correcting him. Always thinking she was smarter than him. Always right.

He was just about to make a clever retort when Fern cleared her throat. He glanced at her, knowing exactly what *that* throat clearing meant. So often Fern could quiet a sharp reply with the slightest look or touch. He lowered his eyes to the bowl of gray, pasty oatmeal. "I was hoping for corn fritters." He could see them cooling on a tray on the counter.

"Not possible," Jenny said. "We're having a comfort quilt bee today."

We, she said. Like she owned the place.

Not one minute later, Hank Lapp burst into the kitchen, desperate for a can of ground coffee. "Edith sent me! We're fresh out of coffee and she's as grouchy as a riled grizzly until she's had her third or fourth cup." He shuddered. "She looks like a grizzly too."

Hank Lapp could be described as a man with no filter.

"I'll get a spare can from the cellar," Jenny said.

"I'd better go with her," Fern said. "They're stacked on the top shelf." Jenny was not at all tall; in fact, she looked like a child to Jesse.

As soon as they disappeared down the steep cellar steps, Jesse whispered to Hank, "Why would a girl show up in a new town, for no apparent reason?"

Hank leaned toward him, reeking of stale cigar smoke. "ONE REASON!" He slammed the table with the palm of his hand. "Husband hunting."

Jesse stilled as worrisome thoughts came too fast, one after the other. The only sound was the pot of oatmeal sputtering on the stove. He thumped his chair down on all four legs and bolted to his feet. "Just as I'd feared. I'm leaving before she returns to cast her web around me." He downed the last of his coffee.

"GOOD FOR YOU!" Hank boomed. As Jesse closed the kitchen door, he heard Hank yell out, "WAIT! WHO'S THE GIRL?"

When Matt Lehman asked David Stoltzfus if he could use the Bent N' Dent after hours for an official meeting, he said yes, of course. Matt said the meeting was open to anyone in the community who was interested in learning the identity of the stranger who died at the Inn at Eagle Hill.

Naturally, nearly the entire church showed up. Hank Lapp and his cronies, Fern and Amos Lapp, Freeman and Levi Glick and their gigantic families, Luke and Sammy Schrock, more Kings, Zooks, Fishers, and all the Stoltzfuses. Three of the five old sisters from the Sisters' House—one was home minding Ella. Of course, Rose and Galen, owners of the Inn at Eagle Hill, had come, as did Jesse's sister Ruthie.

Jesse was glad he had arrived early, because he was able to get a spot in the room where he could watch the reactions of others as people walked in. It was quite interesting. For example, when his cocky apprentice Leroy Glick came through the door, his sister Molly turned bright red. Why was that? Surely, she wouldn't have a crush on the town's most obnoxious boy. That was a distressing thought. What made his sisters have such questionable taste in men?

Patrick Kelly walked in and scanned the room as if looking for someone. Then he spotted Ruthie and Molly, standing in the back, and went right to them.

Luke Schrock sidled up to Jesse. "Who's that guy next to Ruthie?"

"Patrick Kelly. He's supposed to be staying at the inn for a month. Your inn."

Luke didn't look happy. But before Jesse could explain that Patrick wasn't even Amish, he was distracted by the arrival of Jenny Yoder. Was Hank's assumption correct—could Jenny be here to husband hunt? Had she been through all the eligible men of Ohio and now was sifting through Pennsylvania bachelors?

Here was where another worry flew in and landed, right on top of Jesse.

When Patrick Kelly walked into the crowded store and made a beeline for Ruthie, she felt a flutter in her chest. There again was that strange bubble of light around him so that he looked like an angel. She blinked rapidly, thinking there was something wrong with her vision.

"I'm sorry I didn't get a chance to say goodbye after I packed up and moved to the Inn at Eagle Hill," Patrick said, coming toward Ruthie. "I'm hoping we can continue with the Penn Dutch tutoring sessions. It's nice to have someone to work with whose assiduousness dovetails with my own."

Assiduousness. Had anyone before ever appreciated Ruthie's assiduousness? Usually, her family complained about it. Tyrannical, they called her. Dictatorial. Imperious. Never assiduous.

Dovetail. It was such a soft and subtle word, such an unusual implication to describe how two pieces joined together without need for nails or screws, without conflict or strife. Her brother Jesse would like to hear Patrick's eclectic vocabulary. Assiduousness. Dovetail. Jesse fancied himself to be a word collector. *Lexophile!* She could practically hear him correct her.

"I have to confess our tutoring sessions have been the high points of my day," Patrick said, grinning at her.

Her insides melted, and she couldn't help but grin back at him.

"Your ears," Molly said, peering at her curiously. "They're turning red."

"Be quiet, Molly," Ruthie snapped. "Matt Lehman is about to reveal the mystery of the dead stranger."

Dok lunged for her cell phone when she heard the familiar chiming tune linked to incoming calls from Ed Gingerich. "Hello?"

"Hey there, hon. How goes life in the cornfields?"

She tried not to take offense at the slight. Ed thought buying a private practice was ridiculous. Ludicrous, he called it. Feeling guilty about the way she'd been dismissed from the hospital staff, he promised to look for positions for her in other hospitals despite her insistence that private practice was the right step for her. She was doing exactly what she wanted to be doing. He thoroughly disagreed—he told her she was just overreacting to getting fired and he was going to fix that for her. "It's fine. Peaceful. How goes life in the hectic hospital?"

"Exciting. Unpredictable. In fact, that's why I called. There's an opening for an ER doctor in Harrisburg that would be perfect for you. I've got a friend on staff who's been able to pull some strings to get you an interview. You need to be there tomorrow afternoon. I'll text you the contact info."

"Harrisburg," she said in a flat tone.

"Yes, Harrisburg. I know, I know. But it's really not all that far. We'll see each other on weekends." He paused. "Maybe every other weekend."

He completely misunderstood her hesitation. "Thank you, but no."

Another pause. "You can't just say no to an opportunity like this."

Dok's back instantly stiffened. She had a strange flashback: standing in the kitchen on an April morning when she was sixteen years old as her mother told her she had signed her up for baptism class without her knowledge. She had the same feeling that she had now: she was getting pushed too far. "I *can* say no, Ed. I *am* saying no. I keep telling you the same thing and you're not listening. I am doing exactly what I want to be doing."

Ed tried another tack. "Hon, you sound a little tired. Sleep on this. We can talk in the morning."

Not a word of kindness, no thought to ask her how she was feeling.

Evasion.

She had worked with him long enough to know how his mind worked. This was Ed's way of cueing her that he wasn't coming out for dinner, like they had planned. Earlier this morning, she had bought filet mignon, his favorite.

She was starting to feel angry and knew she'd better hang up before she said something she regretted. "I have a meeting I need to get to. I do appreciate what you're trying to do, but I'm confident I won't change my mind."

"Ruth, I think this position is made for you."

She bit her lip. Ed was right even when he was wrong.

"Promise me you'll think it over. I'll call in the morning. Night, sweets."

She heard the click before she had a chance to respond.

What was wrong with them lately? She used to feel like

they were a pair of train tracks, parallel but heading in the same direction. Lately she felt like one of the tracks had slipped out of alignment. Everything with Ed felt uncertain, wobbly, vacillating.

She saw a buggy roll by, then another and another, and grabbed her keys to lock the door. Not that there was much concern of a break-in, but she did have a cupboard that was filling up with prescription drugs. An old saying of her mother's floated through her mind as she locked up: "Even a saint is tempted by an open door."

Her mother. Mammi the Meddler. She loved her mother but knew they were better at a distance. They couldn't be in the same room without sparks erupting. Poor David did his best to try to keep the peace between them. Fortunately, two years ago her mother married a nice, passive-minded widower. Her mother convinced her new husband to move to Ohio because she wanted to be closer to Dok's older sisters.

What would her mother have to say about Ed Gingerich? She could only imagine. Selfish. Arrogant. Controlling. Dominating.

She went completely still. Why, Ed *was* all those things. It wasn't her mother's voice in her head. It was hers! She hurried to balance out Ed's character, as if trying to remind herself of why she loved him. He was fascinating, brilliant, one of a kind. They enjoyed all the same things: classical music, long hikes in the woods, leisurely meals.

Everything was fine. Ed hadn't changed. It was her. She was just going through . . . an adjustment. They'd weathered this kind of misalignment before. Things would settle down between them and get back to a good place soon.

And what place is that? a little voice inside her badgered. *Marriage?*

She pushed the troubling inner conversation to the back of her mind as she picked up her pace. The Bent N' Dent was already overflowing with curious Amish. Good! Dok wanted to hear what Matt Lehman's big announcement was, but she also wanted to meet as many local Amish as she could while she was in the store. Future patients, she hoped.

Matt Lehman had to stand on a wooden crate behind the counter to be seen and heard by everyone in the jam-packed store. "Thanks to the work of Jesse Stoltzfus—"

As those words hung in the air, Jesse changed his mind. He was delighted that Jenny Yoder had arrived at the Bent N' Dent exactly when she did, and not a minute later.

"—who found the stranger's car on Old Spotted Horse Road."

"WHO MURDERED HIM?" Hank Lapp asked in his ordinary bellow.

Matt sighed. "Hank, nobody *ever* said he was murdered. And he wasn't. The stranger died of a heart attack. Natural causes. No murder. I repeat. There was *no* murder at the Inn at Eagle Hill."

Luke let out a breath, slowly, like the air of a leaking tire. Jesse noticed.

The *Stoney Ridge Times* reporter snapped his notebook shut. "Blast it all. Another dead lead."

The bells on the door rang and in walked Dok, Jesse's aunt. Matt was in the middle of explaining that all rumors of a murder were just that, rumors, when he looked over to

142

see Dok and he just stopped talking, midsentence. As if his stream of thought had drizzled down to a drop.

Dok sidled up next to Jesse. "What did I miss?"

"The stranger died of natural causes," Luke said.

Jesse's dad was next to Matt, behind the counter. In his preacher's voice, loud and clear, he prompted Matt to keep going. "Have you found out who the man is? Or, I guess I should say, was?"

Matt jerked to attention, as if he'd forgotten where he was and why he was here. "Yes. We've notified his daughter, who lives out in California. She said she hadn't realized her father had gone missing."

"WHO WAS HE?" Hank Lapp asked.

"His name is Arthur Baumeister. He's a sportswriter. He was covering the Lancaster Barnstormers. Apparently he was taking a few days off in between series."

"No kidding?" The reporter snapped open his notepad and started scribbling down notes.

"Why was there blood on his forehead?" Ruthie asked.

Matt looked to the back of the room, where Ruthie and Patrick stood. "His car veered off the road and into the bushes. The coroner said he must have hit his head pretty hard. Enough to daze him."

Jesse spoke up. "But why? What made his car veer off the road?"

"His car had a flat tire. Must have been a blowout by the way he skidded and swerved. He lost control of the car and ended up deep in the bushes."

The bell on the door jingled. Jesse glanced over to see who else had arrived, but then he realized that Luke Schrock had quietly slipped out.

As soon as Matt finished answering the last question, people set out for home. Within minutes, the store was nearly empty. That didn't surprise Dok—the Amish weren't ones to linger, especially close to suppertime. She had hoped to meet a few people, but she knew her acceptance into the community was going to take a long time. She turned to leave.

"Dok, hold up."

She held the door open as Matt hurried to join her. "Did you hear the news?" They walked out on the store porch.

"Much ado about nothing."

"I thought I'd see more of you now that you've set up a practice in Stoney Ridge. But I think I've seen less of you the last week than I have in the last year." He searched her face. "I haven't seen you at church, either." They both attended the same Mennonite church in Lancaster, though both of their work schedules made attendance erratic.

"It's taken more time than I expected to set up the practice." More money too. Her savings account was rapidly dwindling. If she didn't start having patients soon, she might . . . well, she didn't want to think about that right now. One day at a time, David always reminded her.

"Many patients coming in?"

She shrugged. "Not yet."

"Won't be long until you're so busy, you'll be longing for a day without patients."

A smile lifted her face, and her spirits came along for the ride. "Let's hope you're right." She turned from Matt and walked down the steps.

"Dok, wait. I hoped you might change your mind and go

out with me sometime. Tonight, for example. You know, as long as you have the time. Before things get too busy."

The answer was a definite no—how could she possibly go out with someone like Matt? There was nothing interesting or exciting about him. He was like the men she knew from her childhood church. Kind, yes, but steadfast, boring. Yet how could she ever tell him such a thing? "Thanks, but I have a few more things on my to-do list tonight." She looked at him to see if that was enough answer, but she could see it wasn't, so she got serious. "Matt, I just don't think it's a good idea."

"It's just dinner, Dok. Not a marriage proposal."

His boldness startled her. For a split second, she was tempted. It would be nice to go out with someone who wanted to be with her, only her, the way Matt seemed to want to be with her. But she held on to her wits. She backed a few feet away from him, casually lifted a hand with a "Some other time," then turned and hurried off down the road.

12

David had been wading carefully through the book of Leviticus to prepare for a sermon and was struck again and again by its overriding message: Our destination is holiness. Just as God set apart the Israelites to be holy, he has called all people to pursue holiness. In fact, the very word *Leviticus* was a Hebrew word that meant "and he called."

And he has called *us*, David thought. To holiness. Nothing in us makes us holy; we are holy only if we belong to God. The Old Testament word for *holy* was "kadesh." Its meaning reflected its very sound: cut off. Anti-secular. In the New Testament, the word was *hagios* or set apart. Together, they summed up every obligation of living as a Christian and the demands made on Christians by a holy God. All of life was meant to be holy, set apart, dedicated to God.

It seemed to David that those seemingly minute details of daily life that were given attention in the book of Leviticus revealed God's desire to be involved in daily business. Even a pot on the stove could be considered holy, if cooking were done for the glory of God. Even the bells on a horse's harness, the prophet Zechariah declared.

In a flash of insight, he realized what had been nagging at him lately like an intermittent squeak in a buggy wheel, barely audible. Now he knew what it was: the daily business of the Stoney Ridge church members was growing increasingly secular. How had he missed it?

Just yesterday, at the store, he'd asked Edith Fisher Lapp why she had advertised her fresh eggs for sale in the local paper as Amish eggs.

"Times have changed," Edith had said. "People like everything Amish now."

Edith had given him a broad grin as she explained her logic. Her smile may have appeared innocent to the untrained eye, but David thought he detected a mercenary's gleam in it. "Why," she asked, "should we let the non-Amish benefit from our brand?"

Our *brand*? The very thought chilled him.

It was well known among the Plain People that whenever a product was advertised as Amish, it wasn't Amish. Even if products had been made by the Amish, if advertised as such, the actual retailer was non-Amish, brokering for the Amish. That was their tradition, their custom. To declare a product as Amish, a people set apart, was the very opposite of being set apart.

Something seemed to go missing as the economy of Stoney Ridge started to blossom, then bloom. He saw it clearly now, in dozens of ways.

Families weren't as quick to help each other the way they used to. The most recent example was when the sisters of the Sisters' House finally took a turn to host church, and four neighbors paid a cleaning service to clean in their stead, rather than offer to step in and lend a hand, as was their custom.

He could hear Birdy gently scold him, almost as if she were seated beside him in the buggy. "David, you know what kind of clutter and mess was in that house. Even with your niece Gabby chipping away at it for four months, she'd only made a dent in the clutter. Getting a few rooms ready to hold a church service in it was a miracle. I don't blame the sisters' neighbors. It would've taken them a month of Sundays to get it ready. The professional cleaning crew left exhausted!"

Perhaps the condition of the Sisters' House did present unusual circumstances. Birdy would say David was only looking at the negative signs of prosperity, and she would be correct. Prosperity had its benefits. It was a good thing to see new families moving into Stoney Ridge rather than moving out. It was a good thing to see the relief in his church after such a long, hard spell. It was like the first rain after a prolonged drought.

But in those hard times, those drought years, there was a sense of unusual, heartfelt companionship among the church members. They were all in this up-and-down-and-everything-in-between journey of life together.

He thought back to the love that poured from the community to Ephraim Yoder's widow and son: the property tax bill that an anonymous donor had paid, the gift of a trained buggy horse by Galen King after the old horse went lame, a grocery shower box at the Bent N' Dent that was continually getting refilled, the blacksmith who refused to charge them a cent for horse shoeing, sympathy cards that flooded their mailbox for months, the ice cream cone that

Hank Lapp treated Yardstick Yoder to each time he saw the boy dash into the Bent N' Dent.

When was the last time the church had gathered as one, without having to be asked, to care for one of their own as they had for the widow of Ephraim Yoder? David couldn't remember. Certainly, there were acts of charity and kindnesses. Barns that needed building, fields that needed harvesting. But something essential seemed to have gone missing in their great prosperity and he wasn't sure how to bring it back.

David forced his attention back to the book of Leviticus. It was a time of preparation for when the Israelites would be entering the land of Canaan, a culture that they were perfectly at home in. The Hebrews knew the Canaanite languages, customs, the practice of celebrating many gods. Moses was giving them holy tools to live with daily discernment, to avoid contamination of pagan cultures, and to be fiercely loyal to the one true God.

Moses was teaching them to say no to the culture when they had to.

David leaned back in his chair, floored. Something had to be done in Stoney Ridge, but he couldn't figure out what.

Dok was picking up a package at the post office in town when she saw Matt across Main Street, bending over to talk to a little girl. A red balloon bobbed over his head. "Matt. Hey there, Matt!"

He stood up and the red balloon rose with him. "Well, hey there yourself!" he said, his lips spreading into a broad smile as she crossed the road. If he thought less of her after their last meeting, it didn't show.

"Morning." She was smiling back before she knew it. Something about a grown man not embarrassed to carry on a conversation as he held a red balloon struck her as amusing and she nearly giggled. "I have a favor to ask."

"Okay . . . give me a sec," he replied, as in, *Consider it done*, but he didn't look up at her. He had crouched down to tie the ribbon that held the balloon around the little girl's wrist. "Tiffany just got this balloon from the shoe store, but it nearly got away from her."

"He chased it down the street and caught it, just in time," Tiffany said with a lisp. She coughed once, then twice, enough to catch Dok's attention.

"Where's your mom, Tiffany?" Dok asked.

Tiffany coughed again and pointed to the door of the shoe store, just a few feet away.

"Tell her I'd like to speak to her for a minute."

Tiffany went into the store, balloon trailing behind her.

Dok looked at Matt. "I'm surprised you have time for balloon chasing."

"It's a funny thing about time. There always seems to be enough of it for the things that really matter."

She wondered if that was a remark aimed at her, then dismissed it. Matt wasn't subtle or evasive, not like Ed Gingerich. If Matt had something to say, he'd just say it.

"So, what's this about a favor?"

She handed him her newly printed business cards. "Would you take these to the police station? Maybe, pass a few around?"

"Absolutely."

The shoe store door opened and Tiffany's mom came out with a curious look on her face. With one hand, she held onto Tiffany. In the other hand was a shopping bag filled with shoeboxes. "Tiffany said you wanted to see me?"

"Yes. I was concerned about her cough. It sounds like it might be bronchitis."

Her mother frowned. "I know. It's getting worse. We're new in town. I haven't found a doctor yet."

Matt whipped out Dok's business card. "I just so happen to know of an excellent doctor." He handed her the card. "She comes highly recommended. I go to her myself. If I were you, I'd hurry home and call for an appointment. Dr. Stoltzfus books up fast, but I'll put in a good word for you. Wouldn't surprise me if she could even squeeze in little Tiffany this very afternoon."

The mother read the business card and beamed. "I will! I'll do it right now. Thank you."

Matt winked at Dok and took the bag from Tiffany's mother, then walked them both to their car.

As she watched them go, she thought of Matt's remark about time. *There always seems to be enough of it for the things that really matter.*

Was that really true? The words hovered above her head, like the red balloon that bobbed along with Tiffany. So different from Ed's view of time. He was always in a rush, always planning for the future. His future.

It wasn't Ed's fault, she quickly rationalized. Modern medicine required haste to be profitable, but there was a terrible cost that came with haste. Deep down, on some level, she had to admit that if she hadn't been terminated to protect Ed's error, she would have quit soon. She had been growing increasingly discontent for a long while.

Actually, Ed's error did her a favor. It pushed her out the

door and into her own practice, thanks to a little help from Matt Lehman. She had a chance to be the kind of doctor that patients needed. And now, thanks again to Matt Lehman, she had her first official patient. Two, if you counted her brother David, whom she had forced to come. Three, if she counted Matt, who said he was her patient even though he hadn't come in to her office for anything other than bringing her a caffè latte.

Having Matt Lehman as a friend, she just now realized, was like having your own personal guardian angel.

Jesse stopped by the Bent N' Dent to pick up a package and was horrified to discover Jenny Yoder behind the cash register. "Where's my father?" he asked her in a flat voice.

"Bishop duties. He had a phone call about someone having a problem with his neighbor. He had to go." She snapped her fingers. "Like that. Out the door."

"So he asked you to watch the cash register?"

"Yes."

"Why?"

She answered him in a tone of a mother speaking to a slow-witted child. "Because that's what a store employee does."

"Wait. You work here? At my father's store? When did that happen?"

"Yesterday. I saw the 'help wanted' sign in the store window and asked your father for a part-time job. He said yes." She gave him a smug smile. "I started today."

Jesse felt his shirt collar tighten. Jenny Yoder was everywhere. *Everywhere.* She was closing in on him, like a predator on the heels of its prey. Like a hunter adjusting the rifle's scope to aim at the target. He had a giant red bull's-eye on his back.

For a while she said nothing more, she just stood there looking at him curiously, in a way that made his palms sweat. "Are you okay? Your face is turning red. It's brighter than your hair."

Memories flashed across his mind. Jenny Yoder beating him in the third-grade spelling bee. Beating him out for the fourth-grade math prize. Then, the *worst* defeat of all. She beat him in the fifth-grade fifty-yard dash!

"I have . . . to go." He backed out of the store, bumping into aisle ends as he made his way to the door. Outside, he gulped in fresh air. This was turning into an alarming situation. He felt as helpless as a newborn lamb, left alone in a pasture, with a vulture circling above. Waiting. Just waiting for the vulture to swoop in and make off with him.

The bells jingled as the door opened. Jenny held out his package to him. "You forgot this." As soon as he reached for it, she dropped it in his outreached hands and shut the door in his face.

He looked at the brown package in his hands. For once, Hank Lapp was right. Spot-on. Jenny Yoder was surely here to trap him into matrimony.

David hitched Thistle's reins to the post and went looking for Birdy. He found her out back, pruning her tomatoes. She got to her feet when she saw him, her face bright with good humor.

"Hello there." He gathered Birdy up in his arms, and she rested her face against his neck. "How was your day?"

She pulled back to look at him. "Amazing. Astonishingly wonderful."

He smiled. "What's made it so particularly wonderful?"

"You. You're home early. Let's pack a picnic supper and take the girls to the top of the ridge."

He winced. "I need to head over to the Zooks' to settle a dispute with a neighbor that's getting out of hand. Something about a cow leaning its head through the rails to eat grass."

Her expression fell.

"I'm sorry." He kissed her forehead.

"Don't be." She recovered her composure. "It's part of the package. Everybody needs you. You fix everything, from broken hearts to broken fences."

"Just don't ask me to plow behind eight mules."

For some reason, the thought of him behind eight mules made her laugh, one of her real letting-go laughs, where she couldn't stop giggling. Was it that hard to imagine him as a farmer? Probably.

He kissed her between her giggles and went into the house to change his coffee-stained shirt. Earlier today, Patrick Kelly arrived at the store with Nyna the Mynah. The store was empty and there was some coffee left over in the pot from the morning's fresh brew. Just one cup, he rationalized. He hardly ever indulged himself, but now and then, he couldn't resist the temptation. He was concentrating so carefully on pouring coffee into his mug that he hadn't heard the door jingle to announce their arrival and suddenly Nyna squawked, "Repent, O sinner!" and David swung around so quickly he spilled his coffee.

Did he try to fix everything? Of course he did. A little fixing, anyway. That's what bishops did best.

Abram Zook met David at the turnoff to his driveway. "I have news to tell you, David." Abram's voice was flat and expressionless, and David felt a hitch in his gut.

But Abram's tone could have meant anything, from the celebration of his newest great-grandchild to the death of his favorite dog. Under the best of circumstances, Abram's craggy face was solemn and soulful. His hollow cheeks were fringed by a wiry untrimmed beard, his bald head was ringed by a circle of fuzzy gray hair. His expression never changed.

"Birdy called while you were driving over here. Thelma Beiler is in the hospital. Something real serious. She's going to meet you there, Birdy said."

Abram Zook's fence problem with the neighbor would have to wait.

David was desperately sad as he made his way to the hospital.

He stopped Thistle at the intersection and paused. *Dok*. He wanted Dok with him for this. He had a sinking feeling about what he would be facing. On top of that, he had no stomach for hospitals; he disliked the antiseptic smell of them, the clinical business side of healing, the sorrow and uncertainty that filled the halls. He had never been able to walk into one without awful memories flooding him from that time when Katrina, his oldest daughter, spent weeks in intensive care, recuperating from the buggy accident that had taken the life of his wife Anna.

He made a right-hand turn at the intersection and drove straight to Dok's practice. She was in the middle of setting up her computer as he explained about Thelma. Without a word, she switched off the computer, picked up her keys, and drove him to the hospital. Once there, she went straight to the nurse's station to find out what she could. All business, Dok was, and David was grateful for her professional expertise. He sat in the waiting room, taking a moment to pray.

Within minutes, Dok returned with the on-duty Emergency Room physician.

"You're family?" he said.

"Yes. Yes, she's family." As far as David was concerned, Thelma was like a mother to him.

Satisfied, the doctor explained that Thelma had an aortic aneurysm in her abdomen. "You need to talk to her," the doctor told David. "She's stable, but it's on the verge of rupturing. Immediate surgery is the only option to save her, but apparently she's very uneasy about it." He walked them down the hallway toward Thelma's room. "You'll talk to her, right? Get her to see it's the only way?"

"I'll talk to her."

Dok leaned a little closer to David as they stopped in front of Thelma's room. "They're going to press her hard for surgery, but I have to warn you. It's a big surgery, with a long recovery in intensive care. There's a better than likely chance that her kidneys wouldn't make it, and a minimum 10 to 20 percent risk of death."

David had his hand on the door to push it open, but he didn't push. Not with that additional piece of information. Instead, he closed his eyes and searched his memory for a Bible verse to settle his heart. What came to mind was a verse from a psalm he had read just this morning: "Thou has beset me behind and before, and laid thine hand upon me."

Yes. *Beset*. Around, enclosed, hemmed in.

Lord, thank you for besetting this dear woman, who has been such a significant person in my family's life. Thank you for surrounding her, David silently prayed, *for hemming her in, for enclosing her in your love.*

David walked into the dimly lit room. Thelma looked so tiny and frail, lying there in the bed with the little prayer cap on her head. Birdy sat perched on the side of the bed, and stood as soon as David came in, a relieved look on her face.

"I'm so glad you're here," Birdy said, reaching a hand out to him.

He stood next to Thelma's bed, still holding Birdy's hand, and explained all that the ER physician told him, plus what Dok had added. "Surgery has some risks, but it's the only option to save your life."

Thelma listened carefully, her hands clasped on her abdomen—probably the very site of the aortic aneurysm. She lifted her head and fixed her eyes straight at David. "I don't want surgery. I just want to go home." She had lived a long life, she said. Her health had grown increasingly fragile over the last few years. "I'd asked God to give me enough time to see that my home was in good hands." She lifted a small hand. "And hasn't the good Lord answered that in a wonderful way, David?"

Hadn't he, though. Thelma had taken in David's daughter, Katrina, during a stressful time in her life. She swept Katrina under her wing to help establish Moss Hill as a business of moss farming, and Katrina had become like a daughter to Thelma, who had lost her only son years ago. Then Thelma rewrote her will so that Katrina would inherit the property. And that was before they had any knowledge of the oil traps, sunk deep into the hillside, just waiting to be discovered. Yes, God had provided an answer to Thelma's prayer in a miraculous way.

"David," she said, her reedy voice steady and determined, "I've been measuring my remaining days in coffee tablespoons for the last six months. I don't buy green bananas anymore. I just want to go home."

She didn't mean Moss Hill.

The ER doctor came in and emphasized again that surgery was the only option, that if Thelma refused treatment, she would die. She understood, she said. In that case, the doctor wanted to admit her so that she remained in the hospital.

"I can't," she said. "I don't want to stay. It's not home."

The doctor argued with her, insisting that she would be better cared for in the hospital. David watched the doctor try to persuade Thelma and knew it was futile.

Why did the medical world think that dying was a matter to be managed only by health care professionals? They didn't seem to understand that being cared for in an institution, by strangers, under regimented routines, cut people off from all the things that truly mattered to them in their life. Why couldn't they see that there might be a better approach to face death? At home, cared for with the loving hands of family.

Thelma wouldn't budge and finally the doctor threw up his hands and agreed to release her. He wrote out a pain medication prescription to fill, made her promise to call hospice, and half an hour later Dok drove David, Birdy, and Thelma to Moss Hill.

Her last trip home.

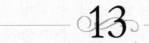

13

David was in the barn, brushing down Thistle after a long buggy ride, when he realized Birdy was standing by the open door. He stilled when he saw her, knowing from the look on her face that she had something important to tell him.

"It's Thelma. Katrina sent word that she thinks the time is short. They want you to come."

He looked down at the brush in his hands. Birdy walked over to him and put her arms around him. "I'll go with you."

"I'd like that." He returned her embrace, grateful for a woman who saw his ministry as hers too. Their marriage was a true partnership, beyond anything he could have ever hoped. He stroked her back. "Will you call Dok and ask her to stop by?"

David asked for a few moments alone upstairs before they left for Moss Hill. He wanted to pray before he did anything else. He knelt briefly by his bed and lifted Thelma up to the Lord. "Precious in his sight is the death of his saints. Lord, Thelma is precious to us and precious to you. Receive her spirit. Restore her soul."

Katrina met their buggy out in the yard with little Anna clinging to her leg and a baby in her arms. "Andy called Dok. She should be here any minute." Her eyes were red and swollen from crying.

"How are you holding up?" Birdy asked.

"Truth be told, I'm exhausted. Between the baby coming and Thelma . . . passing, I've hardly slept."

"What happened to the mother's helper you hired?"

"Someone paid her twice what I had offered to pay her."

Birdy's mouth dropped. "Why didn't you let us know? I would have come right away."

"Everything was happening too fast. There wasn't time. Thelma started going downhill last night."

"Well, we're here, now. I'll send Ruthie right over."

"No," Katrina said quickly. "Not Ruthie. She has no patience with children."

Birdy swallowed a smile. "Molly would love to come and stay with you. She had asked if she could be your mother's helper weeks ago."

Katrina nodded. "Molly would probably be the best choice. I just hoped to have someone with experience. But there's no one available, at least not in Stoney Ridge." She opened the door and they followed her into the living room, where Thelma lay on the couch. "She wants to be in the middle of things, even now."

Thelma's labored breathing filled the small room. David was glad it was morning, with the sun streaming through the windows, and not night. Thelma loved the light.

He pulled a chair to the couch and took Thelma's age-spot-speckled hand in his, noticing how crinkled her skin was, crepe-paper thin. She was lying with her head propped

160

up slightly on a pillow, as if she'd wanted to sit upright but hadn't the strength. Her eyes fluttered half open, lighting faintly with recognition, before closing again.

"Glad you got here in time," she panted through blue lips. "You always did run late, David. Your sermons too."

How he would miss Thelma! She was the one who had convinced her husband, Bishop Elmo, to invite David to Stoney Ridge. She was like a mother and aunt to him, all wrapped up in a ninety-pound package of spunk.

She mumbled something to him.

He leaned closer. "Thelma, can you say that again?"

"The music. Do you hear the music?"

He didn't, but it wasn't the first time he had sat by the deathbed of someone who heard music as the curtain of heaven opened. What was Thelma hearing, seeing, sensing? It was such a holy mystery, this business of dying. Of a soul leaving earth and bound for heaven. He often wondered if unseen angels might be surrounding them, waiting to accompany the soul through the realms, protecting it from the Evil One, until it reached its final destination. Yes, death was a holy mystery, yet one that filled him with reverence and praise for God.

He felt a hand on his shoulder and glanced up to see his sister Dok. He hadn't heard her come in.

"I'd like to listen to her heartbeat," she said, warming the stethoscope in her palm.

Her voice was calm, there was no sign of alarm in her expression. He had to hand it to her—she was not a woman ruled by emotion.

David stood and pulled the chair away to let his sister move in closer to Thelma.

Dok crouched down beside her. "How long has she been like this?"

They all looked to Katrina to respond. "Much worse since yesterday."

Dok frowned. "Why didn't you call me sooner?"

"She wouldn't let us," Katrina said. "She was afraid you'd put her in the hospital."

"She might be more comfortable there. They could give her oxygen that would help her breathe more easily."

"No," Thelma gasped. "No hospital."

"She thinks it will only prolong her dying," Katrina said. "She said she's ready. She's said all her goodbyes. Let her stay, please." She handed the baby to Birdy and little Anna to David and knelt by Thelma, gently massaging her wrists.

David realized that this was a significant moment for his sister. Despite being raised with the Amish view of death as a normal part of living, she had been trained in modern medicine, which perceived death as not normal. This issue was a constant tension between Dr. Finegold and his Amish patients, resulting in having patients avoid calling him unless it was a dire emergency. So this, David knew, *this* was the moment that could endear Dok to the Stoney Ridge Amish . . . or alienate her.

Dok took Thelma's pulse, her blood pressure, listened on her stethoscope to her abdomen, all with her chin tucked to her chest. She lifted her head and looked around the room. "Well, then, let's keep her as comfortable as possible." She nodded to David to follow her and walked into the tiny kitchen. "It won't be long. The aneurysm has burst. Blood is filling her abdominal cavity. I'm going to set up an IV."

"Thank you. You can't imagine how much it means to everyone to have Thelma stay here in her own house and die surrounded by those she loves. If she were in a hospital, she'd be restless and anxious and unhappy. You don't know what it means to us."

Dok looked David straight in the eyes. "Oh, but I think I do." She swept past him to head out to her car. He watched out the window as she bent over the open hatch and rummaged through her medical equipment.

Dok was going to do just fine.

It was a good death. The best.

Katrina and Andy, Birdy and David, and Dok stayed with Thelma through her last hour. David read Psalm 90 aloud, Thelma's favorite, the only psalm written by Moses. As she died, they were all able to be with her, touching her. And God was with them.

When he finished reading the psalm, he looked up and realized that Thelma was unmoving, too still to be sleeping.

Katrina knelt beside the old woman and touched her cheek. "Oh, Thelma, I'll miss you."

Yes. Yes, David thought, fighting back the sting of tears in his eyes, she would be dearly missed.

As the undertaker removed Thelma's body from her home, an osprey circled above the hilltop, giving its distinctive cry. Birdy said she thought it was a special gift from God, provided as a benediction for a life lived well.

Three days later, Thelma Beiler's funeral took place on a beastly hot, utterly breezeless day. The little Amish church of Stoney Ridge stopped their daily obligations and responsibilities to acknowledge the passing of a fine woman.

After the funeral, while everyone gathered back at Moss Hill for a meal, David offered to rock Katrina's baby to sleep in a back bedroom. He tucked the baby into his crib, then sat on the bed, not ready yet to return to the gathering. It was David's third funeral that year, but the loss of Thelma hit him deeply. She'd always had more confidence in him than he had in himself.

After a while, Birdy came in and quietly sat beside him. He took her hand and held it, unable to speak. "All these people had their time to grieve, David," she said softly, rubbing his back with her free hand. "Now it's your turn."

He tried to hold back his tears, then gave in, let them come. For the first time in a long, long time, David wept.

Jesse always thought that the world got two for the price of one in David Stoltzfus. His father put in staggeringly long days at the store, then he would tend to the well-being of others. As busy as he was, as weighed down by responsibilities, you never felt as if he didn't have time for you.

But that only happened if you could find him. It took Jesse four days before his father was available to him. There was the funeral for Thelma Beiler, which meant that everything in town stopped for three days. His father was constantly in demand during the funeral period.

But on the fourth day, Jesse went to the house as soon as he finished breakfast. He found his father in the barn, checking the cow's hoof. "Dad, there's a problem."

His father didn't even look up. "I know. I'm going to have to call the vet."

"Not with Moomoo. With the store." His father looked up from his task. At long last Jesse had his full attention. "Why in the world did you hire Jenny Yoder?"

"Because I need help and not one of my children want to work at the store. Not even Molly."

"Dad, Jenny Yoder has an ulterior motive."

His dad rose to his feet, grabbed a rag from the stall door, and wiped his hands. "Son, just what has got you so tied up in a knot?"

"Jenny's got designs on me."

His eyebrows lifted. "You? You think *you're* the reason why Jenny is working part-time at the Bent N' Dent?"

Jesse nodded knowingly. "It came as a shock to me as well."

His father did not seem to be quite as shocked by the revelation as he had expected. A smile crept over his father's face. "And just what leads you to believe this?"

Jesse lifted his hand and pressed down fingers as he rolled off his reasons. "She arrives out of the blue at a time when Mim Schrock is away. She lives at Windmill Farm where I happen to live. Now she works at my father's store. It's so obvious."

David leaned against a bale of hay. "I thought Mim Schrock was devoted to Danny Riehl."

"Maybe for now, but I'm just biding my time for Mim to come to her senses."

"One thing I've always wondered about your interest in Mim Schrock . . ."

Jesse was all ears.

"It's always seemed like a pretty safe bet, considering she's Danny's girl."

A sense of umbrage poked Jesse's pride. Did his father think he wasn't aware that Danny Riehl continually edged him out with Mim? "What exactly is your point, Dad?"

"Have you ever wondered if you're devoted to Mim Schrock because she's *not* available?"

"Interesting point," Jesse said agreeably, as if he had wondered it himself. He had not wondered. "However, let's not get sidetracked and ignore the crisis that sits before us. Jenny Yoder has set her sights on me."

"Has she said as much?"

"No. But she's everywhere I am. Everywhere."

"It's a pretty small town, Jesse. Hard to avoid anybody."

"Especially when they *live* at Windmill Farm."

David folded his arms against his chest. "And you think she arrived because she heard you were there."

"Yes. Probably."

"Why do I feel as if there's a Hank Lapp 'theory on women' behind this?"

Because there was, but Jesse didn't feel the need to admit that.

"Sounds like Jenny Yoder has really gotten under your skin. She is a lovely girl, isn't she?"

"Yes. No! I mean, she's always been an irritant. A pebble in my shoe. A thorn in my side. A cloud in—"

"I get it. In fact, I well remember. I also remember how bothered you were when she left Ohio that one summer."

"Only because there was talk at the schoolyard that she'd been kidnapped and brutally murdered. I'm not heartless, Dad."

"Obviously not."

"Every time I turn around . . . there is Jenny Yoder. Everywhere. Don't you think it's more than a coincidence?"

"In fact, I don't." His father crossed one ankle over the other and leaned forward. "I don't mean to burst your bubble, but Fern invited Jenny to come live with them at Windmill Farm."

"Oh." Jesse squeezed his eyes shut. This was worse than he thought. "So Fern's in on the scheme with Jenny."

His father rolled his eyes. "Jesse, Fern invited her to come because she needed a little extra help."

"Why?"

"Haven't you noticed that Amos doesn't seem himself lately?"

No, Jesse hadn't. Now that he thought about it, he hadn't seen Amos doing heavy fieldwork in the last few weeks, only hired hands. Did everybody know everything? "Is it his heart?"

"No, thank heavens. It's a back injury. He's in a lot of pain."

"They could've just asked me for help. I do live there."

"And yet you didn't notice Amos hasn't been himself?"

No.

"Jesse, I don't mean to sound harsh, but it's not all about you."

"I know that." Sort of.

"Son, what all are you doing for other people?"

"Building and repairing buggies." He lifted his eyes to the barn rafters. "I'm thinking of getting a sign built for the repair shop: *Stoltzfus Buggies. Built to Last.* Has a nice ring to it, don't you think? Maybe one day your grandchildren will be talking about Stoltzfus buggies."

His father winced. "I don't mean what you're doing for a profit. Only what you're doing for others out of kindness."

Jesse felt his shirt collar grow tight. This physical response to uncomfortable moments was becoming a habit. "Speaking of buggies, I'd better get back to the business."

"Son. Hold up. It feels pretty nice to do something good

for someone else. There's nothing like service to get our minds off ourselves."

The direction of this conversation had veered off into an entirely different direction than Jesse had planned. "Right."

"Jesse, has it occurred to you that all service is worship?"

Oh no. Jesse could sense a sermon about to unfold. One of the many drawbacks of having a father who was a bishop. Sermons seemed to be at the ready, on the top of his mind at all times, just waiting to be delivered to the helpless victim. Jesse lifted a finger in the air. "A scintillating topic for another time. I'm off before Fern goes looking for me. She's been threatening sudden death if I don't fix her buggy's storm front wipers by the time the next rain rolls in. And you know as well as I do, inclement weather can hit at any moment."

As he flung open the barn door, he had to blink hard and fast against the too bright, too hot summer sun.

Ed Gingerich walked into Dok's office unannounced and unexpected, raised his eyebrows, and gave her a *Have-I-got-a-surprise-for-you* smile, one of his facial expressions that Dok found hard to resist. "I've been searching everywhere for you."

Odd. He knew where she was.

He waved two airline tickets in the air. "You. Me. New York City. This weekend."

"Ed, you do understand what I'm in the middle of, right?"

There was a long silence, long enough that Dok thought perhaps Ed hadn't heard her, and she was about to repeat it when he said, "There's nobody in the waiting room. You aren't in the middle of anything but an empty practice." He walked toward her. "Come on, what's one weekend?" He was giving her his sensitive expression now, which she also liked. Ed did have a sweetness to him, although it appeared only rarely.

This one weekend . . . it was Emily's and Lydie's birthday, and Dok was going to do blood pressure screening at the Bent N' Dent on Saturday morning. And then there was church on Sunday. She hadn't been to church in far too long. Dok needed the weekend, to keep moving forward. "I'm sorry, Ed. I can't. I do appreciate the gesture, though."

"You're still mad about that little girl's appendix. You blame me for getting fired."

"No. Honestly, I'm not mad. I would tell you if I were."

"Look, Ruth, I blew it. I admit it. I'm trying to make it up to you. Why do you have to make it so difficult?"

What kind of an apology was that? His terms only, that's what. "Ed, if you really want to make it up to me, then stay here this weekend and help me finish setting up my practice. Go with me to my nieces' birthday party. You've never had time to spend with my family. You've got a free weekend. Spend it with me, here in Stoney Ridge."

He fixed an intense gaze on her. "They're pulling you back in, aren't they?"

"Who's they?"

A horse and buggy rolled by her window and he pointed at it. "Them."

She let out a laugh. "That's what you think this is all about?" She swept a hand around her office. "You think I'm feeling tugged back to the Amish?"

"I do. I've seen it coming for a while. Using Penn Dutch

with patients at the hospital, becoming known in the ER as Dok. There's something inside you that won't let it go."

"Let me get this straight. You think I should let *it* go?"

"Absolutely. You'll never be the doctor you're meant to be if you stay out here in this cow pasture, treating uneducated farmers and their bounteous offspring."

No matter how wrong he was, he was right.

Something had to change between Ed and her. The more time she spent away from him, the more clearly she could see the problems they had.

She tried to keep her voice calm and controlled, though she wanted to smack him. "Ed, have yourself a great weekend in New York City."

A startled look came over his face. He wasn't accustomed to being dismissed. He walked to her door and turned back at the jamb. "I will."

The kitchen smelled strongly of the sour tang of vinegar. Ruthie wrinkled her nose and glanced around, and that was when she noticed Birdy half in and half out of the oven. Her hands were clad in yellow rubber gloves up to the elbow, and she was vigorously scrubbing the interior of the oven with a mixture of baking soda and vinegar.

It hadn't been easy for Ruthie to relinquish being the female head of the household to Birdy, but she didn't miss oven cleaning. Or cooking. Or gardening. Or shepherding her little sisters. Now that she thought about it, there were a lot of things that Birdy took care of that Ruthie would never miss.

Birdy craned her head around and lit up at the sight of Ruthie, cheerful as all get-out. How could anyone be so relentlessly cheerful? Wringing her sponge out in the vinegar and baking soda solution, she returned her attention to scrubbing the oven door.

Ruthie hoisted herself lightly onto the countertop. "Birdy, have I ever told you I'm glad you married my dad?"

Birdy froze. She put the sponge down and slowly rose to her full height, 6'2". Her face started to crumple and Ruthie thought she might be trying to hold back a sneeze—which wouldn't have surprised her because the vinegar odor was that strong. But no! Birdy's eyes flooded with tears. She was *crying*.

"Oh Birdy! I didn't mean to upset you."

"I'm not upset," Birdy said, wiping tears off her cheeks with her yellow rubber gloves. "These are tears of joy." She took a deep breath. "Thank you for telling me that, Ruthie. You've just . . . well, you've made my day." She patted her hand over her heart. Then—back to work!—she took another gulp of air and dove back into the oven to continue giving it a thorough scrub down.

Ruthie sat on the counter, watching Birdy, startled that she was so oddly moved by the compliment. She was so happy, Birdy was. So content. She didn't have huge goals for herself, other than encouraging everyone to become bird-watchers, but she had the ability to focus on whatever task lay before her. Like now. She was zeroing in on that oven like it was the most important job in the world.

But at the same time, Birdy didn't force anything. She waited for it.

Let things come to me instead of rushing at them as I usually do.

Patrick's journal entry danced through her mind, and suddenly she understood what he meant by it.

Birdy let things come to her; she didn't rush at them. She had a sense about what it would take to be a stepmother, a job that couldn't be easy. She met each girl where they were, and offered them what they wanted from her. Nothing more. The twins needed a mother, Molly did too. Ruthie didn't want a mother and Birdy respected that. She never talked down to Ruthie, and gave her the space she needed. Somehow, Birdy seemed capable of absorbing whatever came her way with a gracious acceptance.

A few years ago, Birdy's brother Freeman—at the time, he was the bishop before the big scandal blew him right out of the job—insisted that she quit her job at the Wild Bird Rescue Center, something she loved, and become a teacher. Birdy had zero desire to teach but she stepped up to the task. It wasn't easy for her, Ruthie remembered, especially with Luke Schrock pulling pranks in the classroom that were often targeted at Birdy. But she persevered and, in the end, she was beloved.

Birdy didn't trouble herself with trying to be important or significant. Oddly enough, she was.

"A man's heart deviseth his way, but the Lord directeth his steps." Ruthie thought of her father's words from their talk the other night. *It means that whatever we think might be the right direction for us, the right path, God has the final say.*

Ruthie had a sinking feeling. She did *not* want to teach school next year. She didn't want to do it.

Not at all.

Early Saturday morning, Dok opened the door to the practice and propped it open with a box to get some fresh air in the waiting room. She had just turned on her computer in her office when a voice called out, "Hey there, Dok."

Dok walked out to the waiting room. It took her a second to recognize Matt Lehman because he wasn't in uniform, nor was he in a suit and tie like the one he wore to church. He was wearing a T-shirt and jeans. Normally, he seemed so serious, so official. Today, he looked kind of . . . casual. Kind of cute, actually. "I'm here to build those shelves you said you needed for your supply closet." He lifted his tool-box in one hand, and in the other hand was a caffè latte. He handed the coffee to her as he passed by, heading straight to the supply room.

She followed right on his heels, assuming he wouldn't know where she had stashed the shelving kits, but he found them in her office, grabbed them, hoisted them over his shoulder, and walked to the supply closet. He got right to work, tackling the shelving kits she had bought that promised to be easy for a novice to put together, but proved impossible. They worked together companionably for the rest of the morning. She talked about one of the cases she'd had this week—three children with snakebites from running barefoot through cornfields. He told her about the camping trip to Yellowstone he had planned with his favorite cousins. "It's taken six months of planning," Matt explained. "We had to get special permits to go camping."

As she watched him bolt the heavy shelving pieces together, she wondered why he hadn't remarried after his wife died. And how had she died? She had no idea. Birdy would know Matt's backstory.

By lunchtime, he had built sturdy floor-to-ceiling shelving for her. As he packed up his toolbox, she offered to pay him for his time, but he wouldn't hear of it. He didn't even press her to go out with him, as she thought he might. He just wanted to help, he said.

Matt was simply the best, truest, most excellent guy.

"Matt," she said, as he started toward the door. "Come with me to Emily and Lydie's birthday party this afternoon."

His grin could have lit the room.

~⌒~

David Stoltzfus chopped the corn off each cob, picked fresh from Birdy's kitchen garden, and sautéed it in a large frying pan, adding butter and salt, stirring until the corn was tender. David knew that if any male church member arrived at the door and found their bishop standing at the cookstove with an apron pinned around his waist, bushy eyebrows would be raised in alarm. But David liked to cook, was a better cook than all five of his daughters, though Molly showed promise in the kitchen. And quite frankly, he had always liked to be in the kitchen. It was something else he appreciated about his wife: she gave him the space to do the things he liked to do. Some wives would chase a man out of the kitchen. Birdy welcomed him in.

Today, he was making Emily and Lydie's annual birthday meal, which always coincided with the ripening of the first sweet corn of the summer. The entire meal had a corn theme: sautéed corn, creamed corn, corn fritters, corn pudding. Even a cornbread cake.

His daughters had been talking about it for days and had invited Patrick to attend, as long as he brought Nyna the Mynah. When Patrick arrived, he prompted Nyna to sing "Happy Birthday." David's daughters squealed with delight, as ear piercing as Nyna. Patrick said he had just taught it to Nyna that morning. He said he had discovered that her short-term memory was best—she could mimic best what she learned that day. "But if I don't keep up her vocabulary," Patrick said, "she loses it." They practiced every day and Nyna knew over one hundred words.

Amazing!

But David decided that if he had to spend a lot of time around Nyna the Mynah, he would have to start wearing winter earmuffs. She spewed out constant noise—screeches and whistles and words.

Dok and Matt Lehman had arrived with gifts for the girls, which set off more squeals of delight. As the girls showed off Nyna to Matt, and as David and Birdy finished up with meal preparation, Dok asked Patrick how he enjoyed being around the Amish.

"I quite like it in Stoney Ridge"—and here Patrick turned to look directly at Ruthie—"Everyone's been so extraordinarily kind to me."

David turned toward Ruthie, expecting some snappy retort—"See how you feel about being Amish in the middle of a winter storm when you realize your buggy doesn't have a car heater" or "Talk to me after you've handwashed five hundred dishes after a funeral"—but she was preoccupied doing something he would never have anticipated.

Ruthie was blushing.

14

Ruthie remembered Jenny Yoder as a sweet, solemn little girl. They had gone through a few years of school together, and though Jenny was older than Ruthie, she had been small for her age, and there weren't many girls in that Ohio school-house, so they were knitted tightly together. When Jenny left one summer, without a word, Ruthie keenly missed her.

So when Jesse told her that Jenny Yoder was in Stoney Ridge, living at Fern's for the time being—and Jesse emphasized that fact, as if she needn't bother to unpack her suitcase—Ruthie insisted he bring her along to the youth gathering on Sunday evening. She invited Patrick too, with instructions to meet at the Stoltzfus home at 4:00 that afternoon. He agreed to come as long as Ruthie didn't insist that he speak only in Penn Dutch. Reluctantly, she agreed.

Jenny came over early and the two girls got ready up in Ruthie's room. She was still astounded to have reconnected with Jenny after so many years apart. As they brushed and repinned their hair, they caught each other up on the last few years. Jenny had left Ohio and went to Stoney Ridge with her brother, Chris, whom Ruthie had never met. When Chris married M.K. and moved back to Ohio, Jenny went along with them. It sounded like they moved to Ohio about the time the Stoltzfus family moved to Stoney Ridge. They crisscrossed.

As she watched her friend brush out her long brunette hair and repin it, Ruthie thought there was no need to worry about her own appearance tonight. There was almost no chance anybody would notice her—not with Jenny Yoder in the same room. Jenny might still be sweet, but she was no longer solemn or little. Still petite, she was a confident young woman, beautiful, absolutely beautiful, in a delicate Dresden china sort of way. In their mirror reflection, Ruthie felt like a common dandelion next to a rare rose.

Through the window, she saw Patrick and Jesse lope up the driveway and hurried downstairs to jerk the door open.

"Wow," Patrick said, looking straight past her and directly at Jenny, who had paused halfway down the staircase.

They all turned.

For a split second, Ruthie couldn't remember Jenny's name.

"Jenny Yoder," Jenny supplied, smoothly stepping into the awkward void. Jenny had all the social graces Ruthie had momentarily lost. Another change. The Jenny Yoder she remembered was as quiet as a mouse, painfully shy. "So nice to meet you," Jenny said, shaking Patrick's hand. "Ruthie has told me about you. She said you want to join the Amish. My brother Chris and I did that very thing. We converted."

"Really? Ruthie's been talking about me?" Patrick's eyes twinkled as he looked from Ruthie to Jenny. "Well, I'm sure you've got a lot of advice you can give me."

Advice? Just what had Ruthie been giving Patrick for the

last two weeks? Her best possible advice—don't even think about converting to the Amish—and he didn't take any of it. She could feel herself bristling, but as always, Jesse said just the right thing.

"De alde Leit ihr Rott sott mer nemme."

Patrick looked at Ruthie with a question. "Something about an old man?"

"Close. Good for you. Jesse said, 'If you wish good advice, consult an old man.'"

"With the exception of Hank Lapp," Jesse quickly added. "Avoid any and all advice he might give you. We'd better get going before Leroy Glick helps himself to the entire barbecue."

"It's a little chilly tonight. I left my sweater up in Ruthie's room." Jenny turned and started up the stairs. "I'll run right up."

"So Jenny's an old friend?" Patrick said, watching her disappear up the steps.

"A very old friend, all right," Jesse said, but in an entirely different tone of voice than Patrick's.

Ruthie reached for her sweater. "Jesse, how come you didn't mention she was staying with Fern and Amos indefinitely?"

"Indefinitely?" His face fell. "I didn't know she was even coming until she just showed up."

"You don't sound very happy about that," Patrick said.

"Let's just say that Jenny and I have history."

"They were in school together," Ruthie said. "In fact, I think the two of them made up the entire grade."

"Three solid years of sharing a desk with Jenny Know-It-All Yoder."

"People change," Patrick said. "You might try giving her a fresh start. People rise to our expectations for them."

That, Ruthie thought, was an interesting piece of advice to consider. Was it possible to expect more out of Luke Schrock and hope he might rise to those expectations? Each time she expected more of him, she was disappointed.

Jenny swept back down the stairs like she was gliding on air. Jesse held the door open for her. As she passed him, she whispered, "You're missing a button on your pants" before she sailed out the front door to the waiting buggy.

And she was right! A critically situated button was missing. Jesse looked mortified. It was a very rare occurrence to see her brother's face turn a scalding red, and Ruthie had to bite her lips to keep from laughing. Patrick's eyes crinkled with amusement.

When they arrived at the Zooks', Jesse parked the buggy in the pasture. Ruthie hopped out and turned to wait for Patrick. With one foot still on the booster and one on the ground, he wobbled and almost fell. She reached out to grab his arm and steady him. "Are you feeling all right?" She searched his face. He was pale and a faint line creased his forehead, but his eyes shone more with excitement. A tiny blush of color touched his lips.

"You mean, besides being acutely clumsy?"

She didn't correct him since it was a true self-assessment, and he didn't seem to expect an answer. Ruthie had never known anyone as clumsy as Patrick, not even Birdy. He often stumbled over small things in his path. Yesterday, during a tutoring session, his water glass slipped from his hands and spilled over their paperwork. He laughed off his gawkiness, and because he did, she did too. She was accustomed to boys and men who were thoroughly athletic, graceful in their movements because so much of their life was spent doing physical work. She couldn't even imagine Patrick plowing a field, driving a set of Belgian draft horses to turn over the hard earth.

His gaze surveyed the expansive yard. Three volleyball nets were set up and dozens of Amish teens, boys and girls, were playing. Clumps of girls stood together, chatting and laughing. Some dads manned the barbecue. There was a delicious, smoky smell of chickens on the grill wafting through the air. "Oh . . . this, *this* is wonderful. Everything I thought it would be."

"What? The chicken? It does smell good."

He smiled as though the question amused him. "No. Not the chicken. Not just the chicken, anyway. All of it. All together. A community." He shook his head. "You just don't see what you have, Ruthie. You think this is normal. It's not."

She looked around. It seemed pretty normal to her.

He looked at her for a while, seeming to be searching for something to say to her. "Sometimes, Ruthie, you seem so unclear. Foggy. No . . . not foggy. More like . . . fuzzy. I hope you won't be offended, but you need to get out of fuzzy."

"I don't know what you mean."

"I think you do. Uncertainty, confusion, discontent."

Oh yeah, she thought. *That.*

"You have to get out of fuzzy and reach for something with your whole heart. Live wholeheartedly. Don't waste your life. Don't squander time."

The problem was that the path to get out of fuzzy was, in itself, so muddled.

Jesse called out to him to join in a rotation of players, so

180

Patrick jogged over to him. As she watched Patrick play volleyball, she found herself shocked speechless. She couldn't make herself slide away. Patrick was a terrible player. *Truly terrible!* He lunged for and missed balls that were gently tapped right to him. He managed to jam his elbows into every player's side, completely unintentionally. If Luke Schrock were here, he would be howling with laughter at the sight. Patrick seemed completely wrong here, as out of place among the other sturdy Amish youth as an orchid blooming in the desert. What was so mesmerizing about him was that he acted as if there was no place he'd rather be.

On Monday afternoon, at the end of the day, Dok made a house call to the Inn at Eagle Hill on the guest in the cottage. The young man, Patrick Kelly, said he was prone to migraines, and he certainly seemed to be suffering. As she left the cottage, she felt a tickle of worry about Patrick. "If you're not feeling better tomorrow," she told him, "I'd like you to come in to the office for a checkup."

He assured her that he would be fine, just fine, with a day's rest, but she saw a tremor in his hands. Something in the back of her mind struck her as off-kilter.

She drove across the street to her brother's home. She found Birdy in the kitchen, preparing a recipe from Anna's cookbook, giving the twins tasks to do as they prepared the dish.

"Dok!" Birdy's face lit up as she saw Dok. "Somehow, you always have the most perfect timing. Can you read Anna's handwriting?" She pointed to a word scribbled on the recipe card.

Dok squinted at the card. "Diced onion."

"Oh, of course! Silly me. What's a lamb stew without an onion?" Birdy hurried down the cellar stairs and returned a moment later with her apron full of round yellow onions.

Dok had a déjà vu moment as Birdy disappeared into the cellar. Years and years ago, she had come to David and Anna's home to meet the new twins, then infants, and Anna had made that very stew. The smells took her right back to that moment, as if time had never passed.

Sometimes it seemed as if Birdy was following in Anna's very footsteps, slipping into the groove she had forged and left behind. Was that always the way of it for second wives? Dok wondered. But maybe they didn't mind. There was a groove to settle into, just waiting for the right fit. Dok, on the other hand, never seemed to find her groove.

"Birdy, do you happen to know what caused the death of Matt Lehman's wife?"

Birdy glanced up to the ceiling, as if she was trying to remember details. "Cancer. Caught too late. She was only thirty-three."

"And no children?"

"No. They'd only been married less than a year, as I recall."

"How sad." Dok was leaning against the silverware drawer, thinking about the sharp grief Matt must have experienced as a young husband, when she realized that Emily and Lydie stood peering at her with napkins in their hands. "Ah! Looks like you want to set the table and I'm in your way."

"You'll stay for supper, won't you, Dok?" Birdy asked as she whisked from one task to another.

Dok wasn't planning to stay, but the tantalizing aroma of that lamb stew changed her mind. "I'd love to."

Birdy stopped what she was doing to give her a bright smile. "Excellent." She pulled another plate from the cupboard and added it to the pile on the counter. "Didn't he tell you?"

"Didn't who tell me what?"

"Matt. He and his wife, Kathy, met at a cancer support group. Matt's a cancer survivor." She chopped an onion at a remarkably fast pace, then tossed it into the pot on the stove where Molly stood stirring. "Sauté those onions, Molly. Keep stirring. Don't let them burn." She spun around with the knife in her hand. "Matt's Kathy wasn't as fortunate."

With that news, Dok had been chewing a piece of carrot and stopped, mid-chew. Her respect for Matt grew another notch or two.

Birdy looked up from cutting carrots into circles. "Why do you ask?"

Dok shrugged. "The other day Matt came over to help me set up some shelving at the practice and . . . I just . . . got to wondering."

"Good for you," Birdy said in her cheery way, giving her arm a little pat. "Good for you."

Jenny Yoder was a quiet person. That, Jesse had always known. What he hadn't realized was that she was quiet but not timid. She had settled with ease into life on Windmill Farm, working alongside of Fern like a mother and a daughter. Sometimes, from a distance, if it weren't for their height difference, Jesse could confuse the two. The way they stood, spoke, moved. She was a mini-Fern.

Why did Jenny Yoder have to return to Stoney Ridge? Things had been going along just fine for Jesse. Just fine.

Now, everything was turned upside down. He was turned upside down.

Why couldn't life just stay static? Why did it always have to change?

Take today, for example. Jesse had been taking Patrick out on country roads in the afternoons so he could practice buggy driving. Patrick was a shockingly slow learner, especially for a pretty intelligent fellow, though he'd never been around horses, he had said. Still, he had a difficult time acquiring the reflexes and coordination for negotiating traffic. But Jesse was determined to help him master the art of buggy driving. And it was, indeed, an art.

So it came as a bit of a surprise when Patrick told him today that he was going to need to suspend the buggy driving lessons for the time being. He offered him no explanation as he handed him a week's pay with an apology.

Even more surprising was that Jesse refused the money, automatically, without thinking about it.

"You're a very generous person, Jesse," Patrick had said.

On the drive back to Windmill Farm, Jesse mulled over Patrick's compliment, said with sincerity. Generosity and Jesse were not two words that had ever been placed together in one sentence before. It pleased him, and he was glad that someone, somewhere, felt he was a generous guy. It was quite unfortunate that certain affirmations couldn't be held in reserve, then delivered in front of just the right person, at just the right time. For example, it would be very timely if Patrick could repeat that he thought Jesse was generous in front of his father, who recently inferred that his son didn't do anything unless it brought him financial benefits. He'd like to see that look of shock on his dad's face.

And it would be particularly nice if Jenny Yoder had heard Patrick compliment Jesse. Would it seem peculiar if he asked Patrick to repeat the compliment in front of her? Probably. He could practically hear his sister Ruthie's voice in his head: *Yes. That would be weird.*

He was driving past the Bent N' Dent and pulled the horse into the parking lot. No sooner had he crossed the threshold and been heartily welcomed by the old codgers who considered him to be one of them, that he was annoyed with himself for two reasons. The first was that he'd forgotten it was Tuesday and Jenny Yoder would not be working at the Bent N' Dent today. He knew that.

The second annoyance was that he was here to see Jenny Yoder in the first place.

He'd had to deal with both of these annoyances while being roped into an endless game of checkers with Hank Lapp that he ended up losing, topped off with the realization that he was astoundingly disappointed by Jenny's absence. That, in itself, seemed as strange to Jesse as if a woolly mammoth had appeared in the store, shopping for a box of Froot Loops.

Leaving the store to head home, Jesse flicked the reins over the horse's withers and gave the horse his head, cantering along the road, eager for this disappointing afternoon to end.

It meant nothing, really.

Ruthie found that whenever she was in Patrick's company, she experienced a kind of deep serenity. He was one of the few people who actually listened when she talked and so forced her to think about what she was saying. She knew herself well enough to know she liked talking more than listening. With Patrick, she was learning to listen carefully. To really hear what someone was saying and not let her mind race ahead to formulate her response, as she was inclined to do.

Today, though, she couldn't understand why he said what he did. They were sitting in the shade on the porch steps of Ruthie's home. He had dropped by unexpectedly to ask if he could talk to her. "Ruthie, we need to hold off on the Penn Dutch lessons for a while."

"We what?" Ruthie demanded, unsure she had heard him properly. "Why?"

"You've given me so much to study . . . I need time to catch up."

He didn't look at her as he said those words, though he did say them in a lighthearted way. Ruthie couldn't pinpoint why, but she knew he wasn't telling her the truth, or at least not the whole truth.

Was it her? Had she said something, or done something to offend him? She should have been nicer to him, more patient. She could be nicer! Starting now.

"I could slow things down. We could repeat some lessons." She was talking a little too quickly, a little too loudly. She didn't want the lessons to stop. She found herself wanting to etch out more scenes, fill in the shapes and colors and shadows of Patrick Kelly.

He seemed to be watching something in the distance. "Thanks, Ruthie." He stood up and turned to her, his voice matter-of-fact. "Maybe in a few days or so. I just need to slow down a little."

He reached down for Ruthie's hand in order to help her up. Then, to the surprise of them both, he held it for a minute.

Ruthie looked up at him and made no move to take back her hand. There was a sensation of something surrounding them as he held her hand that Ruthie had never experienced before. It felt as though she were living in two realities at the same time: Ruthie's World, which was jumbled and vague and out of focus, and Patrick's World, which was peaceful and orderly and clear.

She didn't want to leave his world.

15

Luke Schrock, David decided as he drove past him on the road one afternoon and noticed a fishing rod in his hand, was a dabbler. That young man needed something to light the fire inside him, a reason to get him up in the morning.

David thought back to all the jobs Luke had had over the last few years, and realized he'd been fired from every single one. Finally, Galen King, prompted by Luke's mother, tried to take him on in the horse training business but that backfired when Luke kept forgetting to lock the paddock gates. After chasing down horses on a daily basis, Galen concluded Luke wasn't cut out for the job. David wondered if leaving paddock gates open might have been Luke's method to avoid work. Most of his previous employers thought Luke Schrock wasn't very bright, but frankly, David wondered if Luke wasn't the clever one—he sabotaged every employment opportunity and ended up with a lot of free time on his hands, which was, David suspected, exactly the way he liked it.

It was a conundrum. Luke had potential. But how to tap it? It felt a little like the oil traps on Moss Hill. The oil sat there for centuries, just waiting for the right equipment to tap into it. What equipment, what means, could possibly tap into Luke Schrock's potential?

And then David had an idea.

As soon as he reached home, he hunted down Birdy. She was in the garden, down on her hands and knees, weeding the carrot patch. "Birdy, what kind of a student was Luke Schrock?"

She sat back on her heels and wiped her muddy hands on her apron. "What kind of student?"

"Yes. How did you enjoy teaching him?"

She bit her lip. "'Enjoy' might not be the word I would use for being Luke's teacher."

"What word would you use?"

"Challenge. Dare. Trial. Test."

"Ah."

She smiled. "Toward the end of eighth grade, I asked each scholar to choose a life verse to memorize. On the last day, they recited it in front of the entire class. With a perfectly straight face, Luke recited Deuteronomy 32:15. 'Jeshurun waxed fat, and kicked.' The class looked puzzled, trying to understand the deeper spiritual meaning of that verse."

"So he was just being a smart aleck."

"Yes, but he is frightfully smart." She went back to a tug-of-war with an unyielding carrot. "Any reason you're asking about Luke?"

"The school board is looking for a replacement for Danny Riehl. I was thinking . . ."

"Luke?" She gasped, eyes wide. "You are considering Luke Schrock? To shape and mold young minds? To care for little children? To nurture varying intellects?"

To put it mildly, Birdy was flabbergasted. "I thought it might fill his mind. You know, challenge him. Help him find a way to contribute to the community. But from the way you positioned it, I can see that it's a bad idea. Never mind."

"That verse of Luke's . . . I'm not sure he meant it this way, and I have no idea who Jeshurun is, but he sounded a little like Luke. Growing fat and kicking?"

"Jeshurun is another name for Israel," David said, taking off his straw hat and waving it at a bee that hovered too close to Birdy. "And yes, the same thought occurred to me."

Back to the drawing board.

Jesse noticed Jenny Yoder coming down from the orchard at Windmill Farm before she noticed him. He liked looking at her from a distance. There was a sense of purpose, an aliveness in Jenny's stride. She knew what she was about. So different from Mim Schrock's wishy-washiness.

The comparison startled him. When had he ever found fault with Mim? Never! Look what Jenny Yoder was doing to him. Scrambling his head. Tangling his mental wires. It was a dangerous and destructive effect she had on him. The Jenny Yoder Effect.

But, truth be told, Mim *was* wishy-washy. She could never quite decide if Danny Riehl was the one for her and, in her indecision, kept Jesse dangling on a thin thread of hope.

Or could his father have been right? Was Jesse the one who preferred the fragile thread of hope to the ups and downs of a real relationship?

That, too, was an alarming thought. He didn't like to think of himself as one of those guys who avoided commitment. Not like Jimmy Fisher, who managed to dabble with matrimony and avoid it the way a clever fox toyed with a trap.

A trap? A trap. Did that description of matrimony just flip through his mind? The fact that what he had thought felt peculiar made him realize, indeed, he had become a cliché—he was one of *those* guys.

Leroy Glick, the older apprentice, exchanged a knowing glance with Sammy Schrock, the younger apprentice. "I think our boss is sweet on Fern's helper."

"Ooo-la-la!" Sammy whistled. "Jesse has a girlfriend!"

Jesse sighed. It would be easy to lose his temper with these boys, but he knew he should hold his tongue and exercise patience with them. It helped to remind himself that these two boys had very little brain power.

"I never want just one girlfriend," Leroy said. "As soon as I turn sixteen and my dad gets me my own buggy, I am going out with a different girl every night. Lots and lots of girlfriends."

Sammy looked blank. "But that would be a lot of girls to keep track of. Sundays too?"

"Every single night. Different girl."

"That would be thirty or thirty-one girls every month, except for February."

Leroy smiled. "Maybe I would have three dates on February twenty-eighth," he said smugly, "just to keep the numbers even."

This information stretched Sammy's mind beyond capacity. "But then . . . what would you do about leap year?"

Exasperated, Jesse looked at the boys. Where does one start? He considered himself to be an expert repairman, but how could he try to patch the holes in their faulty thinking? Especially when they thought they already knew everything.

Jesse left the two of them as they tried to work out their meager mathematics. They were appalling, those two. He had to have faith in the young girls of Stoney Ridge and hope they were all smart enough to avoid his apprentices.

He looked toward the farmhouse and saw Jenny Yoder climb the porch stairs. Without any warning, right by his side, C.P. let out an ear-busting woof. Jenny turned her face toward the buggy shop and lifted her hand in a casual wave.

Why, if his eyes weren't deceiving him, Jenny Yoder was smiling at him. Jesse's whole being soared upward.

C.P. looked up at him with his big saucer eyes, and he reached down to pat him fondly. Maybe this dog wasn't quite as useless as he thought.

David forgot all about Luke Schrock's smart-alecky life Bible verse for a few days. He sat at his desk and opened the Bible to the thirty-second chapter in the book of Deuteronomy. "But Jeshurun waxed fat, and kicked: thou art waxen fat, thou art grown thick, thou art covered with fatness; then he forsook God which made him, and lightly esteemed the Rock of his salvation."

Luke had missed the point by not memorizing the full verse, which came as no surprise. And didn't that just seem to summarize Luke Schrock? He lightly esteemed the Rock of his salvation. In doing so, he missed the very heart and soul of the Amish life: glorifying God.

Context, context, context. David knew it was dangerous to pluck a verse out of Scripture and put weight on it that it wasn't meant to bear. He turned the pages of his Bible to set the stage for this verse. Who was speaking? And why?

Moses.

It was Moses's last day as leader to the Israelites. God had informed Moses that he was going to die—which David thought was such a gift. It gave him peace to know that God had prepared Moses for his death. A good death. Buried by the very hand of God.

Moses had time to prepare for his death. These last few chapters of Deuteronomy consisted of his farewell address. Pastor Moses preaching the Word of God to his congregation in the desert. The Israelites were poised on the brink of the Promised Land. David's imagination wandered as he pictured old Moses high on a ledge, speaking truth to the two million Israelites in the barren valley below him, his aged voice amplified by the rocks around him in the desert. God had told Moses to teach the people this song, known as the Song of Moses, as a reminder of God's faithfulness and a warning to not abandon their faith once they inhabited the Promised Land.

"But Jeshurun waxed fat, and kicked: thou art waxen fat, thou art grown thick, thou art covered with fatness; then he forsook God which made him, and lightly esteemed the Rock of his salvation."

The thought that followed literally took his breath away. This time the verse struck him, as palpably as if he'd received a blow to his gut. It seemed eerily prophetic of the condition of the church of Stoney Ridge. They were growing fat and lightly esteeming God.

David covered his face with his hands. Without God, the Promised Land was nothing.

193

A summer storm blew through Stoney Ridge, hitting Eli Zook's old dilapidated barn with such strong winds and rain that it collapsed, killing two cows. David sent word around the community that a barn raising was scheduled for Saturday. Ruthie could see the look on Patrick's face when he heard about the barn raising. He'd asked her all about them, which she found to be amusing. How many barn raisings had she seen in her life? Dozens and dozens. To her, they were just a long day of hard work.

To Patrick, the work frolics were a romantic slice of Amish life. Of *community*, a concept he felt the Amish excelled in. She tried to correct his assumption. "You'll see when you come. It's not so much a community as it is a few men bossing everyone around. Everyone has very clear roles."

"They're probably the ones who know what needs to be done. Any construction project needs supervisors."

She hadn't thought of it in that way. "The women stay out of the men's way to get a huge meal ready for them, then spend the afternoon cleaning it all up." She had tried, when she was eight years old, to join the boys as they hammered nails and was shooed away by one of the fathers, told to go back to the kitchen. It was one of her many pet peeves about being Amish. You had to fit in the box.

"The way I see it," Patrick said, "the women's role is the most important one. You're providing nourishment to all of those people, to help them do their jobs. Take away the food and everything else would disappear too. Providing sustenance is the foundation."

She had never, ever thought of providing food like that.

Not once. To her, it was just hard work. The long preparation, the endless cleanup. And people gobbled the food down so fast! Hours and hours of work consumed in fifteen minutes. Here and then gone, just like that.

Patrick smiled. "What strikes me most about a barn raising is that it's a metaphor for the Amish. I'm looking forward to a glimpse into a world where people give without expecting anything in return. They just . . . *give*. Their time, their food, their energy, their supplies. Even their Saturday. All given in love."

But when Saturday came, Patrick thought he was getting a cold and told Ruthie he was going to have to pass on the barn raising. She had to admit that he looked terrible, like he hadn't slept at all. Dark circles under his eyes, and he moved slowly and cautiously, as if he didn't quite trust his body to do what he wanted it to do.

"Should I be worried about you?" she asked. "There won't be anyone around if you need help. We'll all be at Eli Zook's for most of the day."

He smiled at her. "Thank you, but I'll be fine. I just need a quiet day to knock this out." Patrick shoulder-bumped her, a friendly, familiar gesture that felt strangely comforting.

"Is there anything I can get for you before I go?"

"If I think of something, I'll tell you," he said, opening the door and stepping aside for her to go through it.

"Will you?"

"Yeah."

"You promise?"

"Yeah." There was a faint sheen of sweat on his forehead that made Ruthie nervous. She wanted to do something for him—bring him soup, aspirin, something like that. But he seemed to just want to be left alone.

Walking over to the main house at Eagle Hill, she saw Luke sitting sprawled on the porch steps. His head was tipped back to stare at an eagle soaring overhead and he didn't see her approach. Handsome hardly began to describe him. So handsome that it made her a little queasy. She liked his dark hair—nearly jet black—that curled around his collar, she liked his sapphire blue eyes—distant and a little mysterious. She liked the whisker-scruff on his face, his Adam's apple, the tense form of his athletic body.

The wind caught at her skirt, slapping it so that he turned his head at the sound. When he saw her, he looked at her in that intense way that made her stomach swoosh up and down, and she felt warmth spread along the ridge of her ears. He slowly rose to his feet.

"Patrick isn't feeling up to joining us."

"I'm sorry to hear that."

Ruthie lifted one eyebrow. "You're not sorry at all. You are extremely pleased."

"Pleased that Saint Patrick has to stay home and polish his halo?"

"Stop calling him Saint Patrick. He's not like that, Luke."

"Like what?"

"He's not a hypocrite." Hypocrisy was something Luke railed and ranted against, yet sometimes Ruthie thought *he* was the real hypocrite. He disdained everything Amish, yet he didn't leave. Wasn't that a false way to live? Patrick had come to the Amish because he sincerely believed in their way of life. He told her he admired that they worked so hard to safeguard the things that were beautiful and true in the world. She wondered how Luke would respond to that comment. "You haven't even tried to get to know Patrick."

"Not true! He declined my magnanimous invitation to go out with my friends last night." His tone was jokey, but Ruthie sensed he was a little miffed.

"To do what? Look for trouble?"

"I don't go looking for it. Trouble is just so difficult to avoid." The stone-faced stare the comment earned only spurred him on. "Ruthie, if it didn't seem downright laughable, I'd say Saint Patrick is trying to steal you away from me."

Why did that seem so downright laughable? But to Luke, she only said, "He can't steal me from you because I don't belong to you."

"Not yet." He gave her that smile of his, the one that was hard to resist, and she felt herself ease up. His fingers toyed with the ends of her capstrings as he smiled down at her, his eyes twinkling with mischief. "Maybe after the work frolic, we can go to Blue Lake Pond. A couple of guys are meeting up to play kayak chicken."

Kayak chicken. Such a stupid game! She shook her head. "Not after a long day of barn raising." Cooking, serving, and cleaning up hundreds of dishes.

Luke put a finger to her lips. "Don't say no. Let's just see how the day goes."

At Eli Zook's, the strangest thing occurred. Only a handful of families showed up, more children than adults. There was a man in their church, Henry Smucker, who was the architectural brains of barn building—he knew how much lumber to order, knew how to number the boards so there would be an economy of effort in putting the barn together, like a jigsaw puzzle. But on this morning, no one knew where Henry Smucker was. No lumber had arrived from the sawmill, and when Ruthie's father called, he learned that no lumber had been ordered.

Everyone looked to Luke, perhaps unfairly. He lifted his hands in surrender. "It wasn't me! I've been here the whole time!"

They ended up clearing the debris of the old barn off to one side. Ruthie was glad Patrick hadn't come today. There wasn't the usual lightheartedness, the joking between people, the buzz of energy and excitement. People worked quietly, ate quickly, and left soon after lunch had been cleaned up. There was no reason to stay. The barn raising would be postponed, Ruthie's father explained. But he seemed bothered by the day's outcome. Everyone did.

Except Luke. He thought the abbreviated workday was awesome.

16

Luke was waiting for Ruthie outside Eli Zook's kitchen. "Let's go to Blue Lake Pond," he said, as soon as she came down the steps. "Please. It'll be fun. Like old times."

She'd been out with Luke enough times to know how this would play out. "Luke," she said, "I don't think I'm going to go."

He seemed genuinely disappointed. "But . . . I want you there for the games."

The strange thing was that not so long ago, just a few months, she would've been jumping at the chance, pleased that Luke didn't want to go without her. But today, all she could think about was how Patrick was faring, and if his cold was getting worse.

"C'mon," he teased. "You're my good luck charm. I never lose when you're with me."

The pull of old habits tugged hard. It was only two o'clock on a beautiful summer day. She wasn't needed at home. "Fine. I'll go."

But she regretted that decision as soon as she climbed out

of the buggy in the parking area of Blue Lake Pond and felt very . . . uncool. It was an effect Luke's friends almost always had on her. In their company, she felt acutely aware of her tightly pinned hair, her plain dress and apron, her starched organza prayer cap. Most everyone was Amish, from different churches, but nearly everyone ditched their plain garb for the evening and wore jeans and T-shirts. She couldn't let herself go that far.

"Hi!" she said, smiling, as a few girls approached the buggy.

Too loud, she thought.

It didn't matter. Since Ruthie had broken things off with Luke, they never paid any attention to her, only Luke. "Hey . . . Luke!" one girl called to him and he waved back. He wasn't immune to the flirting. She knew he could have pretty much any girl he wanted. So why was she even here this afternoon? Why had she let him talk her into going with him?

Because it was a glorious summer day, she wasn't expected at home, and there was no reason why she shouldn't enjoy the lake. Luke untied the kayak off the top of the buggy roof and lifted it easily over his head, smiling from head to toe. Ruthie got the paddles out of the backseat and followed Luke down the shore to join the others. The beach was already packed with teenagers, kayaks, volleyball. Luke fist-bumped a couple of his friends on the beach, then stood talking to a group of them.

Within a few minutes, Luke had pulled off his shirt and was in the water, paddling out to the center of the pond in his kayak beside a couple of buddies. Ruthie took off her shoes and socks. The soft sand swirled around her toes, sun-warmed on top and cold underneath.

She plopped down on the sand to watch Luke. He and his friends played a game of chicken out in the water. Two boys paddled their kayaks to the center of the pond and faced each other, about fifty feet apart. Someone on shore would blow a whistle and the two kayaks would rush each other. Whoever swerved first lost the game. It was harmless fun, and the worst thing that ever happened was someone's kayak would tip over and he'd get a dunking.

Luke paddled back out for more rounds of chicken. He never lost at kayak chicken and she grew bored of watching. A gentle summer breeze wafted over Ruthie, and she closed her eyes, listening to the sounds of summer at the lake. She was starting to relax, starting to feel glad she'd come.

Too soon, Luke returned. He leaned close to shake water from his hair, the spray pelting her. Someone brought out hot dogs to roast on sticks over an open fire, someone else passed around a big bag of potato chips. Naturally, there was the ever-present, bottomless pit of six-packs of cold beer, which Luke and his friends dove into. He offered her one, but she turned it down.

As the sun dipped down the horizon, guys and girls gathered around the fire, eating, laughing, drinking. Out of the corner of her eye, she saw a small flash of light. Someone was lighting a twig. No, not a twig. Too big. A cigarette? No. It had a brown wrap, like the wrapping of a cigar. The guy who lit it drew a deep breath and held it, before slowly exhaling. A sweet smell, like alfalfa hay, filled the air. Ruthie could see it being passed from one person to another.

"What is that?" she whispered to Luke.

"A blunt."

"A what?"

"It's . . . kinda like a small cigar. Better though." He put it to his lips and inhaled slowly, holding his breath for a long moment, before he passed the blunt to her. She held the wrapped glowing light in her hand . . . wondering what magic this little thing held that made it so enticing.

"Use it or pass it," a boy called to her.

"Go ahead," Luke whispered. "Give it a try."

Ruthie looked at him, then around the circle, resting eyes on the guy who had first lit the blunt. Watching him watch her, she tossed the blunt directly into the center of the fire.

"Hey!" the guy roared. "What are you doing? That cost good money!"

She stood up. "I need to get home."

Luke tugged on her dress sleeve. "Chill out, Ruthie."

"No. I want to leave. You can stay but I'm leaving." She started walking up the shore.

Luke snatched his shirt and ran to catch up. He grabbed her arm to make her stop. "What is with you lately?"

"I've put up with your derelict friends, and I've put up with your drinking . . . but I'm not putting up with *that*."

"Then just pass it along. No one was forcing you to try it."

"You've tried it before, haven't you? That's why sometimes your eyes look weird. Dilated."

Luke blinked slowly, his head tilted as if he was considering the appearance of his pupils. "It's no big deal, Ruthie. Marijuana is legalized in a bunch of states." He cut her off, brightly raising a finger in the air, as if to point to the source of his inspiration. "And you're the one who wants me to drink less."

"Me? You're smoking marijuana to appease me?" She shook her head. "You can justify anything."

"Maybe you should try it before you get so high and mighty. It might loosen you up a little. Geez, you're wound so tight lately. You used to be—"

"Stop it!" Halfway to the buggy, she wheeled around on him. "Don't turn this into my problem." She climbed into the driver side of Luke's buggy.

"Hold it. If I'm taking you home, then I'm driving."

"You're not driving me anywhere. You can either get in the passenger side or stay here and get a ride home from someone."

From down on the shore, a girl called Luke's name. He glanced back at the bonfire.

"I'm sure she'd be happy to give you a ride home. As for me, I'm going alone." She snapped the reins on the horse's rump, perhaps a little harder than she should have, and nearly ran the buggy wheel over Luke's foot as it lurched forward. He ran along and jumped in the open door as she circled the parking area. Once she reached the road, she pushed the horse to a fast trot, jostling Luke as he tried to slide the door closed. He made a strange choking noise, and fearing that he was going to throw up, she pulled over onto the shoulder. Luke slumped against the passenger door. He was drunk. Or worse.

"Luke," Ruthie said. "Don't you dare get sick in—"

But she was interrupted by blue and red lights in her rear-view mirror and one short burst of police siren, which was enough to cause her to cry out. "Straighten up!" she barked at Luke. "And don't say anything."

She put down her window as a flashlight came poking into the interior of the buggy. She looked up. The police officer was Matt Lehman. "Ruthie? Your right taillight is out. Makes it very hard to see a buggy, even with the reflector."

203

"I didn't realize. I'll have my brother fix it tomorrow." Now wasn't the time to point out that this was Luke Schrock's horse and buggy. Matt wouldn't care whose it was.

Matt frowned. "Have you been drinking, Ruthie?"

"Me? No. I don't drink."

Matt poked his head into the buggy and studied Luke, leaning against the buggy window. "Is he drunk?"

"Affirmative," Luke said, without opening his eyes.

Ruthie sighed. She had hoped Luke would pretend to be asleep. She hoped he was asleep.

Matt studied Luke for a second and then Ruthie for a longer second. Finally, he said, "Seems like you could do a lot better than Luke Schrock, Ruthie."

"You're so, so right."

"Hey!" Luke said.

She kept her eyes on the twitchy ears of the horse.

"How's your aunt doing?"

"Good, I think. Over the last week, she had a few more patients come in to the practice. She seems a lot more encouraged."

Matt straightened up. "I could give you a ticket for that taillight. You know what happens when a buggy and a car collide. The buggy always loses."

"I know." She knew all too well.

"You're almost home, so I'm going to let you off with a warning. Be smart, Ruthie. Get that taillight fixed." Luke let out a deep snore. "And maybe give some thought to getting rid of your boyfriend."

"I will," she said. Both.

David was flummoxed over Eli Zook's barn raising . . . or lack thereof. After he left the Zook farm, he went straight to Henry Smucker's, the church's architect of barn building, to find out what had happened to the ordering of the lumber. And to find out what had happened to Henry Smucker.

And then came a shock. Henry hadn't ordered the lumber because he had forgotten all about Eli Zook's barn raising and gone fishing with Hank Lapp. David learned all of this through a visit to Edith Fisher Lapp, sister to Henry, wife to Hank. David interrupted her as she was in the middle of canning cherries in a steam-filled kitchen. David asked why she wasn't at Eli Zook's today, and she pointed a large cherry-stained finger at a counter full of bowls of pitted cherries, as if it was obvious. "When the fruit is ripe, you don't wait."

She gave David a look of mild exasperation when he asked her why she hadn't thought to let anyone know about the fishing trip. She folded her arms across her ample middle section and looked down at him through spectacles perched on her nose. "Am I my brother's keeper?" she snapped.

"Well, yes," David said, which only annoyed her all the more.

Since she was already irritated with him, David went ahead with the question that had been rumbling around his mind for weeks. "Why did you and Hank buy a golf cart?"

Edith sighed a grievous sigh. She never had fully accepted David as the bishop. In her mind, he was too young, too inexperienced. Too everything. "To get the eggs down to the roadside stand."

"And a wagon or pony cart wouldn't suffice?"

"Not with Hank. The way he handles a horse or pony, taking corners too tight, he tips the cart so my eggs jiggle and break. The golf cart has solved that problem. And it runs on a battery, you know." She gave him a look as if to dare him to find fault with *that*.

He wasn't quite sure how to respond, so he didn't.

Tonight, after David saw Ruthie march into the house and go straight upstairs, apparently bothered about something, he sat at his desk and opened his Bible, the best way he knew to settle his mind, his heart, and to seek God's wisdom. He read a passage from Exodus 16, about the manna that rained down from heaven to help sustain the Israelites as they wandered in the desert, slowly making their way to the Promised Land. Two verses kept running through his mind. "And the children of Israel did so, and gathered, some more, some less. And when they did mete it with an omer, he that gathered much had nothing over, and he that gathered little had no lack; they gathered every man according to his eating."

Not too much, not too little. Just enough.

He sat back in his chair, feeling that something had arrived and hovered over Stoney Ridge, like a low-lying cloud.

The church seemed to have lost a sense of "enough." The income from the oil traps wasn't the problem. Money was only a tool. It was the attitude that came along with the income. Instead of drawing a line in the sand on a lifestyle and sharing the abundance, church members had merely erased the line and moved it farther out. A new line, one that included an emphasis on leisure and pleasure. Curiously, it seemed to correlate with a de-emphasis on caring for those in need.

David remembered another bishop once describing that very thing: the more money we make, the less we give away. He thought, surely that couldn't be true for Stoney Ridge, with all the income that was coming in from the oil leases. Surely not here.

But the issue kept poking at him.

Nyna the Mynah had become a local celebrity. Jesse's youngest sisters, Emily and Lydie, told anyone who would listen about Patrick Kelly's talking bird. Even Jesse found himself driving out of his way to drop by the cottage at the Inn at Eagle Hill to hear Nyna's latest wisdom: "Be slow to anger!" "All things are possible!" "A time for everything!"

She was better than a circus show, that bird.

When Edith Fisher Lapp heard about Nyna the Mynah, she sent word to Jesse to bring Patrick over to the house with the bird. She was persistent about it, absolutely relentless, which translated to sending her husband, Hank, over to the buggy shop each day in the golf cart to remind Jesse. He didn't have time for bird visits! He had a buggy shop to run. He had apprentices and a dog to mind. He had to keep an eye on Jenny Yoder.

But it wasn't easy to put off Edith Fisher Lapp.

Luke Schrock dropped by the shop on Monday afternoon when Hank was hanging around. Patrick happened to be there too, when Luke volunteered to take the bird over to visit Edith.

"Only if Patrick goes too," Jesse said, shooting him a look of warning.

"Of course!" Luke said, as if such a thing would never occur to him. He seemed wounded by the implication. "I'll take your scooter home and get the bird, then I'll be right back. Fifteen minutes, tops."

Jesse felt a little bad about always assuming the worst of Luke, but he thought he detected a troublemaking look in his eyes. Maybe that was just Luke's regular look. If he could get Edith off Jesse's back, he would be doing him a favor. Jesse should be grateful, not suspicious. Ruthie had told him Luke promised he was turning over a new leaf. He had promised he would stop drinking and avoid his no-good friends. New leafs were a welcome thing. Jesse should be supportive, not skeptical.

But then, as so often happened when Luke Schrock was involved, disaster struck.

Patrick went with Luke and Hank to take the bird over to Edith's. They returned much sooner than Jesse expected, without Patrick and Nyna the Mynah. According to Hank, who relished giving Jesse and the apprentices a blow-by-blow account, Nyna the Mynah had stared her black beady eyes at Edith and let loose a string of hair-curling cuss words.

Edith was outraged. Patrick was mortified, hugely apologetic, and thoroughly baffled as to how his bird had gained that particular vocabulary.

Hank retold the story twice, doubled over with laughter, as red in the face as a turkey gobbler. The apprentices ran for Jesse's dictionary to try to figure out what the words meant. Luke remained stone-faced, shocked and disappointed by Patrick. Saint Patrick, he called him.

But when Luke thought no one was looking, Jesse saw a look of mirth flit through his eyes. Here and then gone.

Whenever Galen King was away from the Inn at Eagle Hill to attend an auction, Luke would slip into his stable and ride the newest horse, bareback, the one straight off the racetrack, hot-blooded, eager to run. It was Luke's favorite on-the-sly pastime.

On Wednesday afternoon, as Ruthie and Patrick watched from the open paddock, Luke was dashing around the property of the Inn at Eagle Hill on a new Sorrel Bay, a Thoroughbred horse Galen had recently purchased to train as a buggy horse. The horse was lathered up, eyes wild, as Luke yanked hard on its reins and pulled it to a stop in front of them. The horse stomped its legs impatiently, but Luke had the reins pulled so tightly its mouth was stretched.

"How about you, Saint Patrick?" Luke said. "You ready to give this horse a try?"

"Stop it, Luke," Ruthie said.

"What, are you scared?" Luke taunted. "You do look a little pale. Don't tell me you're not man enough to ride this gentle little pony. I got him all warmed up for you." The horse was panting, its nostrils flaring.

"Knock it off, Luke. He's never been on a horse."

Luke smiled that mean smile. "There's a first time for everything. Right, Saint Patrick? You said you wanted to live the Amish life. That includes knowing all about horses."

"Then go get a gentled horse," Ruthie said. "Racehorses are trained to run. This one's barely rideable."

Patrick spoke for the first time, his voice tight. He spoke in English, not Penn Dutch as Luke and Ruthie had been doing. "Thank you, Ruthie, but I can answer for myself." He drew himself up tall. "Perhaps another time." He turned and walked to the cottage.

To his back, Luke shouted, "Farichbutz!" *Coward.*

Patrick swiveled and strode back to Luke. "Socrates was

once asked, 'What is courage?' He responded by saying that there were times when the courageous thing to do was not to persevere but to retreat or even flee." He lifted his palms in the air. "Thus, I am retreating."

"Then you, my friend, have a thing or two to learn from the Greeks," Luke said, arrogance in his voice. "Alexander the Great would have never retreated."

Patrick didn't offer up a retort, though Ruthie could see the forceful jut of his chin. He simply turned and went to the cottage.

When the door to the cottage shut, Luke turned to Ruthie with a smirk. "Imagine that. Quoting Socrates to justify cowardice."

"Imagine who you've become," Ruthie said, furious. "Justifying fun at the expense of another."

David was surprised to see Ruthie standing at the door to his storeroom at the Bent N' Dent. She had spent a few hours helping Dok unpack her office and said she'd come by at closing time to hitch a ride home. Was it five o'clock already? He glanced at the wall clock. It was!

"Come in," he urged.

Ruthie closed the door behind her. "Dad, who was Socrates?"

He put down his pen. "Socrates was a wise Greek man. It's thought that he's responsible for shaping Western philosophy."

"When did he live?"

David rubbed his forehead. "I think . . . somewhere around 400 to 300 BC." He wondered what had triggered her curiosity about Socrates. "Are you asking for any special reason?"

"Patrick said something about Socrates and courage. That sometimes the courageous thing is to know when to retreat."

David nodded. "That's in reference to the *Laches*, a dialogue written by Plato, another Greek philosopher. Two generals had gone to Plato to resolve a question about what true courage is. Socrates kept questioning them to find the faults in their thinking. That's what Socrates did best—questioning and questioning, so the seeker came to his own discoveries. Truth discovered is better than truth told."

"So how does the story end?"

"The generals go back and forth, examining all sides of courage, but they are stumped. It allows the reader to come to a conclusion. Courage is strength in the face of knowledge."

"What does that mean?"

"I think it means that true courage is acting on the truth we find." He could see Ruthie was taking it all in, and he wondered why Patrick Kelly had sparked this particular conversation. But then, he was finding that Patrick Kelly's presence was sparking quite a few unexpected conversations this summer.

17

David waited quietly outside the Wild Bird Rescue Center. Twice a week, Tuesdays and Thursdays, Birdy led a bird-watching class at the center for children. He heard the town bell ring eleven times and knew that she would be finishing up soon.

A stampede of children burst out of the Wild Bird Rescue Center door, escaping into the bright sunshine, which forced David to jump to one side to avoid being trampled. No one paid any attention to him until Birdy came through the door, carrying a large bundle of books that shifted suddenly in her arms and sent her through the doorway at such an extreme angle that David had to put his arms up in order to stop a collision.

"Oh hello," Birdy said, obviously surprised to see him. She struggled to rebalance the tower of books in her arms. "What a lovely surprise!"

David reached out and grabbed half the stack. "I had to get a few things taken care of at the post office and thought I'd grab a ride back to the store with you, if you don't mind."

Birdy's kind face lit up. "I don't mind at all." Her whole face soared upward when she smiled. "In fact, I'd be delighted."

He smiled back. "Why in the world did you take so many books?"

"I wanted the children to identify different species."

David set the books into the back of the buggy as Birdy climbed in the passenger side. "So, what's troubling you?"

He looked at her sideways as he picked up the reins and snapped them to get Thistle started. "How can you tell?"

She nudged him. "You didn't sleep well last night."

He hadn't. "I'm sorry if I kept you awake."

She waved a hand in the air. "Don't worry about me. I can sleep through anything."

That was the truth. Birdy was a champion sleeper. "I just keep getting the feeling that something isn't quite right in the church. I spoke to Eli about the tithing and he said it was a larger amount than usual. Everything looks all right on the outside . . . but something doesn't feel right on the inside."

"Like a polished cup."

He glanced at her with a question in his eyes.

"Jesus said the Pharisees were like a polished cup. Shiny on the outside and empty on the inside."

"Oh, let's hope not."

"If tithing is larger than usual, what makes you think there's something to be concerned about?"

He shrugged. "Just a strange, bothersome feeling I have that I can't shake."

"Well, I think you should listen to it. You have a sense about things that always turns out to be spot-on." She looked out the window. "I think you might be right too. Not sure if you heard, but the old sisters' Second Chance Soup Kitchen might be closing its doors."

"Lack of donations?"

"No. It's got nothing to do with a lack of money. It has to do with a lack of volunteers."

There it was again. That disturbing sensation. Something felt awry. Off-center.

"I wonder if it might be wise to do an audit." There. He said it aloud. It was customary to have the church appoint trustees to do a financial audit of each household in the community every three to five years. It had been over three years since the last audit. It wasn't a popular thing to do—everyone in the church had to provide their financial status, including an accounting of their assets, but it was informative and helpful as the church made decisions.

Birdy remained silent.

"The school board wants to add a new schoolhouse. That alone would be the reason for an audit." The audit would help the trustees decide how much each household would be required to provide to pay the schoolteacher's salary. The information from the audit would allow the adjustment of each family's ability to pay. It wasn't meant to be a burden. He looked at his wife. "Go ahead. Tell me what you're thinking."

"I think it won't be a very popular idea, yet it might give you the answer you're looking for."

But what answer, David worried, was that?

David spoke to his ministers and deacons, and after the service on Sunday, there was a meeting for the church to choose trustees, a team of honorable men. Amos Lapp led the team, which gave David great peace. Amos had wonderful judgment and would lead the team to ask the right questions and nothing more—they weren't coming around to pry and coerce. Over the next few days, the team carefully and respectfully made their way around to each of the church members' homes in Stoney Ridge.

After the audit, David met with Amos in the kitchen at Windmill Farm and learned some surprising facts. The people of Stoney Ridge had grown rich. A few households brought in well over two hundred thousand dollars per year. But the entire church was less generous than it was a few years ago, when the average household income was fifty thousand dollars. Amos pointed out the figures to prove that the actual percentage of giving was lower. "The average household is giving only 6 percent," Amos said. "And the ones who have the most money, they're giving 4 percent."

David was astounded.

"Folks have more money, but they aren't giving in proportion to their income."

"Not like they used to?"

"Not like they used to."

Three years ago, the church had given substantially more to the Amish Aid Society than they did this last spring, when they held communion and collected the monetary gifts. Three years ago! A time when the church had so little to give . . . they actually gave more.

How could that be? How could they have more and give less? "Did you ask them why? Was anyone forthcoming?"

"I did. I asked them outright. Mostly, it came down to fear. They said they were afraid to give more."

"Afraid? How could they justify feeling afraid?"

"Afraid they might need it, mostly. A number of them have gotten themselves into precarious situations. They bought land for their children, but they did it with steep mortgages. A few others had taken out bank loans to expand their businesses. They're concerned about rising interest rates."

It was a disturbing discovery. They were . . . hoarding.

And it wasn't just hoarding money. It was a lack of giving with time, as well. He was still stunned by Birdy's news that the Second Chance Soup Kitchen might close due to lack of volunteers, not a lack of money.

These attitudes—they felt like red flags to David, warnings of things to be concerned about. They didn't reflect the heart of Christ. The church, he feared, had transferred trust from the Giver to the gifts.

As David drove home from Windmill Farm, he thought of an assumption Patrick Kelly had about the Amish. He felt the Amish worked hard to safeguard the things that were beautiful and true in the world.

So how does a bishop safeguard attitudes? He looked through the buggy's storm front to the blue sky above, lifting a prayer. *How can I keep abundance and plenty from turning our hearts away from you, Lord? How can I keep our community whole and healthy . . . and generous in their abundance?*

Jenny Yoder was here at the Leola auction! Jesse could not have been more surprised if he'd bumped into her at some exotic location—at a museum in New York City, or while visiting his aunt in Pinecraft, Florida. Of all the people he could have happened upon at this auction, why in the world did it have to be her?

Perhaps Jenny was following him.

As they approached, she feigned to be startled by the sight of him. "What are *you* doing here?" she asked, the very picture of innocence.

Schauderhafdich. Jesse was shocked silent. Were Jenny Yoder's eyes always that shade of blue? Nearly violet. Those eyes of hers, were they always such a striking contrast to her creamy skin? And when did her skin get so milky? It reminded him of Fern's peaches and cream, served up this very breakfast. The black bonnet framed her face and softened her angular features. He felt a strange interior paradigm shift: as if seeing Jenny Yoder with new eyes. It seemed to him that she had developed curves in all the right places, seemingly overnight. She certainly didn't have *that* shape a week ago. Not even this morning!

He felt struck to the marrow, as vividly as if an arrow had pierced his heart. His mind went completely, utterly blank. It was as if the two hundred other people at the auction ceased to exist.

"Jesse, did you hear me? I asked what you're doing here."

Jenny searched his face for some clue to his thinking. But he had no thinking to speak of.

Fern suddenly appeared at his elbow, frowning at him. She took the large flowerpot of red geraniums out of Jenny's arms and handed it to Jesse. "Where are your manners?"

Where indeed? He had no idea. He hadn't even noticed the bright red geraniums in Jenny's arms. "They come and they go," he said, and then he laughed. His laugh, even to his own ears, sounded nervous, too loud.

"Mostly, they seem to go missing," Fern said. "No wonder the apprentices have such appalling behavior. My work is not yet done."

217

"Right," he said, clearing his throat, thoroughly uncomfortable. He blamed the Jenny Yoder Effect.

Ruthie took off her prayer cap and set it on her bedside table, pulling the pins out of her hair and letting it flow down her back. She scratched her scalp, closing her eyes and enjoying the moment of quiet. Her family was sound asleep. She should have been in bed hours ago, but she started reading a book and couldn't stop. By the time she came to the last page, the grandfather clock downstairs struck 2:00 a.m.

Just at that moment, she heard a frightening sound outside her open window, a moaning and gasping. She ran to the window to look at the sky, expecting to see a flash of lightning or to hear a roll of thunder. Lately, one summer storm ran into the next.

But the sky was still, dark, clear, lit with bright stars.

Then she noticed a shadowy figure trying to hoist himself up on the porch roof by shimmying up the gutter. She slammed the window shut and the intruder looked up in surprise.

Luke Schrock. Of course.

She expelled a little breath and lifted the window. "Luke. What are you doing? You'll break your neck. Or the gutter."

Luke craned his neck to look up at her. "Ruthie! Ruthie, come on down and let me in! I wanna talk to you."

Ruthie flew down the stairs before he woke Molly with his clatter.

She held open the door as he stumbled onto the porch. Luke was clearly drunk, so drunk that just standing still was

218

problematic. "You told me you were going to stop drinking! You promised."

Luke hesitated, giving Ruthie a moment to realize he was— there really was no other word for it—a disaster. Normally, he took great pride in his appearance. He was hatless, with greasy hair and bloodshot eyes and a wrinkled white shirt that hung half in, half out of his pants. His gaze lifted to hers.

"You look terrible."

His bleary eyes focused on her undone hair. "You, on the other hand, look gorgeous," he said, with a flash of his old charming self. "No wonder Saint Patrick is falling in love with you."

Ruthie rolled her eyes expressively. "Stop it, Luke."

"I can tell these things. I know how guys think." He thumped his chest. "I am a guy. I see how he looks at you."

"You need to leave." She opened the door for him.

"What I need to know is what *you* are feeling about St. Patrick."

"What I know is that you need to leave. Now." She kept the door open.

They stood next to the grandfather clock in the hallway, a steady ticking in the silent of night. "That sound!" He boxed his ears with his hands. "It's so loud. Make it stop. It's making me crazy!"

Crazier, Ruthie thought to herself. "Hush. Unless you want to wake up my dad."

That threat silenced him.

She had to get him home. "Let's get you to Eagle Hill."

He made a sudden jerking motion with his shoulders, as if throwing off the weight of his thoughts, and he laughed. "No can do. Galen locked me out."

Ruthie didn't blame Galen. He had a short fuse with Luke's shenanigans. Everyone's fuse was growing short with Luke. "I have an idea. Follow me." *If you can.* She grabbed a shawl off the hallstand, a flashlight from the kitchen, and started down the driveway.

"I thought I could just stay at your house," he said in a slurry voice, falling into step beside her, his long strides tipsy and wavery. "I'll be a perfect gentleman and sleep on the couch."

"My father might have a different opinion of that solution."

"Ruthie, hold on. Let's run away. Let's get married and run away. Tonight." He stopped abruptly. "I'm dead serious."

"Right." Humor him, keep him walking toward Eagle Hill before he turned mulish again. "And where would we go? What would we live on?"

Luke started walking again. "I hadn't gotten that far." He grinned sheepishly. "That's why I love you, Ruthie. You're good with plans. Every couple needs at least one grown-up. Does that make any sense?"

"Perfect sense," Ruthie said.

"Good! Because I might have had a teensy-weeny too much to drink." He pinched two fingers together as he spoke. "Makes me mix up what goes through my head with what comes out of my mouth."

He tripped twice, and started to sing, but she shushed him. She put an arm around his waist as they followed the flashlight beam toward the cottage at Eagle Hill. A soft buttery glow shone through the windows from the Coleman lantern hanging above the kitchen table. Good, Patrick was still up. She tapped tentatively on the door until Patrick opened it, surprised by the sight of the two of them.

"Saint Patrick, how good of you to join us." Luke glanced sideways at Ruthie, mocking laughter in his eyes.

"Patrick, I'm really sorry to bother you, but I need some help."

Patrick backed away from the door and held it open so they could come in over the threshold. He quickly closed the door behind them and pointed to Nyna's empty cage. Ruthie knew he often kept the door open to Nyna's cage so she could get some exercise. With one firm word from Patrick, she would return to her cage. "I'll handle it from here, Ruthie," he said, putting his arm around Luke to steady him. "You can go on home."

But Luke was not to be easily corralled. He lunged for Ruthie and caught her by her free arm. "Not without Ruthie!" he said, his voice soaring. "I'm not going anywhere without my Ruthie."

Patrick shrugged and looked across Luke's head toward Ruthie. "Would you mind?"

Luke glowered at him. He pointed a finger at Patrick's chest. "Do you not realize she's my girlfriend?"

Ruthie rolled her eyes in disgust. "No, I'm not."

"Yes, she is," Luke insisted. "She just won't admit it."

"Well, I can't blame you for wanting Ruthie to be your girl," Patrick said.

Tears pinpricked Ruthie's eyes. She had burst into Patrick's cottage tonight with a drunken Luke, interrupting his peace, and yet somehow, Patrick's peace resisted interruptions. Unflappable.

"She's devoted to me," Luke said. "We have history."

Patrick had far more tolerance for Luke than Ruthie did—she was ready to stuff a sock into his mouth. "What kind of history?" he asked Luke.

"You wouldn't understand."

"Try me."

Luke plopped down on the couch. "Ruthie doesn't mind things about me as much as everyone else."

She suddenly felt a sweep of fatigue; she didn't know what kind of convoluted train of thought Luke was on and didn't care. But Patrick seemed to.

"What things?" Patrick asked gently. "What things do other people mind?"

Luke closed his eyes. "Oh, you know. Things."

"No, I don't know. What things?"

Luke said something in such a soft voice that Ruthie couldn't catch what it was. She thought he said, "Booze."

Then he opened his eyes and spoke again, his voice loud enough for both of them to hear. "She knows it helps me not care. That's what booze does for me, helps me not care."

"Not care about what?" Patrick's voice was oddly gentle.

"You don't know what it's like to be trapped."

"To be trapped?"

"Yes. Trapped!" Luke rolled his eyes in annoyance. "What is the matter with you? Are you deaf?"

"No. I'm not deaf." Patrick remained undisturbed. "I'm just trying to understand. Luke, traps are often of our own making."

Ruthie looked at Patrick with new respect, wondering if he knew he spoke wisdom. It flowed out of him so naturally, so much a part of who he was.

Luke had gone sly again. He stuck a finger in Patrick's direction. "I just want to be clear about Ruthie. You need to back off."

"Got it. Understood. It's good to have things straight between friends."

Luke peered up at Patrick suspiciously. "You think we're friends?"

"Yes," Patrick said, in the same clear, firm voice he'd used for calling his bird. "I am your friend, Luke."

Suddenly, Nyna the Mynah swooped down on the couch next to Luke and pulled a silver flask out of his pocket. When Luke realized what she had done, he tried to swat her, but she flew off and into her cage. From there she squawked, "Repent, O sinner!"

"I hate that bird!" Luke grabbed his flask and held it close with both hands, as if precious to him.

"Sorry, Luke. She's attracted to shiny objects."

Luke slumped over on the couch and murmured, "So am I."

Patrick closed the door to Nyna's cage as she squawked at him. Ruthie had to suppress a grin. If he thought the grandfather clock ticked too loudly, imagine his raw nerves after a night with Nyna the Mynah squawking "Repent, O sinner!" to him. Squawk away! she wanted to tell Nyna. Whistle! Screech! Caw! Have at it.

Ruthie and Patrick stood by the door's threshold in a narrow space. She feared he would hear her heart pounding. "Thanks, Patrick." There was a lump in her throat. "I just . . . he showed up like that and I didn't know what to do with him."

He had a curious look on his face. "It's all the way to your hips. Your hair, I mean."

Her hand went to her hair and she gathered it together to a side ponytail, letting her hands slip down it like a rope. "I was heading to bed when Luke . . . appeared at my window."

Patrick looked over his shoulder to see Luke sprawled out on the sofa. "It's late, you're a lady, and I'm going to walk you home."

Pleasure warmed Ruthie's heart. She dipped her head to hide her flush of pleasure. "All right," Ruthie said. "If you insist." She tried not to sound too happy about it.

"I do insist." He turned, a bit unsteady, so that he had to fling out an arm for balance.

"Are you all right?"

"Yes. Just all thumbs." Patrick smiled down at her and again she felt that wonderfully disturbing sensation of stillness.

~~~

Andy had asked David to stop by Moss Hill, so as soon as time allowed, he left the store in Jenny Yoder's capable hands and drove over. Andy met him at the bottom of the hill, getting mail. "Thanks for coming, David. I just wanted you to know that the land agents have asked to explore a possible oil trap on the other side of the hill."

David looked up at the steep hill. He could see the two oil pumps, slowly rocking their heads. Slower than he remembered. Much, much slower. "Andy, has production slowed down in those traps?"

"Yes, but that's to be expected. The first year is the most productive year, then it drops considerably. That's why I'd like to look for more oil."

"They've offered another lease?"

"Not yet. They want to do some testing, first."

David took a deep breath. "I'd like you to hold off on more testing."

Andy was stunned. "Why? There's a better-than-good chance that this hill holds more oil traps. It's possible that all of Stoney Ridge might have unexplored oil traps."

"I'd like to give this more thought."

Andy looked like he'd been struck by a lightning bolt. "David, do you realize what you're saying?" He lifted his hands. "This moss farm . . . it can't support us. It barely breaks even."

Perhaps, but it seemed that Andy and Katrina had spent very little time growing the moss farm business once generous royalty checks from the oil pumps started to arrive on a monthly basis. Just a few years ago, the notion of developing this moss farm filled Katrina with vigor and imagination, giving her a unique purpose. That focus had recentered her entire life on the Lord. David had never looked at moss the same way—to him, it now held secrets of living, of abundance. The right kind of abundance: a dependence on God.

Clearly, Andy had a different view. He turned left, then right. "David, this land . . . it can't provide for us."

"You're looking in the wrong direction." He tipped his head to the sky. "God is the one who provides."

Andy was flabbergasted. "God *did* provide, by putting that oil into the land! If you turn your back on this oil money . . . it's like walking away from a treasure chest."

"Son," David said, and he did feel like a father to his son-in-law, "I'm trying to protect the treasure."

18

It was a perfect day. Clear blue sky, a steady breeze, and unseasonably cool temperatures after last night's rain broke the relentless heat wave. Ruthie was hanging sheets on the clothesline when she heard someone call her name. She turned around and saw Mim Schrock standing on the walkway to the house, her hands linked behind her back.

"Mim!" Ruthie threw the clothespins down on the pile of wet sheets and walked over to her friend. Well, she wouldn't consider Mim a friend, exactly. The girls were a few years apart in age and Ruthie was always a little uncomfortable around Mim. Partly, Mim was acutely shy; mostly, Ruthie was prejudiced by how she kept Jesse dangling on a thin string of hope. But even if the girls weren't chummy, they were neighbors. "When did you return?"

"Two days ago."

She thought about asking Mim if she liked Prince Edward Island, but from the way she responded to her question, and the way she twisted her hands nervously in her apron, Ruthie could see this wasn't a social call. Even on a good day, Mim

226

had a gift for looking as if the sky might fall. She waited for Mim to say what was on her mind.

"I know your relationship with my brother Luke is none of my business . . . and, well . . . this is a really hard thing to talk about . . ."

"Just go ahead and say it," Ruthie said, thinking she was going to say that Luke had a new girlfriend.

Instead, Mim said, "What I'm wondering is . . . ." After a long pause, she began again, "Have you noticed a change in Luke this summer?"

"Like what?"

"Like . . . he seems to be acting crazy."

"Crazy?" Ruthie said as calmly as she could, switching gears in her mind. "Crazy . . . how do you mean?"

"Sneaky. Belligerent."

"More than usual?"

"Yes. You haven't noticed?"

"No, not really." Other than when he had been drinking. When he was drunk, he was mean. And crazy. But she wasn't sure she should say so to his sister.

Mim looked relieved. "Well," she said quietly. "Maybe I shouldn't have said anything."

"Wait. Let's back up," Ruthie said slowly. "What do you mean when you say he's more belligerent than usual?"

"I know he's always been susceptible to back-acre parties, but he went out last night and didn't come back until dawn. And it was obvious he'd been drinking. A lot."

Ruthie waited. None of this seemed like new information.

"Galen and Luke argued this morning. He told Luke that if he doesn't stop drinking and find a job, he's going to make him move out when he turns eighteen. Luke stormed out."

Still, nothing new.

"I heard my mother cry. She never cries. Luke doesn't realize how he affects our family." Mim looked away. "Or maybe he does."

"Mim . . . why are you telling me all this?"

"Luke can be wonderful. Sweet, thoughtful, funny," Mim said, clearly evading the question. "You know how much you've always meant to him. You've been one of the few who can see the potential in him."

Ruthie didn't know how to answer that.

Mim's hands curled into a tight ball. "Ruthie, does Luke have any reason to be jealous of you? Is there anyone else in your life?"

She thought of Patrick, but didn't answer.

"He does, doesn't he?" she said softly. "That's why you broke up with him. There's someone else."

"No. That's not why and Luke knows it. I stopped going out with him because he drinks too much. I've had enough of it."

Mim nodded, as if she understood.

Just as Ruthie was starting to relax, Mim added, "Maybe he's just misunderstood the situation."

"Misunderstood what situation?"

"He seems to think that there's something between you and Patrick Kelly."

"That's ridiculous. We're just friends." She bit her lip. "Why? What did Luke say?"

"It's not what he said. It's what he did."

"What did he do?"

Mim wrapped her arms against her side, as if it hurt her to say what she was going to say. "He killed that black bird of Patrick's and left it on his doorstep."

Ruthie gasped. Nyna the Mynah? Patrick loved that silly bird. Loved, loved, loved it. Luke killed his bird. *Killed his bird, killed his bird, killed his bird.* Those words swirled around in Ruthie's head. "Has Patrick found out?"

"Yes. He's . . . quite upset."

"I should go find him."

"He left to go bury his bird. I offered to help him, but he said he wanted to be alone."

Ruthie was still trying to absorb this information. Luke killed Patrick's bird? She felt a sick sensation in the pit of her stomach. "How could Luke do such a thing? Why? Why would he do such a thing?"

"He said he saw the two of you together, taking a walk, and it just made him crazy."

Yesterday afternoon. She knew he had seen them leave the cottage. She didn't even mind so much. Luke had been so hot and cold lately that it didn't bother her one little bit if seeing them made him a little jealous. She wanted him to know she didn't belong to him. What had that started, though?

"Patrick said something odd. He said that in ancient Greece, leaving a calling card like that—the dead bird on the doorstep—he said it's a challenge to a duel."

Silence.

"Does that make any sense to you?"

Ruthie thought of Socrates, of courage, of knowing when to advance and when to retreat. "Yes, it does."

Mim looked like she was going to cry. "Please don't tell Luke that I'm the one who told you about the bird. Don't tell anyone about the bird. Patrick asked me not to say anything. I just . . . I felt as if you should know what was going on between them. Just in case . . ."

229

"I won't," Ruthie said, even though she didn't owe Mim any promises, especially not over Luke, especially since Mim had broken her brother Jesse's heart more than a few times. Yet Ruthie would keep the confidence for Patrick's sake. "Well. Thank you for telling me."

"You're welcome," Mim said. And then—"I'm so sorry."

As she finished hanging wet sheets on the clothesline, Ruthie thought about Mim's last words: *I'm so sorry.* There was something about them that was both poignant and telling. She really did sound sorry, although she wasn't sure if she felt sorry for Luke or herself.

The one Ruthie felt sorry for was Patrick.

David was on his way home from the Bent N' Dent one afternoon when he decided to make a quick stop at the cottage next door. He hadn't seen Patrick Kelly in the last few days and it concerned him when Ruthie said that the Penn Dutch lessons had been put on hold, plus the buggy driving lessons. What had dampened Patrick's enthusiasm?

As he reached a hand to knock on the cottage door, it swung open. "David!" Patrick said, a surprised look on his face. "I was just on my way out."

Was it David's imagination, or did Patrick look extremely fatigued? No . . . no, it wasn't how he looked, it was how he moved. Slowly, shuffling his feet like an old man. Before he could ask, he noticed the cage in Patrick's hand. It was empty.

"Where is Nyna?"

"She . . . flew off. The door must have been left open. Just one of those things."

"Oh Patrick. I'm so sorry. I know you were fond of that bird."

"Yes. Yes, I was."

David looked around the trees. "Maybe she'll come back. Have you looked for her? I could help."

"No, David. Thank you. She's gone."

Patrick stepped on the porch and closed the door, then fiddled with the key to lock it. He was having trouble getting the key into the lock, so David covered his hand with his to guide it in and twist it. "These old locks can be tricky." He handed the key to Patrick, who took it without a word.

David didn't like the feel of this. Something wasn't right and clearly Patrick wasn't going to say what it was. He felt as if he was pulling teeth out of him to talk, the way conversations often went with his own children. What would Birdy do? Probably come at it from another angle.

"Patrick, now that you've been here a few weeks, I've been wondering what other things you've noticed about the Amish. Other things than quilt shops open on the Sabbath, that is." He knew that Patrick took long walks around the countryside. He hoped he was seeing the best of the Stoney Ridge church members. The field work, the families working side by side to harvest the garden, the quilting bees.

"I have to admit, I keep coming across things I wouldn't have expected."

David's stomach dropped. "Such as . . ."

"Yesterday, I saw a microwave hooked up to a generator on someone's back porch. An Amish wife was using it to heat up her coffee. And then I saw a group of teenaged Amish girls with iPhones, making selfies. They even had a selfie stick. *That* surprised me."

Selfies? What in the world was a selfie stick?

"Sometimes, to be honest, I don't even know I'm among the Amish." Carefully, holding on to the pole, Patrick stepped off the porch and lifted the empty cage. "I need to get this in the garbage. Makes me sad to see it in the cottage. Thanks for looking in on me, David. You've been very kind to me. You always make me feel . . . better about everything."

David's perspective about everything just went south.

In general, Jesse didn't have much luck when he told others what to do, but tonight, when he found his dad and Birdy and little sisters in the living room, his voice held no room for negotiation. "Luke Schrock has to go." He slapped his straw hat against the tabletop, just to add a touch of drama.

Everyone looked up, surprised by Jesse's sudden appearance or bold pronouncement, or both. Birdy exchanged a look with his dad. She tried to scoop up the twins, but they executed a perfectly synchronized bob-and-weave to avoid her, Emily to the left, Lydie to the right—until David rose to his feet and they trudged upstairs to start baths, grumbling all the way that they were left out of everything good. Ruthie was over at Katrina and Andy's, spelling Molly to give her a good night's sleep, but that meant Molly remained in the living room, looking quite interested, until his dad gave her *the look*.

"What's he done?" His dad sat back down in his chair.

Jesse glanced at Molly's disappearing bare feet on the stairwell, waiting until she reached the top because he knew she had a talent for eavesdropping. He was glad Ruthie wasn't here to hear this news. He lowered his voice. "He killed Patrick's bird and left it on the cottage doorstep." He bumped his fists together and split them apart. "Like it was a twig." The whole thing made him sick. Literally.

"Oh no." His father paled, stricken. "Why?"

"Who knows why Luke does what he does? All I know is that he's kicked up his crazy a notch by killing Patrick's bird. He's skidding off a cliff. Dad, he's gotta go."

"Go where?" his father said.

"Anywhere but here. Everyone in this town has lost patience with him. No one wants to hire him. You won't even hire him at the Bent N' Dent! Galen won't let him near his horses. His own mother has lost patience with him. Have you noticed how worn out Rose looks? Luke needs to go before something else happens and it's too late." He looked straight at his father and boldly pointed his finger at him. "You need to make that call. You're the bishop. Luke needs to leave this town before he ends up knocking off a liquor store and spending the rest of his life in jail."

"No way. Not possible."

"Dad," Jesse said, "when are you going to wake up and see Luke for what he is?"

"And what would that be?"

"A drunk," Jesse said. "A selfish, self-destructive drunk."

"What a person does isn't the same as who a person is," his dad said. "There's good inside of Luke."

Only his father. Jesse glanced at him, impressed by his ability to try to find good in everybody even when there was no good in someone like Luke. Only his father could think like that.

"Tell me one thing, Jesse."

Jesse lifted his eyebrows, all ears.

"Don't you think it's curious that a young man like Luke who fights so hard against being one of us . . . hasn't left?"

It was a testament to Patrick's character that he was still here. Ruthie would have thought he might have packed up and left Stoney Ridge for good after he found Nyna the Mynah dead on his doorstep. She kept Mim's confidence and didn't mention a word to him or to anyone else. Nor had Patrick volunteered anything, and she hadn't seen Luke, which was just as well. She wasn't sure what she would or could say to him. She didn't usually let her temper fly, really fly, but when she did, she often had cause for regret.

Tonight, the sky was filled with colorful streaks of clouds. The sunset would be especially beautiful; her father and Birdy and the girls were over at Katrina's to see the baby, so she asked Patrick if he'd like to go on a hike up the ridge to watch the sun set.

"I'd love to," he said, when she appeared at the cottage door. In fact, it seemed as if he was waiting for her, but she often got that feeling when she was with Patrick. Like he had all the time in the world for her.

Instead of going straight up the hillside, she decided to take the road. It would be slower, but easier on Patrick. The recent rains had made paths muddy. The road meant fewer obstacles to maneuver, less chance of things that caused him to trip. She was convinced he needed glasses but wasn't sure how to bring the subject up.

Patrick brought up a book he'd been reading, a book by Richard Foster called *Celebration of Discipline*, and was explaining to Ruthie about the discipline of prayer when they turned a corner and he breathed out, "Oh boy." They had come face-to-face with Luke Schrock and a few of his friends. They stood on the side of the road, drinking beer from cans, leaning against Hank Lapp's yellow golf cart. She could practically feel Patrick tense up. Even the air around them felt charged, like right before lightning struck.

"Well, well," Luke said, his eyes looking mean. "If it isn't Saint Patrick and the lovely Ruthie Schrock."

Ruthie felt trapped. If she snapped at Luke the way she'd like to, it would only escalate his hostility. He wouldn't lose face in front of his friends.

Luke pushed himself off the golf cart, his boots squelching in the mud, and strode up to Patrick. "Ever heard of a game called chicken?"

"No, I haven't."

"Perfectly harmless game."

"Perfectly stupid, you mean," Ruthie said. "It's a game where there's nothing to gain and pride stops everyone from backing down."

"Not true!" Luke said, eyes fixed on Patrick. "It's a game to find out who is the bravest. We stand in the road and wait for a car to come around the bend. The first one who runs is the chicken." He walked back to his friends in the golf cart and patted the front of it. "We can even practice. Let's try it once while I drive the cart."

Patrick drew in a quick hitching breath.

"Don't let Luke goad you into anything," Ruthie whispered. "Let's leave."

Patrick snapped his head toward her. "I don't run," he said, but he appeared to be trembling. Nearly imperceptible, but she noticed. And then he touched her face. He brushed the curve of her jaw with his fingertips, ever so lightly. He walked over, bold and confident, to Luke, sitting in the golf cart. She looked at Luke's friends, hoping one or the other might stop this foolishness. But that was a foolish notion in itself. An old proverb danced through her mind: Verglaag der Deiwel bei seinre Schwieyermudder. *Don't expect help from the devil's friends.*

She stood rooted a moment, so that she had to hurry to catch up to Patrick.

A slice of fading sunlight fell across the well-scrubbed hospital waiting room. Luke stretched his legs out flat and leaned back on the hard plastic chair. "He should have moved. Why did he just stand there? It was like he was frozen. He should have just run."

"Because Patrick is nothing if not brave," Ruthie said. "He told you. He doesn't run."

"Well, somebody has to move or the game of chicken doesn't work."

And then she realized the truth. A terrible feeling came over her, a feeling that had been poking at her for weeks but she hadn't wanted to face it, to even think it. Her entire body began to tingle as if she were being slowly submerged in boiling water. Slowly she looked up. She had to swallow twice before she could speak.

"Luke, a few weeks ago, were you playing chicken on Old Spotted Horse Road?"

He gave her a deer-in-headlights look, then he slipped on his charming rascal's smile again, but it didn't quite work. He rolled his broad shoulders in a shrug. "I don't remember."

"I think you do remember. I think you're the reason that man drove his car off the road and ended up having a heart attack at the inn."

Luke's smile dimmed. He straightened up and crossed his arms against his chest. His face became subtly guarded. "Ruthie, honey, I know you're upset, but that's a pretty nasty accusation."

She kept her eyes fastened to his. He had a way of making himself look all innocent, a way of making his eyes go sweet and soft as if he were nothing but a mischievous schoolboy. "You did it, didn't you? And you didn't wait to see if the driver was all right. You just ran off with your friends. You left him there, alone. He had hit his head, his car had a flat, and you . . . just . . . left."

"Is that how little you think of me?" He looked over at her now with eyes that were hard and black, staring down at her as if she was nothing more than an annoying insect. "And I think your logic is scrambled because you've got a crush on Saint Patrick." He added a mocking lilt on the last two words.

Patrick had said he didn't run. She wanted to run and keep on running, out of the hospital, away from Stoney Ridge, and to the ends of the earth.

"If Patrick dies, that means you will have caused the death of two people. Do you realize that, Luke?"

His pulled his hat brim to hide his eyes, and his mouth was set hard. "You're talking crazy. I've had enough." He got up and started toward the exit.

"Even if Patrick survives, you could be facing years in jail. Years and years," Ruthie said, but she was talking to Luke's disappearing back. Before he reached the double doors of the exit, she yelled, "Luke!"

Her shout startled him. He spun around, his eyes filled with fury.

She knew she should stop, but she couldn't. "You can't just keep avoiding the truth!"

He stormed back and grabbed her upper arms, their chests inches apart, so she had no choice but to look directly into his face, veins bulging everywhere, his features distorted with rage.

"Let go of me," Ruthie said as calmly as she could with a pounding heart.

"Quit telling me what to do!"

"Then stop doing such stupid things!"

"Stupid?" he said, ratcheting up his grip another notch.

Wincing now, "Luke, that hurts. Let me go!"

She was conscious, suddenly, that he smelled of beer and sweat and blood. Patrick's blood.

19

Ruthie paced nervously in the waiting room of the hospital. What was taking so long? Patrick had to be all right. He had to.

After Luke stormed out, she called her aunt Dok to come to the hospital. Dok asked a few specific questions: Was Patrick conscious when he was brought into the emergency room? No. Did he have a pulse and heartbeat? Ruthie thought so but wasn't sure, and Dok responded by saying she would be right over.

It was all so chaotic and jumbled—Luke ran the golf cart straight at Patrick, expecting him to jump away at the last minute, but he didn't budge. As the golf cart hit him, Patrick crumbled, hitting his head hard when he fell. Then . . . panic! Luke's friends disappeared into the woods like rats scurrying to a rain sewer. Ruthie stayed with Patrick while Luke ran to the nearest phone shanty and called for an ambulance. She cringed as her mind replayed the awful crash, over and over. It all went so fast, yet at the same time, so slowly, like a bad dream. She felt weighted down with nausea, as if an anvil had replaced her stomach.

After calling Dok, she had left a teary phone message on the phone shanty that was shared with the Inn at Eagle Hill, and hoped, hoped, *hoped* that her dad would remember to check messages when he came home from Katrina's. But Rose Schrock must have heard the message, because she was the first to come.

Rose arrived at the hospital and found Ruthie in the waiting room. Her eyes were swollen from crying. "No news?"

"No news."

Rose looked up and down the hall. "Where is my son? Please don't tell me he didn't come with you."

"Luke was here, but he left. A little while ago."

Rose sat down beside Ruthie. "I don't know what to do about Luke. Galen said he doesn't want him in the house after this. He says I'm too soft on him. That I'm too soft on sin." She wiped tears off her cheeks with the back of her hand. "Luke is tearing our home apart. He's tearing our lives apart. The worst thing is that I don't think he even realizes it. And if he does, I don't think he cares. He was always difficult, even before his father died. He tries to blame it on Dean's death, but he was born not wanting to be tethered or tamed. I should have done a better job with him, but I didn't know how."

Whoa. This felt like more information than Ruthie could handle. She was only seventeen! Right now, she felt like a child. She wanted her father. "Soon, my dad should be here. You can talk to him. He'll know what to do. He always does."

Rose nodded. She leaned forward in the chair and covered

her face with her hands. "I love my son. I love him so much. But I don't know how to manage him."

From the way Rose was sitting, with her elbows raised above her abdomen, Ruthie suddenly realized Rose was pregnant—quite, quite, *quite* pregnant. How had she not noticed before? No wonder Galen wanted Luke out of the house.

When Ruthie had prayed for God to open her eyes, she hadn't meant she wanted to see all this.

And then she saw Dok come out of Patrick's room with a very serious look on her face. Ruthie had a moment of tingling, a premonition of something terrible.

Experience had taught Dok to save some good news to give after the bad, so she searched her mind for something positive to deliver to her niece Ruthie. But what? This was pretty devastating news.

During a consult with Ed, together they reviewed the results of some of Patrick's tests and came to the same initial conclusion, which Patrick confirmed.

She went out to find Ruthie in the waiting room. Rose Schrock was with her, but politely excused herself for a moment, which Dok appreciated. She sat next to Ruthie. "Patrick is resting right now. He's going to be admitted so we can run some tests."

One delicate tear trailed down Ruthie's face. "How badly hurt is he?"

"Actually, he's not hurt badly from the crash with the golf cart. A few cuts and bruises, maybe a mild concussion. His forehead was stitched up."

"Then . . . why are you admitting him into the hospital?"

"Ruthie, have you ever noticed that Patrick has some problems with large motor control? Tripping, shuffling his feet, dropping things."

"Well, at times. Not all the time, though. I thought maybe he needed glasses."

"No, he doesn't need glasses. Patrick gave me permission to tell you that, a few months ago, he was diagnosed with multiple sclerosis."

"Multiple sclerosis," she repeated. "I've heard of it, but I'm not really sure what it is."

"It's a disease in which the immune system attacks the myelin sheathing of nerves. It eats away at the protective covering."

"How do you get it? How can you get rid of it?"

"No one really knows why anyone gets it, or what triggers it. It might be hereditary. It tends to present about Patrick's age. Ed is going to run more tests on Patrick. An accurate diagnosis can be difficult to make, because there's no one surefire test that confirms MS, and many other diseases have symptoms that mimic MS. But there's no cure for MS. Not yet. Damage is irreversible. Eventually, Patrick will lose the ability to walk independently."

Ruthie had been digesting this information in silence. Dok waited to see if she had more questions, but then her niece surprised her. Surprised and pleased her.

"He never complained. Despite all that, he never complained." Ruthie wiped away tears, took a deep breath and said, "What can I do to help?"

Dok reached an arm around her to give her a hug. "He needs a friend and I can't think of anyone better than you to be by his side right now. Let him know he's not alone.

He's going to call his parents to come, but he wants to wait until the morning. And . . . do the most important thing of all. Pray."

Ruthie kept her chin to her chest. "Dok, it's not good, is it?"

"No, honey." Dok sighed. "It's not good."

As soon as Patrick was settled into his hospital room, Dok insisted that Ruthie go home and get a few hours of sleep. Ruthie only relented after she promised to pick her up in the morning, first thing, and take her right back to the hospital.

After Dok dropped Ruthie off at her house and gave a brief update to David, she felt the first wave of fatigue hit her as she drove down the dark road. A big yawn slipped out. When she opened her eyes, someone jumped out in the middle of the road and flapped his arms. Dok slammed on the brakes to avoid him.

Luke Schrock!

Seriously? She got out of the car, furious. "Luke! How can you play a game of chicken after what happened tonight? When are you going to come to your breaking point?" And then she saw his face. He wasn't playing a game.

"The horse. Galen's horse. I did something . . ."

"What are you talking about?"

He pointed to the side of the road and it was then she saw a horse lying on its side, one leg twisted grotesquely, moaning the most pitiful wail. *Dear God.* She would never, in all her life, forget the sound of that suffering. It was a terrible, agonizing sound.

"What did you do? Did you try and jump that high fence?"

Luke couldn't answer, couldn't focus. His face looked stark, struggling with some inner torment she couldn't begin to fathom.

Then the crumbling happened. His whole being collapsed as he sank to his knees. "I can't . . . stop . . . anymore. Everything's falling apart."

Dok reached out and touched Luke's arm very gently. "Go sit in the back of my car. I'm going to call for help."

Matt. She needed Matt. She fished her cell phone out of her pocket and dialed. *Please, please be there.*

He answered on the first ring. "Dok?"

"Matt, I'm on Pinecove Road. I need help."

"Stay put. I'm on my way."

"Matt! Wait. Bring your . . . shotgun." Dok hung up and took a deep breath, walked to her car, and leaned in. She took Luke's pulse and noted his dilated pupils. "Luke, are you hurt anywhere?"

He shook his head, but she wasn't sure he could give her a coherent answer. She took his pulse—it was racing—and checked the pupils of his eyes. He had some scrapes, but other than being drunk, he wasn't badly hurt.

Oh, the moan of that horse. It made her feel sick. If Matt didn't come soon, she wondered if she had anything to help ease its pain, anything at all. She squeezed her eyes shut, wishing she could clamp her ears and not hear the animal's agony. She knew enough not to touch a wounded animal, but it felt like her heart was breaking in two. She'd always loved horses.

When she opened her eyes, she saw the flashing lights of Matt's police car pull up. He bolted out of the car. "Ruth! Ruth, are you all right?"

"I'm fine." The relief on his face was palpable. It touched her. "I have Luke Schrock here in the car. From what I can gather, he tried to jump the fence and the horse broke its leg."

"Is Luke hurt? Shall I call for an ambulance?"

"He's fine. He's . . . drunk. And maybe in shock."

Matt checked the horse and went to the trunk of his car to retrieve a shotgun. Dok covered her ears as he readied himself to end the horse's suffering. And then it was over.

"Galen," Luke cried, rocking back and forth in the car, arms gripped against his stomach. "It's Galen's horse. His Sorrel Bay. His new horse. His prize horse." He groaned and Dok worried he might throw up in her new car. And then he started to choke and gag and—"Luke! Get out of the car!" Too late. He vomited all over the backseat.

Matt brought rags from his car and wiped it up as best he could, but the smell . . . it was horrific. Alcohol-related vomitus. And all over the back of her new car! Dok was not normally a retaliatory person, she was a healer at heart— but really, she could smack this kid silly and not think twice about it. Her *new* car!

Luke wiped his mouth on the back of his sleeve. "Galen's going to kill me."

"No, he's not," Matt said calmly. "That's not Galen. I'll help you tell him what happened."

"I'm not going home. I will not go home." Some of Luke's old belligerence reemerged.

Dok knew that sometimes people in crisis needed temporary shelter, and Luke was in a crisis of his own making. "You're coming to the practice. You can stay there for the night."

Luke eyed her suspiciously. "Why?"

Because you've already caused enough damage in this town for one day. "I'm offering you a place to sleep. That's all."

Luke was no fool. "I'm fine. I'll figure out a place to go. I have friends."

Here was something Dok knew from experience: The needier they are, the more they resist. "Luke, you're severely dehydrated. I want to keep an eye on you."

"But—"

"No buts," she said firmly. "You're coming with me." She shut the car door firmly.

"How can I help?" Matt asked. "What should I do?" He glanced at the horse's still body. "Besides taking care of that."

She stood before him, temporarily awed. Matt Lehman was amazing. When she called to say she needed him, he came. No questions asked, no excuses about how busy he was. He was just there, by her side. "Would you mind going to get my brother? Ask him to come to the practice. Tell him I need him."

Matt gave her a brief, businesslike nod. "I'm on my way."

"Matt!"

He spun around.

"Thank you."

He gave her a slight grin and patted her on the shoulder. "All in a day's work."

Dok opened the door to David as if she'd been watching for him, and she probably had. "Come in," she said. "He's back in the exam room."

There, on the cushioned examining table, was Luke Schrock with an IV in his arm. He was asleep.

"He's not in any medical danger, but I'm giving him saline. He's pretty dehydrated after his bender."

David was still regarding Luke. "Well, at least someone in Stoney Ridge is getting a good night's sleep tonight."

Luke opened one eye. "Why not? Excellent accommodations for a bargain basement price," he said. Slowly, he lifted himself up on one elbow to face David.

"Are you having withdrawal symptoms?"

Luke snorted. "I'm not seeing pigs fly past, if that's what you mean."

"Do you know why you're here?"

"Yeah, I do." He rose to a sitting position, looking somewhat fierce. "Galen kicked me out. He's always had it out for me. He's never liked me—"

David cut right through by stopping him abruptly. He knew that a characteristic of self-pity was to make someone else responsible for your trouble. "You can't stop drinking, can you?"

Luke's spine stiffened, briefly proud, then collapsed into wretchedness. He bowed his chin to his chest and covered his face with his hands, weeping, yet silent as stone.

David waited patiently until he was ready to continue.

"I've always been able to manage it. But . . . lately something's changed. It's like the wheels are falling off the wagon."

"Luke, when did you start drinking?"

"After my dad died and then . . . my mom remarried. Everybody was so—" he paused—"I don't know . . . preoccupied with their own stuff. Booze, it helped me get through the day."

"But how old were you?"

"I don't know. Around thirteen."

David closed his eyes. "It hasn't helped you get through it, Luke. All it did was anesthetize you from grieving. Alcohol has kept you stuck." Ruthie had given him a few sentences of explanation when Dok dropped her off, but she was thoroughly exhausted and he sent her to bed. "Would you like to tell me what happened tonight?"

"No." Luke gave a truculent toss of his head. Then he sagged again. "Maybe."

He fell silent. David watched him chew on a nub of a fingernail and waited.

"I'm the reason Patrick Kelly is in the hospital."

"Go on."

"I baited him to play chicken. You know the game—a car comes straight at you. Whoever moves first is the chicken. Patrick didn't move. I didn't either." He held his hands in front of him, one in a fist, one open, and knocked down his fist with the palm of his other hand. "Boom. He collapsed like a house of cards."

"You were driving a car?"

"Not a car. Hank Lapp's golf cart. I stole it."

"I see." But he didn't.

"There's more."

"Go on."

"Back in June, I was playing chicken on Old Spotted Horse Lane. It was the night that guy showed up at Eagle Hill and died."

"You were driving?"

"No. It was a variation of chicken. When someone drove down the road, my friends and I would run in front of the car."

"To make it swerve?"

"Exactly."

"Why?"

Luke looked up long enough to give David the what-a-dumb-question lilt of his eyebrow. "For kicks."

For kicks. The same reason Luke had blown up mailboxes with cherry bombs all over Stoney Ridge. And installed stop signs all over the town. And killed Patrick's bird. And taken Galen's horse for a joyride.

"It's a pretty dull life here," he said, as if that explained everything. Instantly, a tough Luke mask replaced his humbled face.

If this doesn't get dealt with, David thought, *this is exactly what he will look like when he's old. Brittle. Onerous. Hardened.*

Suddenly David got a glimpse of how Moses must have felt when he warned the Israelites of what lay ahead of them in the Promised Land if they didn't toe the line: Moses blasted away at them, he rained down curses on them. His goal was to scare the sin out of them.

What would it take to scare the sin out of Luke Schrock?

The core of the problem was Luke's hard heart. Unless his heart was touched, it would be like a candle that remained unlit. God alone needed to light that wick. God alone needed to touch that heart. David knew he would have to think very carefully about what to do next. He needed time. "So how's this for a plan? You come home with me tonight." He glanced out the window and saw the darkness was fading, dawn would be here soon. A good omen? "Today, I meant."

"I guess I don't have anyplace else to go," Luke said almost crossly.

"You can get some sleep, then later we'll talk to Matt

Lehman, together. He'll be able to tell us what's the best course of action. How does that sound?"

He nodded, somewhat reluctantly.

"You certainly can't go back to alcohol, Luke, without creating more problems for yourself and the ones you love, and you can't go forward without help from other people. If you're ready, I can help."

Luke stared at him. "You'd do that, for me? After . . ."

After vandalizing property of innocent people? After man-handling my daughter? After doing harm to Patrick? Though David did not wish to hear these words of the Lord Jesus in his mind, they spoke to him, nonetheless: "But I say unto you, Love your enemies, bless them that curse you, do good to them that hate you, and pray for them which despitefully use you, and persecute you."

David read confusion, a plea for help, and, yes, hope in Luke's tired eyes. Hope was good. Hope gave David something to work with. "Of course." He fixed his eyes on Luke. "Of course I would do that for you."

20

The sun was rising above the ridge by the time Dok drove David and Luke home. Luke had fallen asleep in the backseat. As the car came to a stop in front of the house, Birdy walked to meet them with a basket of wet laundry in her arms. When she saw Luke in the backseat, jerked awake by the car's stop—which Dok might have made a little more abrupt than was necessary—her eyes went wide. She looked at them with a question written on her face. Caution was there too.

"Luke needs a place to sleep," David said. "I told him it would be okay with you."

"Of course it's okay," Birdy said quickly, back to her old cheerful self. "He can stay in Jesse's room."

David turned around in the car. "Luke, why don't you go in and get a shower before breakfast?"

Birdy shifted the basket from one hip to the other. "Everything you might need is in the bathroom. Help yourself to Jesse's clean clothes."

As Luke trudged into the house, David and Dok got out of the car. "Where's Ruthie?"

Birdy lifted her chin in the barn's direction. "She's milking the cow."

That, right there, Dok thought, was the Amish way. Life might be falling apart at its seams, but the cows still needed milking, the bread needed baking, the laundry needed hanging. They kept going.

"I forgot to ask," David said. "No word on Patrick's tests?"

"Nothing yet," Dok said. "I checked just before we left my office." She had filled him in about the multiple sclerosis diagnosis Patrick had been given by his doctor in Canada. "I'm planning to drop by the hospital this morning. Ruthie wanted to go with me."

"Stay for breakfast first," Birdy said. "I've made your favorite. Baked oatmeal. It's not your everyday baked oatmeal. The secret is adding cinnamon."

David reached out to gently squeeze his wife's arm. "Thank you for letting him stay. It won't be for long. Just until Dok and I can figure out what to do next."

Birdy nodded. "I don't mind, but Ruthie might. David, she has bruises on her arms from where Luke grabbed her."

David and Dok exchanged a look.

"I'll go check on her," Dok said.

In the barn, Dok found Ruthie finishing up the milking. "Did you sleep?"

"Not much."

"Let me see your bruises."

Ruthie set down the milk bucket and lifted up her sleeves. Dok could see an outline of Luke's viselike grip of black-and-blue bruises on both of her upper arms.

"They will get worse before they get better." She gently unrolled Ruthie's sleeves to cover the bruises. "Luke is up at the house. He's showering, then having breakfast."

"What?!" Ruthie groaned. "As if the last twenty-four hours couldn't get any more awful."

"Your dad and I just brought him over."

"I'm not going inside. I don't want to see him. I don't want *anything* to do with him."

"Okay. I'll take you to the hospital to see Patrick right now."

"No. Go ahead and get some breakfast." She blew out a puff of air. "There's a bus heading into town this morning. I'll take that."

"Ruthie . . ."

"You haven't slept at all. You must be hungry after the night you've had. You need to get fortified. Dad, too."

That was true. Ruthie was such an observant girl.

"Talk to Dad. Figure out what you need to do with Luke. And come to the hospital when you can."

Dok was reluctant to let her go alone to the hospital, but she did need to talk to David about Luke's future. She had an idea, but she wasn't sure if her brother would go for it.

For breakfast, Birdy served a French toast made from thick slices of homemade bread with a nice chewy crust, sunny-side-up eggs (of course! so Birdy-esque), crispy bacon, and broiled cherry tomatoes freshly picked from the garden.

When the baked oatmeal was served up, Luke wolfed down his piece as though he hadn't eaten in forty days and forty nights. Seeing this, Birdy, whom Dok suspected was as compulsively tenderhearted as David, quietly switched her own plate for Luke's empty one.

As Luke kept right on inhaling his baked oatmeal without so much as a nod of thanks, Dok was pretty certain he wasn't even aware the switch had taken place.

And wasn't that the crux of Luke's problem, right there?

As tired as she was, Ruthie had hardly slept. All she wanted to do was to head to the hospital and be with Patrick. She saw him for a short time last night, but they didn't talk about multiple sclerosis or his wobbliness or the stitches on his forehead from a game of chicken with Luke Schrock.

They really needed to talk.

She had dressed at first light and gone to the barn to milk Moomoo. It felt good to do something normal, part of her daily routine. Nothing else in her life felt normal. But when Dok had come to the barn to give her a heads-up that Luke was at the house, she felt fury rear up and return toward him. She had no desire to see Luke Schrock, of all people, over the breakfast table.

As she walked down her steep driveway, she saw Mim Schrock climbing the driveway. They met at the halfway point.

"I . . . heard about what's happened," Mim said. "I'd like to see Luke."

Ruthie swept a hand toward the house. "He's all yours."

"Ruthie, he needs help."

"You're so right."

"If anyone can help him, it's you."

Ruthie fought back a pang of annoyance. She lifted her sleeves to show Mim the bruises that ran along her upper arms. "It's not my job to fix your brother."

A look of horror crossed Mim's face as she saw the bruises.

Ruthie thought that would put an end to this discussion, but Mim wasn't finished with her plea. "You don't love him enough to help him?" she asked.

Was she serious? Galen King's new horse had to be put down because of a broken leg, Hank Lapp's golf cart was totaled, Patrick Kelly lay in a hospital room without enough strength to lift a water glass, and Mim Schrock seemed to be entirely focused on what her *brother* needed.

"No," Ruthie said. Her voice sounded unusually firm. She wanted to set the record straight. "I don't love him."

"Because of this, though, right?" Mim said, biting her lower lip. "You don't love him because of this?" She pointed to Ruthie's arms.

"I'm not sure why it makes any difference. But no. I don't love him, period. I cared about him," she said, intentionally using the past tense. "Maybe all I ever cared about was his potential. But even those feelings just aren't there anymore."

Mim's eyes filled with tears. "If you turn your back on him, who's left?"

Luke was running out of people in his corner who made excuses for him, gave him too much margin, expected too little of him. She patted Mim on the shoulder. "Well, that's what sisters are for. Sticking together through thick or thin."

Mim shook her head. "I'm moving to Prince Edward Island."

"To be with Danny Riehl?"

She nodded.

"Have you told Jesse?"

"Not yet." She bit her lower lip again. "I don't want to hurt him."

255

Ruthie lifted her palms in the air. "Jenny Yoder might help him get over it."

Mim's eyes, behind her glasses, went wide with surprise. "Who?"

"I need to get to the bus stop. About Luke . . . being left on his own. Maybe that's what he needs." A quote from Fern Lapp popped into her head and sailed right out. "'When you get to the end of yourself, that's where you find God.'"

Fern Lapp had stolen Jesse's apprentices, along with his dog. She had made a custard base for ice cream and needed help to churn the cranks. The apprentices dropped their tools right on the floor when she asked—right on the floor! They had absolutely no respect for the tools' importance or for the work at hand. Imagine if Jesse were a heart transplant surgeon and Fern walked into the operating room to announce she needed ice cream churners. Those apprentices would drop the precious donor organ right on the floor—*splat!*—and follow her anywhere.

Speaking of nipping at heels, C.P. trotted behind those apprentices as if he belonged to them. Did the apprentices feed C.P.? No. Did they take him out for a walk each night to clear his mind? No. Did they let him hang his head out the window on buggy rides? No. Did they clean up after him? Never.

Jesse was losing control of his domain.

He was going to have to reprimand Fern for apprentice thievery. That was not an easy thing to prepare for, but it had to be done. Fern was a force to be reckoned with. It was only going to get worse.

He marched to the house, jumped the two steps onto the porch, and went right past the two feckless, sweaty-faced apprentices who fought each other for turns at the churn. C.P. sat back on his haunches and looked up at Jesse, cocked his head as if to say, "What's got *your* knickers in a knot?"

Jesse scowled darkly at the dog as he strode past and walked into the kitchen. "Fern," he said firmly.

She was bent over the oven, pulling out a tray before setting it on the counter. Cookies. Jesse's mouth watered.

"Fern. I would prefer if you ask me first if you may borrow my apprentices. It's hard enough to keep them focused on their work. When you wave the promise of food under their noses, they can't refuse. They have no willpower, those two. None at all. Their brains are in their stomachs. And Fern, I believe you know this about them. What you are doing is tantamount to subordinating my role as overseer."

She scooped a cookie off the tray and handed it to him. A hot-from-the-oven oatmeal raisin cookie. He took one bite, just one, and it was delicious. It was . . . *wait*. Wait! This was bribery. Bait and switch. He knew this tactic. He used it often with his sisters. "Fern, you once threatened my very life if I didn't get new storm front wipers on your buggy before a rainstorm. Just now, we were working on Edith Fisher Lapp's brake pads. Would you like to be the one to tell Edith that her buggy won't be ready for another day? You know as well as I do that she was born to bristle." Edith looked and acted like a sour lemon. Like a lemon that didn't like lemons. He took another bite of the cookie. How did Fern get those raisins to be so plump?

Evidently Fern could read minds. "Soak the raisins in beaten eggs and vanilla for an hour. That's the secret."

Oh. He would have to tell Molly. Her oatmeal raisin cookies tasted like sawdust.

Wait. She had done it again! "Fern. Please pay attention. You may not steal my apprentices for your household chores without asking me first."

Fern finished scooping oatmeal raisin cookies from the tray, set it down, and turned to him. "It's supposed to be nearly one hundred degrees this afternoon. Those boys need something to look forward to." She wiped a strand of gray hair from her forehead and looked at him with concerned eyebrows, sparse as they were. "You do too. You need to stop mooning and start courting."

"What are you talking about?"

Fern stood at the counter, slid her glasses down her nose, gave him a look. "Stop mooning over Mim Schrock and start courting Jenny Yoder."

Jesse was speechless. Struck dumb. He felt Fern was looking straight through him, that she could see everything, knew everything.

Then a thought floated through his mind and he caught it. "Would she even want me to court her?"

"How will you know if you don't try?"

A few hours later, Jesse stopped at the Bent N' Dent. Jenny Yoder was sweeping the cereal aisle, where a box of oatmeal had tipped off the shelf and spilled everywhere. She looked up at the jingle of the door.

"I heard," she said. "About Patrick Kelly. About getting MS."

It was astonishing how quickly the Stoney Ridge grapevine's news traveled through town. Faster than a telegraph. Faster than a cell phone. Faster than a—

"I'm so sorry. I know he's your friend."

"He is," Jesse said. Suddenly, he felt a terrible constriction in his throat, like a pinecone was stuck halfway down. His heart was pounding so hard it was like a drumbeat thrumming between his ears. What was happening to him? The Jenny Yoder Effect, that's what it was. Jesse Stoltzfus, a man who considered himself something of a silver-tongued wordsmith, a man who was the Stoltzfus family Scrabble champion, a man who read the dictionary for fun, could not seem to extract more than two words from his head to his mouth whenever he was near this woman.

She pointed to the pink box. "Something from the Sweet Tooth Bakery?"

"Yes," he said, one octave too high. *Mortifying*. He handed her the pink box.

She gave him a curious look, then unwrapped the string and opened the box. "You got me a cinnamon roll?"

"I did." His throat felt slightly less constricted, a mild easing up. "This morning. It was the last one in the case." The dam was breaking loose.

"And you didn't eat it?"

He feigned horror at the thought. "What kind of a man would do such a thing?"

"A hungry one." She dipped her head. "Saving a cinnamon roll isn't for the faint of heart." She glanced up at him with a shy smile. "Thank you, Jesse."

"It was nothing." Well, it was something.

Their eyes met. Met and held.

21

David knew that Luke Schrock needed professional help, more than anyone in Stoney Ridge could provide.

Dok was familiar with a residential facility east of Harrisburg that was designed for Mennonite and Amish patients, supporting their faith and lifestyle, including counselors who were fluent in Penn Dutch. Dok had called ahead and there was a space available for Luke if he arrived today. All that was needed now was for Luke to be willing to go.

David waited until Luke got a few hours' sleep, but when he heard sounds of him stirring upstairs—the gift of squeaky floorboards—he went to Jesse's old room to talk to him. "Dok knows of a place for you to go, Luke, that will help you get better." David showed him the brochure Dok had given to him.

Luke opened the brochure and glanced through it. He handed it back to David with a scoff. "Nope. No way. Not happening."

"Why not?"

Luke leaned back on the bed's headboard and lifted his arms behind his head to rest it. "Too drastic."

"Yes. Drastic is just the right word for it. We need to take drastic measures to try and help you. Your life can't go on the way it's headed. You're going to end up hurting someone. You already have."

"I've stopped drinking. I won't pull any more stunts. You've got my word on that."

"That's a good place to start, Luke. A great place, in fact. You're taking responsibility for yourself. But drinking is only part of the problem." He glanced at Dok, who had come up behind him. "Dok suspects you have undiagnosed depression."

Luke smirked. "I'm *not* depressed."

Dok spoke up. "Anger is often a mask for depression. The other day you told me that you felt angry most of the time."

Luke shrugged. "Sometimes I do. But not all the time."

"Ruthie has bruises on her arms from the way you grabbed her."

Luke kept his eyes on his stocking feet at the end of the bed. "I lost my temper. It won't happen again." More to himself, he said, "It will not happen." He glanced at David, a plea in his eyes. "Please don't make me go."

"Luke, I believe this is the best step for you. You need more help to work through your problems than we're able to provide. The treatment center will help give you tools to get a handle on drinking."

His old belligerence reared up. "I won't go. You can't make me."

Actually, they could. Rose had already signed the paperwork. The facility had faxed it to Dok's office and she had taken the papers to the Inn at Eagle Hill. However, David understood Luke's stubborn streak well enough to know that if he thought he was being forced to go to the treatment center, he would resist the treatment. "No, I won't make you go. But if you choose not to go, Matt Lehman said you might be facing charges for the damage you caused. He said that could result in time spent in juvenile hall, unless the judge decides to charge you as an adult."

After breakfast, while Luke slept upstairs, Matt had come to the house to help David sort through legal issues. Hank Lapp wasn't going to charge him for theft of the golf cart. Patrick Kelly wasn't going to charge Luke for reckless endangerment. Galen King wasn't going to charge him for stealing his horse. But, Matt said, he had the capability to dig up a few justifiable misdemeanor charges to nudge Luke in the direction of admitting himself to the residential facility. Minor in Possession of alcohol, for one.

David heard Luke inhale sharply as it dawned on him that he had only two options. He looked suddenly troubled. He wanted to make this whole matter go away, but there was no ignoring this. Luke picked up the brochure and skimmed through it. "This joint looks pretty pricey. Who's picking up the tab?"

"The church. The people who love you. We all want you to get well, Luke. To be the man God wants you to be."

Luke looked at him with an odd gravity. "And what kind of man is that?"

David smiled. "Let's find out."

David walked Luke out to where Matt and Dok were waiting for him in the car. Matt's car. They didn't want to drive over an hour in Dok's car due to, Matt said very diplomatically, "the insinuating fragrance the interior of the car is infused with." In other words, Luke's vomit.

"Luke," David said. "I want you to listen to me. When we feel frightened and guilty, our tendency is to avoid God completely. Do the opposite. Seek God out. Pursue him. Get to know him. Don't avoid God. Go towards him. He's the lifeboat in any crisis."

Luke looked away. "You're sending me away. My family wants nothing to do with me. None of you care. Why should I believe that God cares?"

"It may seem that way to you now, but this is the merciful thing to do. Yes, you're facing some serious consequences for your behavior. But, Luke, if you seek God in this hard time, you'll realize you have far more reason to hope than to despair. This is a second chance for you. A fresh start." Since Luke wasn't looking at him, he circled so he could observe his expression. " I'll be praying for you each day. I'll come to visit, as soon as the therapists say you're ready for a visitor. We can talk more then."

"How long do I have to go to this place?"

"One month. Maybe two. I think that will depend on you, your therapists, and the progress you make."

"Then what?"

Even Dok, listening to the two through the open car window, looked to David for that answer. "Then, if you're agreeable, Fern Lapp wants you to live at Windmill Farm. To help Amos on the farm."

A light snapped on in Luke's dull-looking eyes. "Fern?"

"Fern?" Dok echoed.

"Fern," David repeated. Luke needed hard and satisfying

work that wore deeply on the muscles. "She works wonders with wayward boys. Just look at Jesse."

Dok was intrigued. "What's her secret?"

"She has a theory that boys aren't busy enough. It's as pure and simple as that."

Luke's face took on a resigned "my life sucks" expression. He stood stiff and resentful as David reached out to embrace him. "I don't want to go," he croaked into David's ear.

"I know," David whispered back. "But you need to go."

Sullen and angry, Luke climbed in the back of Matt's car and away they went. David felt his heart pierce through as he watched the car drive down the road until it was out of sight. "Let this be Luke's new beginning, Lord. Let this be the first day of a fresh start for him. Don't let him go. Hold tight to him, Lord. Shower him with your mercy. Give him as much of you as he is able to receive." It wasn't a typical thing for David to do, yet he couldn't help but lift his hands, palms open, as he prayed the prayer for Luke.

Then he turned and walked back inside.

⁓

Luke asked Dok if they could stop by the hospital so he could talk to Patrick.

"Why?" she asked, suspicion in her voice. "Why do you need to see him?"

"To apologize," Luke said, through a mouth that was tense.

She hesitated, not at all sure if Patrick wanted to see him, but she did want to check on him. She also thought of something David often said, and that convinced her to accommodate Luke. "An apology is the best place to start." Lord willing, today was Luke Schrock's new start.

Matt and Luke sat in the waiting room while Dok checked in with the nurses. She was so grateful for Matt's help today. Without even asking him, he had offered to drive with her to the residential facility. And he insisted on driving in his car because her car still reeked of Luke's vomit. He promised to stick like glue to Luke while she did what she needed to do in the hospital. That was the thing about Matt—he had such respect for her time. And her work. "Gifted in true doctoring," was the phrase he often used to describe her.

As Dok walked into Patrick's room, she smiled to see that Patrick and Ruthie were laughing over something, a private joke. Patrick looked happy, which was pretty amazing, all things considered, but Dok had a feeling it had something to do with Ruthie's presence. She was sorry to interrupt their lightheartedness as she gave the headlines of Luke's last twenty-four hours. "He wants to apologize to you. But I won't send him in if you don't want to see him."

Ruthie's hands drifted protectively to her upper arms, but her eyes, Dok noticed, were on Patrick.

Patrick was the first to speak, and Dok thought she caught a new slur in his pronunciation of "s."

"Of course. Of course we will see him. Send him in."

Dok glanced at Ruthie to make sure she was okay with that, but her eyes remained fixed on Patrick. She appeared to be regarding him with something very close to admiration. Maybe something even more? "Okay. Matt Lehman will stay right here with him. I'm going to track down Dr. Gingerich and see what's going on with your test results." She patted Patrick's leg.

He was a good guy, that Patrick Kelly. He didn't deserve what was coming next.

⁓

Luke stood awkwardly at the edge of Patrick's bed, rocking from foot to foot. He had his hands clasped behind his back, like a man ready to bolt. A bundle of raw nerves. But his eyes were dark sad circles. Self-pity, Ruthie thought. She could see it all over his face. She knew him so well.

"Say what you came to say, Luke," Matt said.

Luke was so tense, he nearly snapped at Matt, but then he clamped his mouth tight. He glanced resentfully at Matt and then looked away. "I just . . . wanted to say I'm sorry about . . . last night."

Patrick fixed Luke with an intense gaze. "I don't blame you, Luke. I should never have taken part in that chicken game. I put myself in a dumb spot. I knew I couldn't move fast enough to get out of the way. I knew it, but my pride got in the way."

"And your bird. I'm sorry about that too."

"Are you?" Ruthie kept a hard glare on Luke. "Are you, really?" *Because I don't think you have an empathetic bone in your body!* she felt like shouting at him. *Are you really sorry for all the trouble you've caused people in this town, people who have been so good to you, people who have given you chance after chance after chance. Are you really sorry, Luke, or are you just sorry you've been caught?* But she kept those thoughts quiet, which was good in a way.

"Yes," Luke said, turning to Ruthie. "Yes, I really am." He glanced at her arms. "And I'm sorry I grabbed you so hard. So very sorry, Ruthie." He took a breath and blinked rapidly in the way that people blink when they're about to cry. He tried to say more, but couldn't. Then he looked up at the ceiling and blinked some more until she could see that the rims of his eyes were turning watery, red.

Ruthie felt a sudden surge of sympathy for him. He was a mess, inside and out. A complete, total, unequivocal mess. If this residential facility didn't work, Luke would be back in the same cycle again and again. He would hurt others, including some other misguided girl who couldn't resist his charm and his handsome looks. She felt sad, but nothing more. His hold on her was broken.

Patrick reached a hand out to shake Luke's, his expression was undeservedly kind.

As Luke pumped Patrick's hand, Ruthie realized that her dad and Dok made the right decision for Luke to go to this facility. She couldn't believe he was actually doing something that wasn't his idea. Maybe there was a tiny glimmer of hope for Luke Schrock.

And then, suddenly, awkwardly, there was nothing more to say. "Well," Matt said. "We should go."

After Luke and Matt left the room, Ruthie turned to Patrick. "You were kind to Luke. You didn't even show that you were angry."

"I wasn't angry," Patrick said. "What's the point of being angry? What good would it do? Luke was sorry. That's the important thing."

How was he able to be so forgiving? Patrick saw things she didn't see. He had such a calming effect on her; even lying there in a hospital bed with a bandage on his forehead, he radiated peace, an acceptance of whatever was coming at him. How? It mystified her. Patrick mystified her.

The world had shrunken down to just the two of them. For the first time in Ruthie's life, time felt like an hourglass, with sand that was running out. She felt tears prick her eyes and blinked hard to hold them back. She was trying not to cry. "Patrick, aren't you frightened?" How could he not be? His present circumstances were monumental.

"Of what?"

Tears were falling now. "Of dying."

He honestly seemed surprised by the question. "No. I'm not." He looked placid, almost philosophical.

"But what . . ." She had to stop and brush away tears rolling down her cheeks.

He waited patiently for her to continue, though she almost wished he would just interrupt her.

"What about when you first heard you had MS? You must have been shocked."

"No. Even when I first got the diagnosis, I didn't feel frightened. In some ways, I have even felt fortunate. Knowing my future is short, I know not to waste a minute of it. Maybe that's why I can't hold anything against Luke. That kind of negativity is just not worth it. I guess I have an appreciation for what's really important in this earthly life that I didn't have six months ago. I've learned to revel in every day. And then there's another life to look forward to." He rubbed the palms of his hands together as if he was cold. Or maybe excited? "Sometimes I feel like I've been given a rare glimpse of what lies ahead. As if I'm on my tiptoes, trying to peek over the windowsill to peer into the future.

"One of the lessons I've been learning from this illness—the most important lesson, I think," he said, "is that some of the best things in life come out of the worst."

The door opened and in swept the professionals. Dok, holding a file, Dr. Gingerich following right on her heels. They both pulled up chairs and sat down. "The results of the MRI are back." Dok glanced at Ruthie and lifted her eyebrows.

Ruthie caught her hint. "I'll give you some privacy."

"No, Ruthie," Patrick said. "Stay put. You can hear this. I want you to hear it."

Dr. Gingerich clasped his hands together and settled back in his chair, then launched right in. "There are lesions in the brain that are running down the spinal cord."

"What does that mean?" Ruthie asked.

"That there's definitely a problem with the central nervous system."

Dok frowned at Dr. Gingerich. In a softer tone, she said, "Patrick, how long have you noticed something wasn't right?"

"Six or seven months ago. I started having anxiety. I've never struggled with it before. Nothing like that. Everything I did brought anxiety, worry, concern. It was difficult to do anything. I was having trouble keeping up with friends."

"Have you struggled with depression before?"

"Ups and downs here and there, like anybody does. But not depression. Not anxiety. I went to my priest and he told me that I needed more faith. If I had more faith, I wouldn't feel anxious. All I could think was, 'Oh great, a new flaw in my character.' But I tried. I tried to have more faith. I tried to manage anxiety through exercise, sleeping well, eating well. I did everything I could to keep a lid on it."

"When did the physical symptoms first present?"

"About three months ago. I woke up one morning and felt some numbness in my pinkie toe. I thought that was strange.

The next day, I woke up and my hands were tingly. I figured I had slept weird. Over the next several days, the numbness and tingly feeling spread up my arms and feet. I went to see a chiropractor and he gave me an adjustment. But it didn't make a difference. That's when I went to see a doctor."

"What did he tell you?"

"That he wanted to do a bunch of tests, but he gave me the probable explanation."

"What did he tell you?"

"That my symptoms and my age were pointing to multiple sclerosis."

Ruthie had to sit down but there weren't any empty chairs. She went to the window and leaned against it. She felt dizzy, a little nauseous, an overwhelming sadness.

Dr. Gingerich looked down, fiddling with the leather watchband around his wrist, as if he were in a hurry to leave.

Dok kept asking questions. "Patrick, did you get any tests to confirm the diagnosis?"

"No. I would have had to go into the city to get the tests. I'm not proud of this, but I went straight to the library and read up on MS and . . . I panicked. I decided that my life was ending and I was going to do the things I wanted to do before it was too late. I told my parents that I was going to Lancaster for a month."

"They have no idea that you're not well?"

"No. Other than the anxiety. They thought the trip might be good for me. They knew I always wanted to live among the Amish. They agreed to let me go for thirty days. They thought I should just get it out of my system. The Amish, I mean."

"Have the symptoms been progressing?"

"They were actually better for a week or two, when I first got here. I thought that maybe the doctor was wrong. But last week, I had trouble trying to talk . . . stumbling over w-w-words." He tried to smile. "Like now. I couldn't even write my name. I couldn't walk in a straight line. There were times when I could only shuffle. Yesterday m-m-morning I reached into my pants pocket for the cottage key and couldn't tell if I was holding a coin or a piece of paper or keys."

Dok leaned forward in her chair. Softly, she said, "Patrick, were you trying to get yourself killed while playing chicken?"

Patrick's eyes went wide. "No! Not at all. I . . . couldn't move."

Dr. Gingerich flipped the chart shut and rose to his feet. "We're going to start you on steroids right away. That should help manage the more acute symptoms."

Dok took the chart from him and flipped through the pages, running her finger down the test results. Then her finger stopped. "His vitamin B-12 came back at .66."

"No, no way. Can't be. Must be an error. It should be around 200–900 picograms per milliliter." Dr. Gingerich glanced where she was pointing. "Let's get a redo. Patrick, when did you last have something to eat or drink?"

"I guess . . . a few hours ago."

Dr. Gingerich looked at his watch. "We can't do a blood test until you haven't eaten or had anything to drink for six hours."

"Patrick," Dok said in a soft tone, "have you called your parents yet?"

"No. Not yet. I wanted to wait until you had the test results."

"Would you like me to call them?" Dok asked.

Patrick shook his head. "No. I need to be the one."

"Family can be good medicine."

The corners of Patrick's lips lifted slightly. "It's plain you haven't met my mother. She knows what's best for everyone."

A laugh burst out of Dok. "She sounds a little like my mother." She winked at Ruthie.

Dr. Gingerich held the chart in the air and pointed it toward him. "On a brighter note, once you get that blood drawn to redo the vitamin B-12 test and pick up your prescriptions, you're free to go."

"I'm discharged?"

"Yup," he said cheerfully. "There's nothing more we can do for you."

"That's *not* true."

Ruthie was surprised by the sharp tone in Dok's voice, even more by the pointed look she gave Dr. Gingerich. His brusque manner thoroughly intimidated Ruthie.

"Patrick, there's a lot we can do for you," Dok said. "We just need to get all the facts first. Getting discharged only means you don't need to be hospitalized. We're going to figure this out and help you manage the disease. I want you to have hope. There are medical breakthroughs happening every single day. Don't give up hope."

As soon as they left Patrick's room, Dok turned to Ed Gingerich, furious. "Why would you say such a thing to him?"

"What?"

"That there's nothing more that can be done for him?"

"I've prescribed massive doses of steroids for him, Ruth. Massive. Those should do the trick."

Massive doses of steroids. That's how MS was combated.

Patrick's symptoms were severe. His strength was slipping away—Dok could see a difference from last night. "And if they don't?"

"Then, it's best not to give him false hope."

She looked at him, dumbfounded. "Ed, there's always hope."

He gave her a patronizing smile. "That's what I love about you. An eternal optimist." He glanced at his watch. "I'm late. I'd better dash. Let's grab dinner tonight."

Over Ed's shoulder, she saw Matt standing with Luke by the exit, patiently waiting for her. "I can't. There's someplace important I need to go today and I probably won't be back until late."

Ed turned to see what had caught her attention. "Where are you—"

"Don't forget to get that vitamin B-12 test redone," she said as she started down the hall. "Call me the minute it comes back."

22

Ruthie's dad arrived at the hospital just as Patrick was finishing up getting discharged. He had the taxi wait so that the three of them could be driven back to the Inn at Eagle Hill. Her dad had to help support Patrick as he walked from the taxi to the cottage porch. As Ruthie unlocked the door, her dad said he wanted to go up to the house to talk to Rose for a few minutes.

"Go ahead, David," Patrick said. "I can manage." He put a hand on the porch railing to steady himself.

David hesitated, but Patrick was insistent. "Okay," he said, looking at Ruthie. "I'll be right back. Just shout if you need help."

Ruthie unlocked the cottage door and opened it. Patrick had to lean on the porch railing just to slowly make it up the three steps to the threshold. After all he'd been through, she wasn't surprised he was feeling wobbly. "Do you want to go right to bed?"

"No," Patrick said. "Not to bed." But his voice was slow and drifting.

"You shouldn't be up at all," she said. "What Dok will

think, I can't begin to imagine." Yet even as she was protesting, she was helping him into a chair. He lurched when he went to sit in it, so that she had to help him, and for a moment they were side by side, her arm around his waist. But then he was in the chair and she had taken a step back from him.

He reached his hand out to take Ruthie's hand and gave her a little tug so that she crouched down beside him. "You've been a wonderful friend to me." He held her eyes and smiled at her, and her heart fell to the bottom of her stomach. "Thank you," he said, measuring each word.

The sight of him fighting to form words pierced her heart.

"My parents are on their way to Stoney Ridge. They've come to take me home."

"Away from Stoney Ridge," she said.

"Away from here."

"Away from me," she said.

"Away from you."

"But," Ruthie said cautiously, eyes on their hands, "you do like me."

He leaned forward, so that their foreheads were almost touching. "Oh, Ruthie," he said, "I more than like you."

Ruthie could feel her ears flaming red.

After Patrick's parents arrived at the cottage, David and Ruthie walked home. They were both exhausted. He was so proud of his daughter. Despite her fatigue, she was a steadfast caretaker for Patrick. Calm and steady. He wouldn't have expected to see the gift of caretaking come out of his Ruthie.

"So, Dad," she said, as they started up the steep driveway to their home. "You sent Luke away."

"Just for a short time. He'll be back."

"He might not come back."

"I think he will."

"Why would you think that? He was always trying to convince me to leave."

"If Luke really wanted to leave, why hasn't he gone by now?"

She shrugged. "I don't know. Money, I guess. No job."

"Then why didn't he take the GED with you?" David felt the same assurance about Ruthie. If she was going to go, what was stopping her? He hoped it was because, deep down, she didn't really want to go.

"But nobody wants him in Stoney Ridge."

"I do. I want him here. It might surprise you, but I see something remarkable in Luke."

Ruthie gave him the wishful-thinking look.

"He has a rare leadership ability." As long as David had known Luke—four or five years now—he had seen how boys tagged along behind him, looked up to him, did what he said, acted the way he acted. Why, a few of them even adopted the unique Luke Schrock swagger in their gait.

Ruthie's face went blank. "Leadership? Luke? Dad, you've always said that if you want to see who is a spiritual leader, look around and see how many spiritually minded people are following a man."

"True. That's one of the ways I've known who to vote for when it's time to choose a leader for the church. But it's also true for any kind of leadership. If you've got the goods, people follow."

"What kind of goods does Luke have? The types that follow him are lowlifes. Felons-in-training."

David smiled. "For now. At this time in Luke's life, he's all about action without wisdom. Knowledge without discernment. But that might change. He was willing to go to the facility." He still couldn't believe that Luke had agreed to go. That was another sign to him that Luke's defiant posture was only skin deep, that his heart was still pliable. "Let's hope the best for Luke while he's at the facility. He said he started to drink after his father died, that alcohol helped him not to care. He also said he wanted to die, that his life wasn't worth anything." He put a hand on her shoulder. "Pray for him, Ruthie. Pray for him every day. He's in urgent need of our forgiveness, our love, our prayers. Luke has a long haul ahead." A very long haul.

"Okay," she said. "I'll say a prayer for him, but I don't want anything more to do with him. I'm done."

David would never say it aloud, but that was the best thing he'd heard all day. Even better than Matt's news that Hank and Edith's yellow golf cart was damaged beyond repair.

A nasty headache descended on Ruthie, only it was a headache that included the heart, not just the head. She was tired, she was worn out, and she was in the worst emotional pain she'd experienced since her mother's accident.

She remembered the cold nights in their home when she was a girl—how her mother piled quilts on top of her and Molly. How peaceful it seemed under the quilts. Then it seemed like sleep was one of the most wonderful things in life.

Now, she lay in bed dreading the long night ahead. Morning would come in less than six hours, she'd barely slept more than a few hours the night before, yet she didn't feel at all sleepy.

She couldn't believe how life had gotten so tangled and sad. Patrick was seriously ill. He was leaving Stoney Ridge.

And then there was Luke the Drunk.

As infuriating as Luke could be, she didn't want him to suffer. He looked so pitiful today in the hospital. Beaten, that's how he looked.

She had no idea that he had been so affected by his father's death in such a way. Dok said that whenever someone started on the road to addiction, it meant that his emotional maturity was arrested at that age. Luke was, in his head—where it really mattered with judgment and common sense—stuck in adolescence.

Dok said that Luke had told him he wanted to die, that his life was worthless. He acted like he wanted to die too. Reckless, devil-may-care, foolhardy.

What a contrast to Patrick. He valued life so much. Yet Ruthie could see his strength ebb away, practically hour by hour. Tonight, his words started to slur, as if forming words clearly took more effort, more control of the tongue, than he could give.

Ruthie couldn't imagine the kind of life that Patrick was facing, and yet somehow, he found God's grace in the most horrible events. How was Patrick able to see the divine in everything?

She had asked him how he had the courage to come to Stoney Ridge when he knew his health was in jeopardy. "There was a point when I had to decide whether my fears or my hopes should matter most." But then they were interrupted by the arrival of his parents and he never told her which he'd chosen. But then, maybe she knew.

She tossed and turned, completely distraught and distracted. She couldn't bear the thought of a world without Patrick Kelly.

She wanted light to spill into her darkened mind, she wanted something luminous to see by. All these thoughts tumbled around in her head. She finally gave up on sleep and went downstairs.

In the kitchen, she found Birdy at the table, eating a snack. She looked up in surprise as Ruthie stumbled into the kitchen. "Can't sleep?"

Ruthie shook her head and slipped into a chair.

Birdy pushed a plate of crackers toward her. "Want one?"

Ruthie took a cracker but only ran a finger along its sharp edges. She glanced at Birdy, who was polishing off the rest of the crackers. "Birdy, help me make sense of this. Luke wants to die and Patrick wants to live."

Birdy put her hand over Ruthie's and squeezed. "My gut feeling is that it will be just fine," she said. "Hold on to that, Ruthie. Everything is going to be all right. I promise." She threw out the empty box of crackers and kissed Ruthie on the top of her head before she went upstairs.

It will be just fine. Ruthie had to admit that Birdy's instincts were often uncanny. Sometimes it seemed as if she could see certain things before they happened.

Everything is going to be all right.

What did that *mean*? Did it mean that Luke would overcome his alcoholism? Would he finally get his life together?

Did it mean that the massive amount of steroids Patrick was taking would slow down the fast-moving march of that awful disease through his body? That the drugs would give him time? Because he was running out of it.

There was no time to waste, for either Luke or Patrick.

Time.

It dawned on Ruthie that time was the real issue here, the lesson that was trying so hard to be taught. Time was precious, it was fleeting, it was not in her control. She had been wasting time, treating it as infinite. Not valuing the life she'd been given, coveting what she didn't have. Wasting time. Wasting it! Time should be cherished. Every single day.

Isn't that what Patrick was all about? Cherishing the life he had, the time he had left. Every single moment.

Ruthie remained at the table until darkness ebbed away outside the kitchen window. Pale red and orange clouds streaked the morning sky, as lovely a sight as she'd ever seen. A strange peace enveloped her, slowly at first, then filled her from head to toe. What was this? It was so real. Nothing she could touch or see, but a certainty that settled into her soul. Everything was going to be all right.

Could this feeling be trusted? Or was she just hoping so much it was true that she had imagined it?

Hope could be like that.

But not without trust in God, her father always said. They're inseparable, like a man and his shadow.

Over the weekend, the steroids had no impact on Patrick. Dok tried to connect with Ed Gingerich to see what he planned to do next. Her call went to his voice mail after the eighth ring, which was very typical. Why did it take Ed so long to answer his phone when he kept it with him at all times? Today, she had no time to speculate.

Ten minutes later, Ed called. "Hey there!" he said, his voice chipper. "Did I miss your call?"

He hadn't bothered to listen to her voice mail. So why did she bother to leave them? Perhaps unreasonably, she found this carelessness to be infuriating. "The initial dose didn't work."

"What?"

"Patrick Kelly. The steroids aren't working."

"Ah. The MS patient." She could practically hear his mind pulling up the Kelly chart. "Okay. Let's try another round. I'll send down the order."

"Ed, you're giving him massive infusions of drugs. It's not even making a dent."

"I know what I'm doing, Ruth." He sounded testy. "I'm waiting for a final MS test to see if there's a certain protein present."

In the background, she heard a nurse ask Ed some questions and could tell his attention was distracted. "I'll let you get back to work. Just let me know when the test results come back in."

He assured her that he would, but she doubted he'd remember. Instead, she called his office manager, Phyllis, his right-hand man—in this case, a woman—who adored her boss but sympathized with Dok over how hard it was to track Ed down, and asked her to call as soon as Patrick's test results came in.

Dok spent the afternoon researching the latest studies on vitamin B-12 deficiency in every online medical site she could track down. When Phyllis called to give her the test results, she knew she was on to something. "Phyllis, where is Ed right now?"

"At the hospital."

She drove straight to the hospital and found Ed on the surgery floor.

When he saw the look on her face as she walked toward him, his smile faded. "You've got news."

"I don't think he has MS," she said.

"Who?"

"Patrick Kelly. I think he has hypocobalaminemia."

Ed stopped. "Tell me more."

"That low B-12 vitamin number—the second test came back with the same result. I did some digging today and I think it might be possible that his low B-12 has precipitated subacute combined degeneration." She handed him the articles she found.

Subacute combined degeneration, caused by a vitamin B-12 deficiency, was a disorder of the spine, brain, and nerves. It mainly affected the spinal cord, but its effects on the brain and the peripheral nerves were the reason for the term "combined." At first, the myelin sheath covering of the nerves was damaged. Later, the entire nerve cell was affected. As the disorder progressed, it spread to muscle weakness, abnormal sensations, mental problems, and vision difficulties.

Ed's face went blank as he skimmed through the articles, then he went into action. "Give me a few minutes to get some supplies, then meet me at my car." He headed toward the elevator.

"We're going to see Patrick?"

He pushed the button and turned around as it opened. "We're going to see Patrick."

23

Rose King met Ed's and Dok's cars as they caravaned to the Inn at Eagle Hill, a worried look on her face. "I'm so glad you're here," she said to Dok, relief in her voice. "Patrick's mother wants to take him to the hospital and I think she's right. He seems to be getting worse."

"Where's Ruthie?" Dok asked. She wanted her to be a part of this, for Patrick's sake.

"Patrick's mother sent her home. She's rather . . . protective. A little austere for my liking."

Patrick's parents sat in chairs by Patrick's bed, looking as if they'd seen a ghost. And in a way, they had. Their son was a ghost of his former self.

Even Ed seemed alarmed at Patrick's declining condition, and he was not easily alarmed.

"What's happened to our son?" Patrick's father said, his voice cracking in a way that sounded both sad and desperate.

Ed took the lead. "We think Patrick might have something other than multiple sclerosis. It's very possible that he has developed a vitamin B-12 deficiency. I'm going to give him a

B-12 injection." He opened his medical bag and pulled out a syringe, then filled it with the vial of B-12.

"Why?" Patrick's father said. "What would have caused such a thing? A few months ago, he was fine."

"For some reason," Ed explained, "there's an enzyme in Patrick's stomach that stopped absorbing B-12. We don't know why it happened spontaneously but the consequences are dire. You can see that for yourself. Your son's entire nervous system is shutting down. Ceasing to function. He's on track to die."

Appalled by Ed's abrupt bedside manner, Dok hastened to soften his harsh words. "But these injections will hopefully reverse that track. If this works, and we think it will, Patrick will see strength returning. The lesions will heal."

"Do you mean . . ." his mother asked, her voice incredulous, "he might be all right?"

Dok gave her an encouraging smile. "A full recovery will take months, plus he'll need physical therapy. But, given enough time, it's very possible he will be just fine."

Ed swabbed Patrick's upper arm with a cotton ball dipped in rubbing alcohol and gave him the injection. "I have to warn you, we're not sure if this is the answer to your son's malady. But if we're right, you'll know pretty soon." He disposed of the syringe and packed up his bag, then turned to face Patrick's parents. "He'll need injections every two weeks for the rest of his life, but he will be able to live a normal life." He rose to his feet. "I need to get back to the hospital. Dr. Stoltzfus will take it from here. She can answer any questions you have."

Patrick's father, unable to speak, shook Ed's hand up and down.

"Thank you so much," Mrs. Kelly said. "You've given us hope. We arrived here with no hope."

"Well, put that way," Ed said, obviously delighted by the commendation, "you're very welcome."

Ruthie waited until a reasonable hour, then hurried over to see how Patrick was doing this morning, to see if the vitamin B-12 injection made a difference. Dok had stopped by the house to update them, but suggested she wait until today to visit Patrick. That wasn't hard; she was uncomfortable in his parents' presence. Not so much his father, but his mother. All yesterday, his mother remained stone-faced, processing the news of her son's sudden and devastating illness. But Ruthie could see herself responding the same way if she found herself in a bleak situation.

Still, her heart sank when his mother opened the door to her knock. "Is he stronger?" Ruthie blurted out.

"Not stronger."

She shrank back. "Isn't there any improvement?"

Mrs. Kelly squared her shoulders in a gesture Ruthie was already coming to recognize. A way to indicate that Patrick's well-being was really none of Ruthie's business. "My husband thinks he seems more coherent. Less confused. But I think it might be that he feels better in the morning."

"Is your husband in with him?" She hoped to be invited in, but from the grim, stern look on Mrs. Kelly's face and the way she was blocking the door, it wasn't looking like an invitation was forthcoming.

"He went to town to purchase some food."

Ruthie remained on the doorstep. "I brought Patrick a

gift." She bent down and picked up a birdcage with a black mynah bird sitting on a perch. "His other bird . . . Nyna . . . she had an untimely accident. This is a replacement. I thought it might cheer him up."

One of his mother's stiff eyebrows lifted. "With so much going on yesterday, I didn't even think about that ridiculous bird. He loved that bird." A thin smile started, then took on fuller life. Ruthie, in that instant, knew she had made a tiny bit of progress to win her over. "You go on in. The company will do him good."

Birdy had brought home the mynah bird from the Wild Bird Rescue Center. It didn't look exactly like Nyna, but close—black as coal, and every bit as noisy. Ruthie barely slept last night for its unceasing racket. She knocked on the bedroom door and let herself in. Patrick had pillows propping him up. His Bible was open and on his lap.

"Am I interrupting?"

"You're never an interruption," he said shakily. He tried to give her a smile, but it ended up looking weird. He was so pale, so terribly tired looking. Even his lips were white. His voice, though, sounded a little stronger. Certainly more clear, more distinct than last night. When she had asked Dok why Patrick had trouble enunciating, she explained that his muscle control was affected, and the tongue was the strongest muscle in the body.

"I brought you something." Ruthie went back to the doorjamb and reached around it to pick up the birdcage. It was heavy and bulky and she needed both hands to hoist it up on the nightstand beside his bed. "Birdy said this mynah bird was brought in to the rescue center. She thinks it's young, so you can train it." She looked down at his Bible, with so many verses underlined in it. "Maybe you can teach it Bible verses, just like the other one."

Patrick's face was pained. He was silent for a long time.

Had she made a mistake? Too soon? But . . . there was no time to waste. Hadn't she been learning that very thing from Patrick? If you wanted to do something, you should do it. Don't wait.

He kept his eyes averted from her, but his Adam's apple kept bobbing. "Ruthie, thank you . . ." His voice trailed off and she was surprised to see tears fill his eyes.

She sighed in relief. "I'm so glad you want it. I wasn't sure. I know it's no substitute for Nyna, but I thought . . . I hoped it might help pass the time while . . ." While what? While he lost more ability to move? To walk? To talk?

She had no idea. All she knew was that this was one thing she could do.

He hesitated, seeming to choose his words with care, slowly and ponderously. "It's perfect, Ruthie."

She went to the little kitchen to get a water bowl for the mynah bird. It took her a moment to find the right-sized bowl. She filled it with water and carefully brought it back to Patrick's room, then stopped abruptly at the open door. Her mind started racing. It was strange how when you were looking hard enough, when you really wanted to seek out information, you could find what you were looking for. Even in a person's tiniest gesture.

"Mrs. Kelly," she said softly. "Would you come here a minute?"

Patrick's mother appeared at the bedroom door. "What is it? What's wrong?"

"Look."

"What?"

"He's holding the bird."

It dawned on Patrick what he had done. Leaned over, opened the cage—which required twisting the catch—putting his finger out for the bird to climb onto it. "I did it without thinking . . ."

"I'm going to call Dok."

As Ruthie ran to the phone shanty, a rush of crazy possibilities whirled in her mind. Was Patrick going to be all right? Or was this just a spurt of energy, a path of twists and turns as the disease progressed? There was no way, no way at all, that Patrick could have picked up the bird last night. Or twisted the lock on the cage. Or leaned over to open it without help. No way. Or could he have? She didn't know! She was shaking as she dialed Dok's number and blurted out what she'd observed as soon as she answered.

"On my way," Dok said, all business.

Within minutes, Dok arrived and went straight into the bedroom to examine Patrick, closing the door behind her. Ruthie and Patrick's mother waited anxiously in the living room. His father returned with a bag of groceries. His mother filled him in on what had transpired in the last thirty minutes. When he finished putting the groceries into the cupboards, he sat on the couch next to his wife and held her hand.

Finally, Dok opened the door. "Come in," she urged. "Come in." They surrounded Patrick's bed, his parents on one side, Ruthie on the other. She realized she was holding her breath.

"Sometimes," Dok said, "there's a simple explanation to a complex problem." At the end of the bed, she smiled at Patrick. "Go ahead. It's your news to tell."

Ruthie heard a little high-pitched gasp escape from her own throat. There were more emotions swirling around inside her than she could hold back. Her heart was pounding so hard it hurt. It actually hurt. She felt as if her heart might just explode.

Patrick laughed, then gulped in air, then laughed, then gulped in air. "Mom, Dad, Ruthie . . . Dok thinks the vitamin B-12 is working. She says everything's going to be all right."

A bubble of unbridled joy, of sheer relief, rose up inside Ruthie, but she pushed it down, was almost afraid to let herself feel happy quite so soon. It was a quietly miraculous moment, a moment she knew she'd never forget for as long as she lived. "I have chills," she said, half laugh, half sigh.

"Me too," Patrick's father said, as a rush of breath left him. He was struggling to contain his emotions.

From the other side of the bed, Ruthie could see the sheen of tears in Patrick's mother's eyes, tears she was doing her best to hide. She was a private person, not comfortable with showing her feelings. Something else they had in common.

Dok felt no such compunction. She looked jubilant. Victorious. Triumphant. "This," she said, "is why I love medicine."

Two days later, Dok stopped by the cottage to check on Patrick and was amazed to find him standing in the kitchen with his dad, working on a crossword puzzle together. She had warned his parents that it was going to take a while for Patrick to get back on his feet. And there he was, *on* his feet! She was astounded by his rapid recovery, by the return of his physical strength, by his healthy appearance. Gone was the look of utterly debilitating fatigue, the dark circles under his eyes, the countenance as meek as a lamb. Today, Patrick was radiant.

This one went into Dok's Miracle Box. She'd seen a few over her years in medicine, but this might be the best one of all.

Ed mocked her Miracle Box, insisting that everything had a scientific explanation. Even vitamin B-12 deficiency. Maybe, she agreed, but what about the timing of the discovery? Not a day to spare. That credit, she knew, belonged to God alone. That was a direct answer to heartfelt prayer.

And wasn't it also a miracle to see the ravaging effect on the body from the absence of one vitamin? Just *one* vitamin. Without the absorption of B-12, Patrick could very likely have been dead by now. Instead, he was standing in the cottage kitchen, chewing over a crossword puzzle, trying to find a six-letter word for *consolation*.

"Relief!" Dok blurted out, struck by its irony.

Patrick and his father had a good laugh over that. Even his mother offered up a rare smile. It was a word that should have been on the top of everyone's mind.

As Dok drove away from the cottage, she let her mind drift over the intricacies of the human body. They never failed to enrich and expand her faith. It was what made medicine so meaningful to her—it drew her to a genuine awe and delight in the Creator.

That afternoon, with Ruthie's help, the last few boxes in Dok's office were unpacked and everything was good to go. All Dok needed now was more patients.

Each day, more and more Amish called the office to make appointments or to ask Dok to swing by their home for a house call. It was going to take time, but she had the time to give it. The time *and* the patience, two qualities she'd never experienced together.

Ruthie stood at the doorjamb of the one exam room with a big box in her arms. She lifted the box. "Cotton balls and tongue depressers. The UPS driver said he wished all boxes were this light." She set the box on the counter. "Patrick is improving leaps and bounds each day."

"Funny, I was just thinking about Patrick. I couldn't be more pleased about the outcome."

"Dr. Gingerich was certainly pleased. I noticed he didn't bother to correct Mrs. Kelly's assumption that he was the one who had discovered the correct diagnosis." Ruthie fixed her eyes on Dok. "You figured it out."

Dok waved that concern away. "Getting credit is unimportant. And Ed did play a part. He ordered the tests, he tried to help manage or relieve Patrick's symptoms. In the end, Patrick got the help he needed before it was too late. That's all that matters."

"Jesse is taking Mrs. Kelly on a buggy ride later this afternoon." Ruthie smiled. "We're trying to show her the best of Amish life, to soften her up a little."

"She's as sour as a pickle, isn't she? But I can't blame her. She's almost lost her son twice—once to a culture, once to a disease. I think I'd be a mama bear too."

Chin tucked, Ruthie twisted her hands in her apron. "As soon as you give Patrick the all clear to travel, she's planning to leave. All of them."

She knew, she knew. The way Patrick was responding to the B-12 injections, it wouldn't be long before Dok felt confident his body could handle the long drive back home. Most likely in the next few days.

Ruthie lifted her head. "If there's nothing else, I'd like to head over to the Inn at Eagle Hill and see how the buggy ride goes."

"There is one more thing." As Ruthie looked around the exam room for the one more thing, Dok said, "I'd like you to consider coming to work for me."

Ruthie's hands flew to her face. "You want me to be your nurse?"

Dok smiled. "No, no. I want you to be my office assistant. Help with phones, paperwork, billing."

"Can I take vital statistics? Draw blood?"

"Hold on. Let's just start with areas I need help with." She thought of the more-empty-than-not waiting room. "I hope I will, that is."

"I'd love it! I want to do something important, something that matters. I don't want to teach school and I don't want to work at the Bent N' Dent. Oh Dok, I want to be just like you."

Dok pointed to a stool to have Ruthie sit down. "Ruthie, if there's one thing I wish someone had told me when I was your age, it was that I should be careful not to confuse wanting to matter with what really matters."

"*You're* doing what really matters," Ruthie said carefully. "You're making a difference. You're healing people. You're important. You matter."

"There's lots of ways to do what really matters. Your dad is doing what really matters by providing a store to the people in Stoney Ridge. Your brother is providing buggy repairs so the people can get around town. Rose King is providing a place for visitors to rest. All work matters to God. What I'm talking about is what drives a person to work. You're not going to get what you want out of any work—as a doctor or a store clerk—if you want the work to define you. Wanting to matter is a conversation you have to have with God alone. When that part is lined up, you'll make a difference in any work you choose to do."

"Okay, okay, I get the message," Ruthie said, a touch irritably. "But you have to admit that being a doctor is important."

"Believe me, I know plenty of highly educated, overpaid doctors who don't make any difference at all. They're still striving for personal significance. Ego is like a hungry animal that can never be satisfied."

Ruthie's face fell. "You think I have a big ego?"

"Yes," Dok said bluntly, truthfully. "So do I. So does most everyone. Maybe not your dad, but most everyone else. I certainly had a huge ego when I was your age. I was sure I knew what was best for me. College, I thought. And then medical school."

"Wasn't that the best?"

"Twenty years ago, I would have said yes. Ten years ago. Even five years ago. But the older I get, the more I realize that my choice caused the people I love tremendous pain. To be entirely truthful, I'm not really sure it was worth it." She looked down at her hands. "Maybe that's why I'm here. In Stoney Ridge. Trying to make it right."

"I'm pretty sure Dad wouldn't want you to feel that way."

"No, he wouldn't. It's not coming from outside. There's something inside of me that wants to make amends."

"So is this job offer to become your medical assistant your way of trying to persuade me not to leave the church?"

"Office assistant," Dok corrected. "And not at all. I'm offering you the job because I think you'd be good at it and I'd like to work with you. The thing is . . . I just don't want you to romanticize life outside of the Amish church. Being alone . . . it grows weary." All at once, Dok realized the deeper thing that bothered her about Ed Gingerich, the thing that made a relationship with him not just frustrating but increasingly intolerable: even when she was with him, she was still lonely.

"So if you were seventeen again, would you choose differently?"

Dok looked straight at Ruthie. "I think I might have." That truth shocked her. She slapped her hands on her knees. "But that was then and this is now. 'Press on,' Saint Paul said. Forgetting what lies behind, we press on." She smiled. "I've already spoken to your dad about the job. He gave it his blessing."

Ruthie grinned. "So I'm going to be a medical assistant."

"An office assistant," Dok corrected. "Big difference."

But Ruthie wasn't listening.

Her whole being, it seemed to Dok, had begun to glow.

There was a meaningful silence, for David at least, as he stood to give an announcement after the Sunday church service ended but just before dismissing everyone. He took a moment to let his gaze hover over each church member, men and boys on one side, women and girls on the other. Individuals he had grown to love so genuinely over the last few years. Hank Lapp, who had nodded off during the first sermon and jerked awake with a startled shout during the second one. Next to him was Amos Lapp, David's trusted friend. Beside Amos was Patrick Kelly, the miracle of Stoney Ridge. Then came his son, Jesse; beside him were his apprentices, who were winking at girls across the room. And there was Freeman Glick, the former bishop, sitting stoic and oblivious to his son Leroy's constant eye twitching.

His gaze shifted to the women's side, past his Birdy sitting with his girls. There was Ruthie, his darling daughter. Something was different. He could see it in her face. Some emptiness, some restless discontent had been filled in her. A wound had healed, perhaps? He might not ever know the specifics, because Ruthie was not one to confide her deepest thoughts, but he knew Whom to thank. This summer, Ruthie had been transformed.

Beside Ruthie was Fern Lapp, sitting so straight it seemed she had a rod down her back. Next to her, sitting every bit as bolt upright as Fern, was Jenny Yoder. Rose King sat in the bench behind Jenny, her sorrowful heart written on her face. Out of the corner of his eye, he saw Edith Fisher Lapp, fanning herself with a folded newspaper. And there were so many others here, and a few he was missing. Thelma Beiler for one. Luke Schrock, for another.

He was their bishop, and he loved them, each one. But sometimes love tasted bitter. He braced himself for what was coming next.

"There's something important that I need to bring up," David said. "After a great deal of thought and prayer, I am asking each and every landowner to place a conservation easement on their property with help from the Stoney Ridge Farmland Trust. This will preserve the land for future generations to farm, and only farm, on it. You will still have ownership of your land, but allowing the Trust to hold the easement will restrict development for commercial use."

The room was silent, then whispering began. Edith Fisher Lapp spoke first. "What will that do to the oil leases?"

She was a sharp one, that Edith. "It will mean no more signing of new ones, no more renewal of leases, no more exploration for oil traps."

There was a collective gasp, then whispering began immediately.

"Birdy and I have already done it," he said.

"But you don't have oil leases on your property," someone blurted out. Ida King, he thought.

"No, I don't. Giving the Trust the easement to your property will be voluntary." David was a great believer in freedom. How could he not, when God gave each individual such freedom? "But I am asking you to consider it."

Birdy stood up. "There are federal tax benefits to doing so."

"I LIKE THAT!" Hank Lapp boomed and Edith frowned sourly at him from across the room.

Andy Miller rose to his feet. "You're asking for a difficult thing, David. We would lose thousands of dollars a year." He looked around the room. "Why? For what reason?"

"Because I believe that we are threatened with losing the essence of community through such easy prosperity."

"God put that oil in the ground," Andy said. "Is it so wrong to take it? To use it? Haven't we seen great benefits from the wealth?"

"Some benefits, yes. I'm not putting a value on the oil. Only on the wealth it brings. We are more in danger of losing what's truly important than from what benefits the oil brings to us. I'm not convinced that our generation has the wisdom to manage it. Perhaps, in the future, another bishop will make a different decision." He cleared his throat and concluded this topic in what Birdy called his Old Testament prophet voice. "But as for me, for Birdy, for our household, and I hope for our church, we are saying no and asking each one of you to say no. Not now. Not yet."

David gave a benediction and most of the church members scattered out of the barn like untended sheep. Edith Fisher Lapp pierced him with her trademark hawklike stare and muttered, "This is why I liked the old bishop."

That old bishop, Freeman Glick, remained on the back bench, the place where he had sat since his ordination had been revoked two years ago, and waited until the room emptied out. Then he walked up to David. A tall man with an impressive beard, gray and flourishing, that conferred considerable authority. "High time that you started acting like a bishop. It's a lonely job."

David looked around the room. No one remained. "Yes, it is."

"I told you, did I not, that it is easier to hold an empty cup than a full one?"

"Yes. I remember."

Freeman reached out his hand. "Well done, David."

24

Dok finished up a phone call with an Amish mother whose toddler had jammed peas up his nose. "Bring him in this afternoon," she told the mother. As she put the phone down, she saw her niece, Ruthie, poking her head around the office door. It was Ruthie's first day as an office assistant and she took her job very seriously.

"There's someone here to see you."

"Show him into the exam room."

"Not that kind of someone. Not a patient, I mean." She pointed to her head. "The brain doctor. He's here with flowers."

Dok went into the waiting room and there was Ed Gingerich, a dozen perfect long-stemmed red roses in his arms, her favorite. He smiled brightly when he saw her and held the roses out to her. "For you."

She took them from him and breathed in their delicate scent. "They're lovely, but why?"

"Because I've taken you for granted lately."

"Lately?"

Ed tipped his head back and forth. "Maybe more than lately."

"Ed, do I like coffee or tea?"

"Tea. You only drink tea."

No, she didn't. He did.

"I came by to ask you to go out to dinner with me."

"Thank you for asking," Dok said. "But no."

Ed frowned. "What about tomorrow?"

Dok thought about the next day. She had patients booked for most of the day, her first full day. She couldn't wait! "I don't have time."

This was met with an expression of extreme skepticism. He wasn't used to her saying no to him. "Are you trying to punish me for working so hard?"

"Not at all." She handed him back the roses. "I don't want them."

He sighed. "You're mad."

"No," Dok said. "I'm not. I'm not mad. I'm just finished. With us. I'm finished with us."

"With us?" His eyes opened wide. "Are you saying you don't love me anymore?"

"Whether or not I love you doesn't matter," Dok said. "I'm tired of waiting around for you to love me the way I want to be loved."

"But I do," he said. "I love you."

"Ed, why? Why do you love me?"

"Because you understand me in a way no other woman ever will. I love you for that. Ruth," he said. "Please. I want you to be my wife." He sank to the ground on one knee. "Will you marry me?"

"You don't mean it," she said.

"I do! I want to marry you. Isn't that what you want too?"

Dok teetered. She wobbled. This was her heart's one desire. Coming true after all.

Ed Gingerich was saying all the right things, and it was true that she loved him. But something wasn't right.

Suddenly, Matt appeared in the open doorway, holding a decaf caffè latte.

Dok thought of how Matt had come rushing out to Pinecove Road that night, after she nearly ran into Luke Schrock, to see if she was all right. How often he stopped by the office to check on her. How he brought her decaf caffè lattes. How he looked at her and how she felt like she was the most beautiful woman on earth. He always made her feel special, treasured.

She looked at Ed. "No," she said. "It wouldn't work."

"Ruth," he said. "I know you've wanted this for a long time."

"I did want it, for a long time, but not anymore. I'm sorry, Ed. Now get up, please."

"Ruth. Honey. Sweetheart. You don't mean what you're saying."

"Dr. Gingerich," Matt said, suddenly sounding very much like a police officer. "I believe the lady wants you to leave."

His head swiveled around. He saw Matt, and recognition came into his eyes. He looked back at Dok, then at Matt, then back at Dok. "You're trying to tell me that you're happier with Officer Do-Right than with me?"

She glanced back at Matt. "It was never a contest." She looked down at Ed. "Please stand up."

He got to his feet.

"Ed, I'll walk you to your car," Matt said.

Dok closed the door behind them and turned to see Ruthie watching her in a thoughtful way.

"You said no." She tilted her head. "Why?"

Dok nodded. "I wanted more for myself." She walked past her niece and put a hand on her shoulder. "You taught me that."

The cloudy end-of-July morning turned into a stormy afternoon. David was signing off paperwork for the UPS delivery man as Ruthie bolted into the store. "Dad! Come quick. It's Birdy. Dok wants you to come right away. Birdy's fallen and hurt herself."

David followed behind Ruthie, overtaking her as he ran down the road to Dok's office. Birdy was on the clumsy side of clumsy, prone to accidents, but there was fear in Ruthie's eyes. As he burst into the waiting room, he called out for Dok.

Dok peeked her head out of the examining room. "David, hold on a minute. I'll be right there."

Ruthie came in behind him. "Is she dying? Concussed? Bleeding to death? Do you want me to bring you the defibrillator? Should I call for an ambulance?"

"No, no!" Dok shouted, frowning at Ruthie. "Ruthie, I've told you before not to make medical diagnoses . . . oh, never mind. Just . . . give us a few minutes." She closed the door with a firm click.

David and Ruthie exchanged a look. "Tell me what happened."

"Birdy came in for a doctor's appointment. I had just shown her to an exam room, and suddenly, she was on the floor, out cold."

"Why had she made a doctor's appointment?" She hadn't mentioned anything to David about not feeling well.

"No idea. Dok won't let me ask any questions of patients until I've taken some medical assistant classes." She gave him a sideways glance.

"Not now, Ruthie. What else can you tell me about Birdy? Did she seem to be feeling all right when she came into the practice?"

"I think so. Honestly, Dad, I'm not sure. I asked her how she was and she said—and I quote—'Downright jolly.' The next minute she was on the floor." Ruthie shuddered. "Her head made a hollow thump sound when it hit the linoleum."

David clenched and unclenched his fists. He could feel the muscles of his throat pulse with tension. What could be wrong?

It seemed like hours before Dok came out of the examining room, though it was only a few minutes.

David jumped up when he heard the door open. "Is she all right?"

"She's fine," Dok said. "You can go in."

Ruthie followed behind her father, but Dok plucked her sleeve as she passed by. "Ruthie, there's some filing work for you to do."

David went into the exam room and there was his Birdy, sitting on the examining table, an oddly serious look on her face. His apprehension grew. "Birdy, vas in die Velt?" *What in the world?* He put his arms around her, pressing his cheek against her ear. "What happened? Are you all right? Are you hurt? Ruthie said you passed out."

"I did. Silly me, I fainted!" she said over his shoulder. "But there's something I need to tell you."

He lifted his head, girding himself for bad news. She pulled away a little, to give herself some room. Then she took his hands in hers and held them to her heart. "David Stoltzfus . . . come Christmastime, we're going to be given a very precious gift from God."

He cocked his head in confusion.

She took a deep breath. "I'm going to have your baby," she whispered, almost reverently.

There was a silence. And then David whooped for joy.

Matt Lehman did the kindest thing anyone had ever done for Dok. Early one morning, he took her car and had it detailed, inside and out, so clean and shiny it was nearly as good as new. No more vomit smell! When he returned the car to her, it dawned on her that he shouldn't even be here today. He was supposed to be on a camping trip to Yellowstone with his cousins.

"They went without me," Matt said. "I wanted to be here. The last week has been pretty intense for you."

"I just . . ." Dok didn't know quite how to express her feelings. "Why would you do that for me?"

"Don't you know?" Color creeped up Matt's cheeks. "Don't you know by now?"

"No. I don't. You love to go camping. You've been planning this camping trip with your cousins for months."

Matt's face was cherry red now. "Because as much as I love camping, I love you more."

Her eyes widened. "You love me?" she said, making sure she heard him correctly.

"I do. I always have. From the moment I first met you. And

I always will." He cleared his throat and looked down at the tips of his shoes. "Is there any chance . . . any at all . . . that you might love me? Even a little?"

Did she love him?

She felt safe with Matt. He was a man she could trust. A man she could lean on. So different from the way she felt with Ed. It felt solid, real. Good. It felt good. She felt happy when he was around. Whenever he stopped by her practice, they talked about her work, they talked about his work. They were both intent on building something in their lives that was going to last. With Ed, she had felt as if she was trying to build a house of cards in the wind. She looked into Matt's coffee-brown eyes. Steadfast, calm, trusting. Ed's eyes, she realized just now, were the color of Earl Grey tea. Not a solid color, uncommitted, a little bitter.

She had always preferred coffee over tea.

She was pretty sure her heart just flipped over.

Did she love him? Could love be that simple?

"You know what?" Dok said. "I believe I just might."

The sun had set and a blanket of darkness had settled over the countryside. Ruthie emerged from the barn after checking on Moomoo's sore hoof, her gaze on the ground, nearly missing the allure of the night sky. The low-lying gray clouds of the day had been blown away by a late-day dramatic thunder and lightning storm. What was left was equally dramatic: a velvet-black sky studded with sparkling diamonds.

Awed, she stopped and leaned against the white fence railing, feeling small. Swallowed up by the vastness. She was struck speechless by the stars. The Milky Way galaxy had never looked so bright. Jupiter was out, or maybe Saturn, she wasn't good with planets. She needed to learn more from Patrick about planets, stars. About everything.

She cupped her hand in the sky and identified the Big Dipper, then the Little Dipper, and there it was: Polaris. The North Star.

Fixed. Established. Anchored. Unmoving.

This summer, she had found her North Star. It was within her, not outside her.

Another light caught her eye, this one bobbing up the steep driveway. It was Patrick! Searching the dark with his flashlight. Watching him regain his strength was like watching a flower bloom, like watching a miracle unfold. Just a week ago, he was on the brink of death . . . and here he was climbing the driveway to her house. To her.

His almost handsome, overwhelmingly dear face stood before her, and she couldn't help but smile at the sight of him.

"Hello there, Ruthie." In one hand was a flashlight, in another hand was the birdcage with the mynah she'd given him.

She felt oddly breathless. "Have you picked out a name for your bird yet?"

"Yes. I'm going to call her Nyna Two." Nyna Two squawked, then whistled. "So far, she's stolen my dad's hairpiece right off his head and told my mother to chill out." He hastened to add, "I didn't teach her to say 'chill out.' Someone else did."

"We can't blame Luke Schrock for that one." Her dad was planning to go see Luke in the next few days, his first visitor at the facility.

"Actually, I think my dad might have taught her." He set the cage down on the ground and turned off the flashlight.

"I wanted you to be the first to know. My parents are leaving tomorrow. My parents have to get back to work."

The smile left her face. "Thirty days are up."

"Yes. It's been thirty days. Thirty amazing, wonderful, unforgettable, and highly dramatic days."

She knew this moment would be coming; she'd been expecting it every day since his parents had arrived. She had tried to prepare herself for it, continually reminding herself how glad she was Patrick had a future at all. But she would miss him terribly. This wonderful, selfless young man had woken up her world, helped her to discover what was right in front of her.

"So," Patrick said, reaching out to take her hands in his, "you know what this means."

"Yes," she said, struggling to be cheerful. She looked down at their hands, joined together. They fit so perfectly together. She'd always felt her hands were swallowed up by Luke's big hands. A metaphor, she just realized now, for how she always felt with Luke. Swallowed up by his . . . stuff. There was no room left for her. "I'll miss you." Her voice wobbled a little, and she felt weirdly teary.

"Ruthie, look me in the eye," he said, giving her hands a gentle squeeze.

After a moment, she lifted her head. "I'm looking." Tears loomed in her eyes.

"What it means," he said, "is that we're going to need to double up on the Penn Dutch lessons. To make up for lost time."

She stilled. "Wait. Aren't you leaving with your parents?"

He grinned. "No. They agreed to let me stay on."

"What?" She was genuinely confused. "But . . . what about

your mother?" His mother didn't seem to appreciate anything about being in Amish country. Not a thing. When Jesse took her on a buggy ride, she complained that it smelled of horses.

"I'm giving Dok full credit. She put my mom's mind at ease by promising to personally give me the vitamin B-12 shot every week. And she promised to give my parents regular updates." He squeezed her hands again. "Pretty special aunt you've got there. It was no accident you were named for her. You're so much alike."

Ruthie's mind was still reeling. Patrick wasn't leaving? He was *staying* in Stoney Ridge? They looked at each other for a long moment, neither breathing, neither saying anything.

Patrick tilted his head. "Ruthie, say something. Anything."

Something welled up inside of her and burst out with "I love you!" But the moment the words left her mouth, she wished them back. She had always prided herself on being composed, filtered, tight-lipped. *What* had she just blurted out?

The truth.

Her feelings for Patrick were very genuine. She was in love with him.

Patrick Kelly wasted no time. He never did. He said, very softly, "Oh boy." And then he gently cupped her chin with his hand, and he kissed her.

David had been looking forward to an evening of preparing for next Sunday's sermon, but just as he was digging into Exodus 23, a knock came at the door. It was Eli Smucker, wanting him to come and pray for his mother-in-law, who was ill and refused to see a doctor.

Birdy was asleep when he finally crawled into bed, long after midnight. She stirred and gave him a drowsy kiss before turning away from him, onto her side. He heard rain start on the roof, gently at first, then changing to a steady patter as it came down hard. He liked hearing rain drum on the roof, liked it especially when he was home in his own bed.

He didn't know when he dropped off to sleep, but he and Birdy startled awake at the same time as a clap of thunder broke directly over the house. She raised her head and propped it on her elbow to face him. "Did you convince Eli's mother-in-law to see Dok?"

"I think so. But not until the morning, she said. She's as stubborn as Eli."

They lay in bed, listening to the rain tapping overhead. "David, I had a brilliant idea today. Positively brilliant."

"You've got my full attention."

"What would you think about asking Patrick Kelly to teach school?"

He turned toward her. "He's staying?"

"He is. He told Ruthie tonight. Patrick's been gaining strength every day. Hour by hour. It's the most miraculous thing I've ever seen in all my life. His parents have agreed to let him stay. His mother says he's crazy to go Amish, but she'd rather have a crazy son than a sick one."

David let Birdy's news sink in. It was the best news he'd heard in a long time. "Interesting. Patrick Kelly as a schoolteacher. A teacher doesn't have to be baptized." He gave her a nudge. "Let me give that a little thought and prayer." He kissed her cheek. "Thank you for being such a wonderful bishop's wife. For taking on my problems as your own."

"Absolutely. We're in this together." She gave a laugh.

"Though I'm glad you're the one who has the frightful work schedule." She took in a deep breath. "David, there's something else I have to tell you."

"Nothing bad, I hope. I'm wrung out." He settled a little deeper into the bed.

"Just the opposite. Good news."

David stilled. He turned to her.

"Dok heard the baby's heartbeat today, loud and strong. She said I should tell you. She said that when you get a heartbeat like this one, the chance of miscarriage is small."

"Ohhhh," he said, with genuine awe. A slow smile began in David, starting from his heart. He reached for his wife, to show her, in the best way he knew, how much he loved her.

Later that night, David tried to let his own breathing fall in with Birdy's, imagining his wife's rhythm could help him sleep and they would be synchronized through the night. It was love, he thought, to lie like this, listening to his wife so near.

But he couldn't sleep. Finally, he went downstairs to read. He lit the lantern on his desk. It cast a golden glow in the room as he reached for his Bible and opened it to Exodus 23. His eyes landed on verse 30: "By little and little I will drive them out from before thee, until thou be increased, and inherit the land."

By little and little. God was referring to the enemies that the Israelites would have to face and defeat in Canaan—a land rampant with paganism and idolatry. Every age would encounter worldly enemies to face and defeat. What was God driving out from the Amish of Stoney Ridge? Greed, selfishness, materialism. And yes, he thought, for Luke Schrock, substance addictions.

By little and little.

Like the Israelites wandering in the desert, David realized, the journey toward developing a moral, godly life is a long and difficult one. It wasn't going to take place overnight, but "by little and little." It was the work not of a Sabbath Sunday, but of a lifetime. God was reminding the Israelites that this was a life of patient endurance, and those words were meant for today's believers too. Lifelong obedience.

David turned off the light and went upstairs to bed. There he fell asleep musing on the many blessings of this life of his, where he felt simply, and easily, at peace with the world.

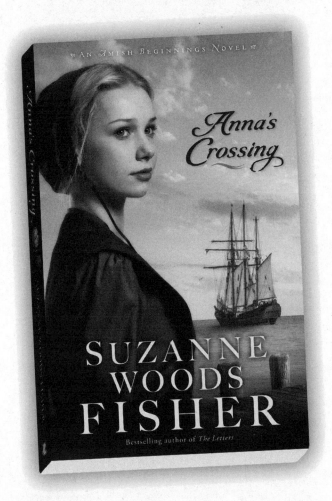

1

It's a hard crossing, they'd been warned. Eight weeks in a wooden tub with no guarantee they'd ever get there. Anna König crouched beside a bed of roses, breathing deeply of the freshly turned loam. She had done all she could to avoid this treacherous sea journey, and yet here she was, digging up her rose to take along with her. She jabbed her shovel in the ground, mulling all the reasons this voyage was fraught with ill.

It meant leaving behind her grandparents, her home, her church in Ixheim, Germany. Her people. It would be the end of everything she'd ever known and loved.

"Some endings are really beginnings," her grandfather had said when she told him that Christian Müller, the minister, asked—no, insisted—she join the departing families. "If you don't remember anything I've ever tried to teach you, remember that."

Despite misgivings and forebodings, Anna relented. How do you say no to a minister? She was the only one who could speak and understand English. And that's why she was stabbing the earth with her shovel, digging up her most precious

313

rose to take on the journey, hoping that the hard winter and late-to-come spring meant its roots would still be dormant. If she was going to go to this strange New World, she was going to bring this rose. And she was going. Tomorrow.

Tomorrow! The crack of doom in that one word.

Anna had begged her grandparents to join the emigrating group, but they wouldn't budge. "It's a young man's sport, that sea journey," her grandfather said, shaking his head, ending the discussion. She couldn't argue that point. The voyage was filled with risks and dangers and uncertainties, especially for the very young and very old.

Anna sat back on her heels and looked around. In a few years, who would be left in Ixheim? Who would care for her grandparents in their final days? Who would bury them and tend their graves? Tears welled, and she tried to will them away, squeezing her eyes shut.

This little valley that hugged the Rhine River was supposed to be their home, for good, for always. Here, they had tried to live in peace, keeping to themselves in secluded hills and valleys, where they could farm the land and their sheep could graze and they could go about their daily life of work and worship without worry or hassle. This valley was dear to her, peaceful and pastoral.

Yet beneath the surface, life had started to change. A new baron held the Amish in disdain; much of the old conviviality of the village was disappearing. It was time to leave, the bishop had decided, before tensions escalated as they had in Switzerland, years ago.

Carefully, Anna wrapped the root ball of the dug-up rose in burlap. She glanced around the garden filled with her grandmother's roses. Their survival was a testament to her people's story: roots that adapted to whatever soil they were transplanted into, thorns that bespoke of the pain they bore, blossoms each spring that declared God's power to bring new life from death. As long as the roses survived, her grandmother said, so would our people. Her grandfather would scoff and call her a superstitious old woman, but Anna understood what she meant. The roses were a living witness to survival.

The sounds of hooting and hollering boys stormed into her thoughtful moment. She caught sight first of eight-year-old Felix, galloping toward her, followed by his older brother Johann. Felix frightened the chickens that scratched at the dirt in the garden, scattering them in a squawking cloud of flapping wings and molting feathers.

"A letter from Papa!" Felix shouted.

Behind him came Johann, holding his father's letter in the air, red faced and breathing hard from the exertion of climbing the hill. His eyes, bright from anticipation, fastened on Anna's face. "My father wrote there are twice as many immigrants leaving for Port Philadelphia this year as last. And last year was three times as many as the year before. He said we must make haste to join him in Penn's Woods and settle the land." He skidded to a stop behind Felix.

"Just think, Anna. Deer, turkey, rabbits, all easy to obtain. And with a little more effort—" Johann pretended to aim and shoot a rifle at an imaginary beast—"elk and wild boar to put up for winter provisions." Naturally, Johann, at age thirteen, knew everything.

But Anna, practical and skeptical and older than Johann by six years, held a different point of view. "I hear that the New World is a land of poisonous snakes, lions, tigers. And black bears and mountain lions. Gray wolves sweep down from the mountains in packs." A wolf pack frightened her most of all. When the wolves here grew desperate for food, they would attack her woollies.

Johann wasn't listening. He never listened to her objections about America. "Good water springs, lumber for building cabins."

"I've heard stories that settlers have seen red men. Many times."

Johann shook his head as he came up to Anna in the rose garden. "Friendly Indians. Curious ones. Fascinated with shiny brass kitchen kettles and knickknacks. Papa said he has found a place for us to settle." His eyes took on a faraway look and she knew he was off in his head to America to join his father. Jacob Bauer, the bishop of their church, had gone ahead to the New World last spring, to claim land and purchase warrants for those who intended to join him this year.

Anna turned to Felix and couldn't hold back a grin. A riot of curly hair peeped from beneath a tattered black felt hat, blue eyes sparkled with excitement, and a big smile showed more spaces than teeth.

The Bauer boys were like brothers to her. Felix was round and sturdy, with carrot red hair that matched his temperament. Johann, blond and thin, had never been hale and was afflicted with severe asthma. His heart and body might not be strong, that Johann, but his mind made up for it. What he carried around in that head of his was what mattered.

Now Felix was another story. Two black crows cackled from a nearby tree and he stared at them with a distant look in his eyes. "There's a crow's nest on the ship that's so high, you can see the curve of the earth."

Smiling inside, Anna said to him, "It's really that high?"

"Even higher." With a sweep of his hand Felix showed the curve of the earth. "Johann told me so."

Anna didn't know where Johann got his information. He'd had no schooling and owned no books except the Bible, but he knew all sorts of things. Solid-gold facts, he called them. She delighted in each nugget, whether true or not.

Then the twinkle in Felix's eyes faded. "It's a great pity I won't be able to find out for myself."

"The Bakers changed their mind and aren't going, so Felix wants to stay behind too," Johann explained. "That means that Catrina Müller is the only one aboard close to Felix's age."

Felix's scowl deepened. "I'm not going if I have to be stuck on a ship with her. I'll stay here and live with the Bakers."

"I don't think you have much of a choice, Felix." *Nor do I.* Anna would never voice it aloud, but she dreaded the thought of spending the next few months in confined quarters with Catrina and her mother, Maria. Those two had a way of draining the very oxygen from the air. She set down her shovel. "Is your mother ready to go?"

Felix shrugged. "She's packing dishes into barrels."

"She must be eager to see your father."

He tilted his head. "She's humming. That's good. She wants to see Papa." Then he took off running along the narrow sheep's trail that led up the hill.

"I wish I could find a reason to go. Better yet, to stay."

"Change is coming, Anna," Johann said with annoying professorial patience. "It's in the air. We can't stay here and live like sheep in a pasture."

Anna looked up at the hillside. "I like sheep."

He crossed his arms in a stubborn pose. "I mean there is a whole new world out there. Just think of the mountains and valleys and unknown places we'll see."

"Filled with savages and the beasts. Your father has said as much in his letters."

"He also says there is land waiting for us which has never before been claimed, surveyed, or deeded. Land, Anna. We can live in safety. We can *own* land."

"Maybe there's no place that's truly safe for us."

He shook his head hard. "That's not what William Penn said. He offered a place where we can go and live in peace."

Johann didn't understand. He was moving toward someone—his father. His mother and brother would be traveling with him. Anna was moving away from those she loved. "My grandmother says it's wicked to want more than you have. She wants to just stay put and thank God."

Johann laughed. "Your grandmother is a frightened old lady who's had a hard life. Doesn't mean you should be scared of new things."

"I'm not." *Yes, I am.*

"Everything changes. That's the way of life. This Greek fellow Heraclitus said there is nothing permanent except change, and I think he was right." He leaned forward and whispered in a conspiratorial voice, "Your grandmother has made Maria promise to find you a husband in the New World. She said that Ixheim has only old toothless men and young toothless boys." He lifted his voice an octave or two, warbling, to mimic her grandmother. "Anna must have Her Chance! She is pushing twenty without a man in sight."

Anna laid the rose in her basket and stood, sobered by the thought. With each passing birthday, her grandmother grew increasingly distressed. The New World, she decided, was Anna's only hope to find a like-minded bachelor.

Johann was watching her carefully, and then his eyes took on that teasing look of his. "If there's no one in the New World who passes Maria's muster, and if you don't mind holding off a few years, I suppose I could marry you."

She laughed then, and her mood shifted instantly from solemn to lighthearted, as it always did when she was around Johann. "I'll keep such a heartwarming proposal in mind."

"With fair wind and God's favor," Johann said, with his usual abundance of optimism, "we'll reach Port Philadelphia by the end of July."

When Anna pointed out that he was basing that assumption on all conditions being ideal and how rarely things ever turned out that way, he rolled his eyes in exasperation. "It's God's will. Of that my father and Christian have no doubt."

And how does anyone object to that? How in the world?

He wiggled his eyebrows and winked at her, then hurried up the hillside to join Felix, who was already on the top, to reach the shortcut that took them back to their house. Midway up the hill, Johann stopped and bent over to catch his breath. When he topped the hill, he turned and doffed his hat at her, flourishing it before him as if he were going to sweep the floor. She grinned, and then her grin faded as he disappeared down the other side of the hill and she was left with only her worries for company.

Tomorrow. Tomorrow!

Like it or not, the journey would begin. They would travel down the Rhine River to Rotterdam, board the vessel a shipping agent had arranged as passage for them, and then they'd be off to the New World.

Anna stretched her back and moved out of the shade to feel the afternoon sun on her face. The muscles in her arms and shoulders ached from spearing the shovel into the cold earth, but it was a pleasant ache. She'd always loved working outside, much more than she did the washing and cooking and keeping up of the house, the woman's work. The drudgery, she thought, and quickly sent an apology to the Lord for her ungrateful heart.

A furious honking of geese in the sky disrupted her reverie. Heading north for summer, she presumed. Her gaze traveled up the green hillside dotted with ruffs of gray wool. Her woollies, each one known to her by name. Her heart was suddenly too full for words as she let her gaze roam lovingly over the land she knew as home: over the rounded haystacks, the neat lambing sheds, the creek that ran almost the year round. The steep hills that brought an early sunset in summer and broke the wind in winter. It grieved her that she wouldn't be here this year for spring, as the lambs came and the wool was sheared and the ewes were mated and then the lambs would come again. She gazed at the hills, trying to engrave it in her memory. Where would she be next spring? She wondered what home would look like, feel like, smell like. She glanced down at her basket and gripped the leather handle, hard. At least she had her rose. If it survived, so would she.

A few hours later, Anna heard the whinny of a horse and came out of the house to see who was driving up the path. She shielded her eyes from the sun and saw Christian Müller on a wagon seat, Felix beside him.

Why would Felix be riding with their minister?

She noticed the somber look on Christian's usually cheerful face, the way Felix's small head was bowed. She crossed her arms, gripping her elbows. The wind, raw and cold, twisted her skirts around her legs. *Something's wrong.*

There came a stillness as if the whole world were holding its breath.

Let it be nothing, she entreated silently, let it be another meeting tonight to talk about the journey, or to let her know that Johann stopped to visit a friend. Let it be something silly. With every squeak of the wheels, she felt the lump in her throat grow bigger, the apprehension build.

A gust of wind swirled up the hill, flapping Anna's dress like a sheet on a clothesline, whipping the strings of her prayer cap against her neck, and she shivered.

Christian hauled back on the reins and set the brake on the wagon. Slowly, he climbed down and waited beside the wagon, bearded chin on his chest. Felix jumped off the seat and threw his arms around Anna's waist, shuddering with sobs.

Anna's gaze moved over Christian's pale face. Behind him, in the back of the wagon, was the shape of a body, covered by a gray wool blanket.

"Christian, who is it?" An icy feeling started in Anna's stomach and traveled up her spine. "C-Christian?" she whispered again, her eyes wide, her throat hot and tight. It was then she saw tears running down Christian's cheeks. The awful reality started to hit her full force and she pressed a fist to her lips. *Dear God,* she thought. *Dear God, how can this be?*

Christian turned away with his chin tucked down, then, almost lovingly, gently folded back the top of the blanket. His eyes lifted to meet hers. "The Lord has seen fit to take our young Johann from us."

Discussion Questions

1. How did Ruthie's shallow faith as a "preacher's kid" change? Compare her faith journey with that of her aunt Dok's.

2. Let's look at the two young men in Ruthie's life: Luke Schrock and Patrick Kelly. How did each of them view Ruthie? How did they influence the way she viewed herself?

3. Patrick Kelly said that he had learned to revel in every day. What does that attitude look like? Who is a person in your life who revels in every day? What kind of effect does he or she have on others?

4. Cherishing time might be another way to describe Patrick's intent to "revel in every day." Ruthie discovered the importance of cherishing time. How do you perceive time in your own life—is it a gift or a burden?

5. In what ways did Ruthie and Dok lead parallel lives? How did they inspire each other?

6. To quote Dok: "Sometimes there are simple solutions

to complex problems." Can you share an experience in your life when you found Dok's words to be true?

7. The story of the vitamin B-12 deficiency is based on real events of a man in my church. It was quite a dramatic, about-face story! When have you had an experience when circumstances seemed so dire, so hopeless, and then they flipped on a dime? What lessons did you glean from that experience?

8. David Stoltzfus might have been the only one left in the church of Stoney Ridge who found redeemable qualities in Luke Schrock. "What a person does isn't the same as who a person is," David said. What are your thoughts about Luke? Is he a lost cause? (If you're interested to learn more of Luke Schrock's backstory, read The Inn at Eagle Hill series.)

9. Did it surprise you to read about a residential facility that was customized for Amish and Mennonite patients? That's not fictitious information; there are such places popping up around heavily populated Amish areas, and they provide a wonderful resource of counseling help for their patients.

10. David Stoltzfus planned to bring Luke Schrock back to the community as soon as he was released from the residential facility. David's intention resounds of being Amish—they want their people under the protective wing of community. How would you have handled Luke? How would your church community handle him?

11. If you could write the next chapter in Luke Schrock's life, what would it be?

12. Dok gave some advice to Ruthie. "If there's one thing

I wish someone had told me when I was your age, it was that I should be careful not to confuse wanting to matter with what really matters." How would you describe the difference?

13. *Why do they keep needing more?* David wondered, as he thought of his church's growing dependence on the oil leases. Why do any of them keep needing more? That's a very provocative question. "Enough" is a rare concept in our consumer-minded world. Do you have limits in your life? What is "enough" for you?

14. Jesus said, "For where your treasure is, there will your heart be also" (Matt. 6:21 KJV). How was the truth of this verse demonstrated among the Amish in Stoney Ridge, Pennsylvania? How is it true in your own life?

15. "Without God," David said, "the Promised Land is nothing." The dictionary defines the Promised Land as a longed-for place or situation where happiness or satisfaction is achieved. What represents your version of the Promised Land? And where is God in your life? Where does God fit in?

Note to readers: Consider yourself invited to share your thoughts from these discussion questions with me. Or maybe you've got some questions of your own? I value your feedback: suzanne@suzannewoodsfisher.com.

Birdy's Baked Oatmeal

This is a favorite breakfast dish you'll find at any Amish restaurant. Birdy's recipe is a little unique because she adds cinnamon, walnuts, and raisins. So like Birdy.

½ cup	butter, melted
1 cup	brown sugar
2 eggs	beaten
½ teaspoon	cinnamon (optional)
3 cups	quick oats
2 teaspoons	baking powder
1 teaspoon	salt
1 cup	milk
½ cup	walnuts, chopped (optional)
½ cup	raisins (optional)

Cream together butter, brown sugar, and eggs. Add the rest of the ingredients to the creamed mixture. Bake in a 9" × 9" pan at 350° for 20–30 minutes (depending on your oven). Can be mixed the night before and baked in the morning. It might take a little more time to bake if the batter isn't at room temperature. Enjoy!

Acknowledgments

My warmest and most sincere thanks to the following people:

Thanks to Ben Joyce, for sharing his story about the misdiagnosis of multiple sclerosis with me and the subsequent true diagnosis of vitamin B-12 deficiency. So glad you're doing well!

The Revell family, who works diligently to provide good books, from content to cover, and to get them in the hands of readers. A special thank-you to Joyce Hart of Hartline Literary Agency, for being such a supportive agent. And to Andrea Doering and Barb Barnes, for adding their special editing touch to the story.

My faithful first readers: Wendy How, Amanda Fisher, Lindsey Ciraulo. You help me find the weak spots of the story while giving me encouragement, all at the same time. Amazing!

A curtsy to my special friend Nyna, who loaned me the use of her name for Nyna the Mynah. A childhood nickname, Nyna told me once, and I filed that info away. (This is why I make my friends so nervous. Everything is grit for the oyster. Everything.)

And, of course, my love to my entire family, whose essence is in the Stoltzfus clan.

Heartfelt thanks to my readers, who are incredibly supportive and dedicated. You really matter to me, and I value your feedback.

Finally, my hands lift in praise to the Almighty, who opens doors for me to write stories about how faith and life intersect. He gives me a fresh wind along the way for each new manuscript, and always prompts me to do my best.

To God be the glory.

Suzanne Woods Fisher is the bestselling author of *The Letters*, *The Calling*, the Lancaster County Secrets series, and the Stoney Ridge Seasons series, as well as nonfiction books about the Amish, including *Amish Peace*. She is also the coauthor of an Amish children's series, The Adventures of Lily Lapp. Suzanne is a Carol Award winner for *The Search*, a Carol Award finalist for *The Choice*, and a Christy Award finalist for *The Waiting*. She lives in California. Learn more at www.suzannewoodsfisher.com or connect with Suzanne on Facebook at www.facebook.com/SuzanneWoodsFisher Author.

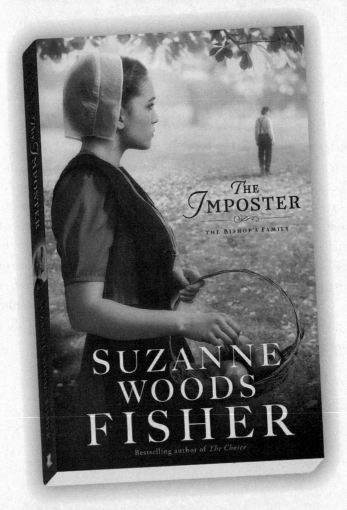
 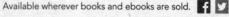

IT WAS A WELL-LAID PLAN—
BUT IT WASN'T HER PLAN . . .

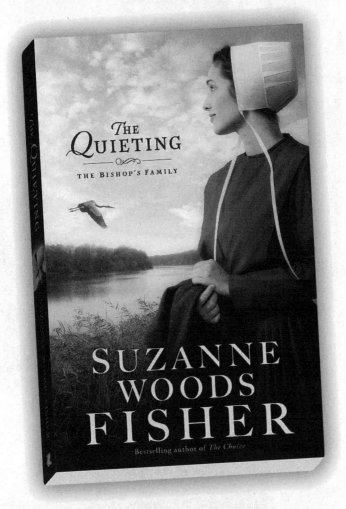

There are no eligible bachelors in Stoney Ridge, barring one,
and he's all wrong. How will Abigail handle the attention?

Revell
a division of Baker Publishing Group
www.RevellBooks.com

Available wherever books and ebooks are sold.

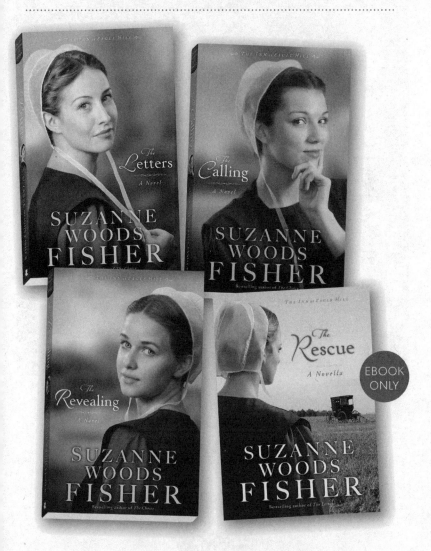

Meet Suzanne online at

 Suzanne Woods Fisher

 suzannewfisher

www.SuzanneWoodsFisher.com

Download the
Free **Amish Wisdom** App